About the Author

John Steinberg spent many years in business before becoming a writer in 2007. Since then, he has co-written and produced comedies for the stage and has created a series of books for children. *The Temple of Fortune* is his fourth novel. He is married with three children and lives in North London.

D1614433

By the same author

Shimon
Nadine
Blue Skies over Berlin

THE TEMPLE OF

FORTUNE

John Steinberg

2QT Limited (Publishing)

First edition published 2020
2QT Limited (Publishing)
Settle, North Yorkshire BD24 9BZ

Cover concept & illustration by Balcony Art & Design Studio

Printed in Great Britain by IngramSparks UK

All characters in this book other than those clearly in the public domain
are fictitious, and any resemblance to real persons, living or dead,
is purely coincidental.

A CIP catalogue record for this book is available
from the British Library
ISBN 978-1-913071-66-0 Paperback
ISBN 978-1-913071-67-7 eBook

Part One

1

North London, late autumn 1990

The red Jaguar XJS, its wipers working overtime against the persistent rain, pulled away from the deserted industrial estate and joined the flow of traffic heading towards Central London. Stanley Rose gazed in his rear-view mirror at the estate agent's *For Sale* board planted outside the old brick factory as it receded in the distance. As the boss, he was always the last to leave – but today it would be for the last time. There would be no more getting in at 8 a.m. to the welcoming hum of the bandsaws, or the distinctive smell of cellulose from the latest prototypes, fresh out of the spray booths. H. & A. Rose Limited, manufacturers of high-quality dining-room furniture for over half a century, had finally gone broke.

The 100-strong workforce were now without jobs – and he, Stanley Rose, was responsible for that.

Stan had personally supervised the disposal of all the stock and sundries to ensure that the creditors got back what was owing to them. His reputation for honesty and fairness was still important to him, even at this low point. Unfortunately, despite his best efforts there was a shortfall of close to a million pounds – a sum which kept him up at nights.

As he drove away, the sense of relief that he had anticipated, now that the worst was over, failed to materialise. Panic took over instead as the reality of his situation began to sink in. Stan knew that the past six months of stress had taken their toll on his looks, as well as on his nerves. His mother often remarked on his resemblance to Omar Sharif, since he was tall and dark, not yet forty, and had the same sort of moustache as the handsome Hollywood star. Now, however, Stan reckoned he looked more like Moe, one of the more miserable characters from *The Simpsons*. And just when he needed to keep up appearances too.

Stuck in the midday traffic, hemmed in by two huge trucks, he thought about the shell of a business he had just left.

It was his Uncle Harry who had started the company after World War Two, partnered by his less able older brother Arnold – Stan's father. Stan had a sudden memory of Harry directing production from the factory floor, immaculately dressed in his usual navy-blue suit, a large cigar in his mouth. The firm had provided the brothers with a decent standard of living, but years of under-investment, coupled with industrial action from workers who hated change, had gradually brought H. & A. Rose to its knees.

Stan knew he had made the wrong choice. He should have completed his accountancy qualification and made his own way in life, instead of taking the easy option and joining the family firm when his father died twenty years ago. Look where it had got him! He cringed at the thought of his Uncle Harry's reaction when he learned of the demise of the business, which he had built up single-handed.

Seeing the road sign for East Finchley, Stan was relieved and terrified in equal measure at the thought of going home. Switching on the car radio to pass the time, he rehearsed again the speech he planned to give to his wife Carol. Stan groaned aloud. He had tried to remain positive for the sake of Tara, their fourteen-year-old daughter, but with the burden of all his business worries, he knew he hadn't given either his wife or daughter the attention they deserved. Diagnosed with breast cancer eighteen months ago, Carol had been through a very difficult time. The loss of the business would, Stan feared, be the last straw.

Carol had left the car in the small car park behind the stately home of Kenwood House, while she and Tara went to have lunch at the Spaniards Inn over the road. The sixteenth-century pub, former haunt of highwaymen, was a family favourite, especially now in the chilly weather when the roaring fire and cosy little nooks made it the ideal place to while away an afternoon.

Tara finished her salad and took a sip of her Diet Coke. Her mother, she noticed, had barely touched her salmon.

'You know, you really shouldn't have taken time off school to come with me for my check-up,' Carol told her daughter.

'Well, Daddy wasn't going to take you. Anyway, Wednesdays are our half-day at school, so I won't have

3

missed much.'

Carol examined the olive-skinned girl, already a resilient young woman, who reminded her so much of herself at the same age.

'It's not his fault,' she said. 'He had something to do at the factory that he couldn't put off.'

'Sounds familiar,' Tara quipped.

'That's not fair – your father does what he can. He's actually a very kind man, deep down.'

'You'd have to dig quite deep!'

They both burst out laughing.

'It's not his fault that he finds it hard to show his feelings; in my experience it's endemic in the male species,' Carol said.

'You mean he's emotionally retarded, due to being the only child of an overbearing mother,' Tara said.

'I thought you got on so well with Grandma?'

'She's all right in small doses, I suppose,' Tara conceded, finishing her drink.

Carol yawned. The visit to the Royal Free Hospital that morning had tired her out. Then she perked up, saying, 'I know – let's take a stroll down to Kenwood House and look at the view across to the lake.' She loved it so much there, and something told her she might not be around long enough to see the rhododendrons there bloom in the late spring.

'All right, Mummy, if you're sure you're feeling up to it,' Tara replied, happy to put off her English essay for a little longer.

*

The landscape of tatty housing estates and rundown shops had by now given way to the lush open spaces of Hampstead Heath. Without even thinking about it, Stan had bypassed the route home, thereby avoiding the confrontation with his wife, and driven straight to his mother's house. He was hoping for some sort of comfort and advice – but even as he rang the bell, he knew it had been a mistake.

The door opened and a perfectly groomed woman, dressed in a maroon cashmere coat and kid leather gloves, looked at him in surprise.

'Darling, what are you doing here?' Elaine Rose said in her well-spoken voice, dabbing a few drops of her favourite Cabochard perfume behind her ears. 'You've just caught me on my way out to lunch at Fortnum's with Stella and then I'm off to the Royal Academy. And would you believe it, I'm out again tonight?'

'I just wanted a quick word,' Stan replied, disappointed but trying to keep his spirits up. He badly needed to share his troubles. Maybe for once his mother would reassure him that everything was going to be all right.

'I don't suppose you'd mind taking me, would you?' Elaine asked, not giving her son a chance to refuse as she passed him on her way out of the house that he'd grown up in. 'Trying to find a meter in Piccadilly can be impossible at the best of times and I shan't want to be late.'

'Yes, all right,' Stan agreed, trying not to let his lack of enthusiasm show. He helped her into the passenger seat and drove off.

'This car is lovely and comfortable – is it new?' Elaine Rose enquired, checking her make-up.

'It's a couple of years old, you've been in it before,' Stan reminded her.

'It's important for a man to have a nice motor car,' Elaine said comfortably. 'It gives a good impression. The first thing I noticed about your father was his car. I remember it was a black sports car with a wonderful smell of new leather.' She sighed.

Stan pictured his father sitting behind the wheel of his immaculately polished Humber Snipe, proudly waiting outside the house to take him to St Anthony's, his prep school in Hampstead.

When it came to his family, nothing was too much trouble for Arnold Rose.

The day that Stan was ushered out of a gym lesson and taken to the Headmaster's office, to be informed that his father had passed away, still seemed surreal, two decades later. Arnold had gone to bed the previous night, feeling slightly unwell, and had never woken up. The post mortem showed that he had suffered a massive stroke. He was just fifty years old.

'Of course, it's different these days,' Elaine was rambling on. 'For someone independent like me, a car's an absolute necessity. I'm sure your wife has one, doesn't she?'

'Sorry, Mother, what were you saying?' Stan asked distractedly.

'A car!'

'Yes, of course, but Carol hasn't done much driving since she's been unwell,' Stan replied, irritated by the way his mother had of always putting him on the defensive.

'I thought the mastectomy operation was successful? I do hope that isn't the reason you came to see me. And Tara, she is all right, isn't she?' Elaine said, showing genuine concern for the first time.

'Carol went for her three-monthly check-up this

morning,' Stan informed her. 'We are hoping that she's still clear, but it's been hard on Tara, seeing what her mother's been going through.'

By avoiding the side roads, he was now on a clear run to the West End. It was time to grasp the nettle.

'It's the business,' he said, coming right out with it.

But Elaine was ferreting in her handbag and didn't pick up on his tone. 'I'm sure that it's just the time of year, Stanley dear. You can hardly expect people to buy furniture in this weather. Your father used to say, "any excuse for the public not to buy".'

'I'm afraid it's more serious than that.' Stan cleared his throat. 'The company has closed down. We tried everything to keep it going, but the bank withdrew their support.'

Elaine finally found what she was looking for and began to file one of her long pink nails. 'There are bound to be others who would be only too pleased to acquire a business like ours. Don't worry, you'll see – it'll sort itself out,' she replied, apparently unable to absorb what was being said to her.

Stan cursed himself for wasting his breath. It wasn't her fault that she had no grasp of financial affairs. His mother came from a generation of women who rarely worked, got married off and left it to their husbands to support them.

Stan turned into Duke Street, the network of art galleries and antique shops so discreet that they always appeared closed, and let his mother out at the side entrance of Fortnum's.

Nothing had been accomplished.

He put on a tape by the Allman Brothers, the American rock band who had blown him away the first time he heard their classic 1970 album *In Memory of Elizabeth Reed.*

Indulging himself in thoughts of what might have been, had he been allowed to follow his dream of becoming a fulltime musician, gave Stan a little respite as he turned the car round and headed back home to face up to his troubles.

It was past six that same evening when Elaine Rose arrived home. She paid the taxi driver and went briskly into the house. Switching on the lights, she picked up the telephone and dialled the number in Spain that was lodged firmly in her mind.

'What!' a man's gruff voice said at the other end of the line.

'Harry, it's me,' Elaine replied, using her free hand to undo the buttons of her coat. 'We need to talk – it's important.'

'Why, what's wrong?' her brother-in-law asked, annoyed at being interrupted during his weekly bridge game in Marbella.

'It's Stanley. He needs help – the business is in difficulty.'

'So, what do you expect me to do about it?' Harry snapped back.

'He's got a wife with cancer and my granddaughter to support. Do you think for one moment I'm going to see a child of mine out on the street?'

'All right, all right, I assume it's money you're after.' There was a short pause while Harry relit his cigar, giving himself time to think. 'How much?' he barked.

'I was thinking that fifty thousand would help keep him going until he gets back on his feet.'

'*How* much?' Harry repeated in shock.

'Small change compared to what you milked the company for, all those years,' Elaine said coolly.

Harry exploded. 'So I paid myself dividends when we were doing well. What's wrong with that?'

'Nothing – except you made damn sure that Arnold never got his share,' Elaine butted in.

'That was different and you know it. He was never involved in running the business.'

Elaine ignored him. 'And then, when you'd drained any goodness that was left, you couldn't get to that flat in Spain quick enough.' Her voice turned bitter. 'How convenient for you, to have Stanley there to pick up the pieces and shoulder the blame.'

'Trade was tough! Anyway, it was time for the boy to show what he was made of,' came the blustered response.

'Harry dear, do I need to remind you that it was *my father's money* that set you up in business in the first place? Arnold was entitled to half of everything. The fact that he was too good-hearted to ask for it is quite beside the point. Giving it to Stanley now is only making up what was due to him.'

'I see. I suppose I don't have a choice,' came the resentful reply.

'Write this down,' Elaine instructed. Reaching into her crocodile handbag for her cheque-book, she read out her bank details.

'All right. The funds will be transferred first thing tomorrow,' Harry confirmed, beaten.

'I shall put Barclays on alert to expect it,' Elaine told him, replacing the receiver. That money, she decided, could stay in her account until she deemed it the right time to help her son without making him feel as if it was a hand-out. She would then pass it off as 'family money'. Satisfied, she hurried upstairs and quickly showered and changed, in preparation for her evening engagement.

When the Mercedes limousine drew up outside, Elaine appeared, wearing a black evening dress and elegant high-heeled shoes. She was, as ever, ready on time.

The chauffeur tipped his cap and opened the rear passenger door.

'Good evening, Paul,' she said, getting in next to a distinguished older man.

'My dear, you look absolutely stunning,' he announced in his thick European accent, reaching across to kiss her.

Elaine took the flute of champagne he handed her and clinked it against his own. Relaxing for the first time since her son's visit, she said archly, 'Well, it's not every day I receive an invitation to the opera at Covent Garden – *and* dinner at the Ritz.'

2

Stan woke early, to the sound of church bells ringing. It was Christmas Day, but any sense of holiday feeling was far from his mind. He glanced at the woman lying peacefully beside him. Carol had finally got to sleep after being up half the night. Despite receiving the all-clear again very recently, the pain in her side had gradually got worse, telling her that things were far from all right.

Stan lay fretting, trying to calculate yet again how long they could hold out at their current rate of expenditure without any money coming in. What on earth had possessed him, to spend the days following the factory closure driving there at the usual hour, as if nothing had happened? But he already knew the answer to that. The fact was, he couldn't face telling Carol the truth.

There was a gentle knock at the door and Tara entered the room. The one thing that had been asked of him, Stan had forgotten to do – to take his daughter's gifts from his office along the corridor and put them outside her bedroom.

'How is Mummy?' Tara asked stoically, peering over at the sleeping woman, her large brown eyes anxious.

'Best to let her sleep, sweetheart,' Stan whispered, getting himself out of bed. 'Go back to your room and I'll bring in your Christmas presents.'

'I don't need presents. I just want Mummy to get well,' the girl replied passionately.

'We all do,' her father agreed, both of them tiptoeing away.

'I pray every night that she will get better,' Tara went on, 'although I often wonder whether G-d takes any notice.'

Stan would have liked to have been able to offer his daughter some spiritual reassurance, but he had always taken his religion for granted and not put any effort in.

'Right, who's coming for lunch?' he asked, changing the subject.

'There are going to be seven of us, including Inge.'

'I thought she would have gone home for Christmas to be with her family?'

'Inge's got a new boyfriend. He's from Jamaica,' Tara revealed.

Hearing this, Stan experienced a momentary pang of jealousy. The au pair had a naturally flirtatious manner, and he had kidded himself that this was for his benefit alone.

'I suppose it's a stupid question to ask whether Grandma will be coming?' Tara wanted to know. Being an only child, her grandparents were important to her, but she knew that her father's mother Elaine, and her mother's father Ben didn't get on. Elaine had never made a secret of the fact that she couldn't abide Ben, whom she regarded as 'nothing but a common barrow boy'. As far as Tara was aware, her parents' wedding, and the time she was born were the only occasions on which Elaine Rose and Benjamin Miller had been in the same room at the same time. To make matters worse, Elaine also disapproved of Carol. Her daughter-in-law was, she said, too self-opinionated and far too worldly to be a suitable wife for her only son.

Not waiting for an answer, the girl set off downstairs, her arms piled high with gifts, her short ponytail bouncing on her shoulders.

Upstairs, Stan went over to his desk and stared out of the window at the grey sky. This time of year, when businesses shut up shop and normal life was put on hold for ten days or more, was the last thing he needed.

He was just browsing through the *Cabinet Maker* trade magazine when Carol stormed into the room. She was deathly pale and looking ready for a fight.

'I hope you're not thinking of working today,' she hissed, her drawn face full of contempt. Stan was sure that if she had had a lethal weapon in her hand, she would have attacked him with it.

'No, of course not,' he blustered, doing his best to avoid another argument. 'I was just going down to breakfast.'

But Carol was ranting on. 'You're the bloody limit, Stan. Would it really be too much to ask you to spend some time with your daughter? She's off school for three weeks. The least you could do is try and be a proper father for once, instead of sneaking off here at the first opportunity. Tara has two parents, you know! Why does it always have to be down to me? I can't be there all the time,' she whimpered, breaking down into a flood of tears.

Stan went over and took her in his arms. He felt terrible. What had happened to them? The effervescent young woman with the mass of black frizzy hair who had captivated him, twenty-one years ago had, through a cruel twist of fate, become like a vulnerable child in need of the love that she herself gave in such abundance to everyone else.

If he was truthful, he had always felt slightly in awe of his wife – intimidated, even. Carol was strong, independent and fearless, so different from any of the other women Stan had met. Carol had had to grow up quickly, no doubt through having to keep house for her widowed father, while Stan had been pampered and over-protected.

Now, although she hated to admit it, Carol was dependent on him – and he couldn't deal with it.

'You will take good care of Tara, if anything happens to me?' she mumbled now.

'Nothing *is* going to happen, you'll see,' Stan responded, trying to put a lid on his own emotions.

After a few moments, Carol wiped her eyes and straightened up. 'Right, I've got to put the turkey in the oven. Our guests will be here in a few hours. I'd like you to give Tara a hand laying the table. She knows who's coming and has prepared place cards. Can I leave it to you to put the wine in the fridge?' She gave her husband a stern look. 'And, Stan, put on a happy face, please? I for one am certainly going to enjoy myself.'

Carol then went away, trying to ignore the shooting pain in her side.

It was four o'clock by the time they got up from lunch and went into the lounge to watch the television. Carol, in a great deal of discomfort by now, had excused herself and gone up to bed, before the Christmas pudding and mince pies.

'Stan, do you think she's going to be all right?' asked their guest Alison in her mild Scottish accent. A good-looking woman with short ginger hair, Alison was unmarried, currently single and had come on her own. She and Carol had worked together in advertising and remained close ever since. Stan was aware that his father-in-law had a soft spot for Alison; in fact, Ben had spent the last fifteen years trying to persuade her to be more than just friends.

'She's gonna be fine,' a cockney voice called out from behind the hand of rummy that Ben was playing with his granddaughter. A thickset man in his early seventies, Ben Miller's lop-sided face indicated that at some time in the past, he had suffered a palsy. 'Under the best doctors, she is,' he went on. 'I've checked them out myself.'

Suddenly, Mrs Schwartz, the ninety-year-old spinster for whom Carol occasionally shopped, passed wind while fast asleep in an armchair, sending the room, led by Tara, into a fit of giggles.

'We'll know more tomorrow after the latest scan,' Stan said, trying to keep a straight face.

'Right, young lady, now you've taken me to the cleaners, I'd better settle up what I owe you,' the child's grandfather said, struggling to his feet. Reaching into his back trouser pocket, he withdrew a thick wad of notes. Taking Tara aside, he placed twenty pounds in the palm of her hand, shutting it tight before anyone else noticed.

'I've got to be off. Lovely meal!' he exclaimed, going to retrieve his coat. 'You sure you're all right for money?' he said, turning to his son-in-law who had followed him into the hall.

'Yes – why?' Stan replied, wondering about the reason for Ben's sudden concern.

'A fine business like that, I just don't understand it,' the older man said, shaking his huge head. 'There was a write-up in the *Gazette* a few weeks back.'

Stan felt ashamed. His attempt to withhold the news

of the closure in tatters, he berated himself for being so naive.

'Does Carol know?' he asked fearfully.

'She hasn't mentioned it, so I guess not. If I were you, I'd try and keep it that way,' the other man said. To Stan it sounded more like a warning than a piece of friendly advice.

'Ben, fashions change, there's not the same demand now houses are getting smaller and people eat in the kitchen,' he replied, trying to justify himself. And then he added: 'Actually, I was wondering, now I've got more time on my hands, whether I could come in with you?'

The horrified expression on his father-in-law's face said it all. Ben blamed him for the demise of the family firm, Stan could see, and was making it abundantly clear that he didn't want him anywhere near the portfolio of fifty properties that he managed by himself.

Poking his head around the entrance to the lounge, the older man called out, 'Alison, can I give you a lift?' knowing full well that her VW Golf was parked in the street.

'Thank you, Ben,' she answered with a big smile, 'but I'm going to stay on for a while. I will call you tomorrow.'

'Bye, Grandpa!' Tara sang out. 'When are you coming again?'

'Next Sunday, as usual,' he shouted back, striding to the front door. 'But watch out – this time I won't let you beat me!' A few seconds later there was the purr of a car's engine as the gold Rolls-Royce reversed slowly out of the drive.

*

On a bright morning during the second week of January 1991, a large crowd dressed in black gathered in the small prayer hall of the North London cemetery, waiting for the arrival of the hearse carrying the body of Carol Rose.

Stan stood rigidly, his arm around his daughter, oblivious to the steady stream of condolences that appeared just as muffled sounds in his head. The scan had confirmed their worst fears. The cancer had spread to his wife's liver, which explained her excruciating pain. It had been just a question of time.

Trying to find a way to break the news to their daughter was the hardest thing he had ever had to do. But Stan needn't have worried. Tara was already aware of the situation and had only kept up the optimistic facade, she said, out of concern for him.

The screeching of wheels brought him back to the present as the draped coffin appeared, strapped on to a flat trolley and pulled slowly along by a sombre-looking man with a long black beard and a wide-brimmed hat.

The door was closed and a simple service began, conducted by the same rabbi who had married them seventeen years previously. After he had recited from the Book of Psalms, Tara, who had asked to be allowed to say a few words about her mother, took out a neatly folded piece of paper from her coat and began the eulogy that she had written herself.

Seeing the bereft girl, her perfectly controlled voice saying goodbye to the most important person in her life, proved too much for the tearful Elaine Rose. Her gentleman friend, Paul Klein, had to offer his support, while her suntanned brother-in-law Harry, fresh off the flight from Malaga, stood looking on impassively. Ben,

Carol's father, was nowhere to be seen. Stan, his attention fixed only on the young woman who resembled her late mother in so many ways, had never felt so humbled.

The cortège then followed the coffin out into the cemetery for the interment. Here, Carol Rebekah Rose was laid to rest, with those who had loved her looking on.

Still in a daze, Stan returned to his car, expecting Tara to be following behind. But when he looked around, his daughter was nowhere to be seen. Thinking she had gone back with her grandmother, he was just about to get into the silver Renault 5 he had purchased after the Jag had been returned, when he changed his mind. He retraced his steps across the cemetery lawn and found the girl at the graveside, bent over in grief. Her eyes were bloodshot from crying.

'Daddy! It's so unfair,' she wailed, weeping uncontrollably for the first time.

'I know, darling, I know,' Stan said inadequately, short on comfort for the distraught child.

For a few precious moments, father and daughter remained together, lost in their own thoughts but both wondering how they were going to fill the huge void left by the woman they had loved.

By two-thirty, the last of the guests who had joined them back at the house in Hampstead had gone, leaving Tara dozing on the sofa in front of the television and Alison and Inge busy doing the tidying up.

'I don't know what I'd have done without you,' Stan said to his wife's closest friend.

'It's the least I could do,' Alison replied miserably. As

she was putting on her coat, she divulged, 'Carol and I spent a long time discussing what needed to be done after she died.'

'In what respect?' he asked, bemused.

'Things like her funeral – letting me know who would want to be there. Making sure that she had the burial plot next to her mother; instructions concerning Tara. She'd recorded every detail, even down to what sandwiches should be served afterwards, written out in copious notes from her hospital bed.'

'But I never knew about any of this!' Stan said, shaken.

'You are lovely,' Alison said gently, taking his hand. 'Carol was a very special woman. It might surprise you to know that she was always fatalistic about her own life after her mother died. After all, Livia was also only in her thirties. Carol didn't ask anything of you because she didn't want to upset you.'

Stan didn't know whether it was the strain of the day getting to him but he suddenly felt overwhelmed with tiredness and had trouble taking in what Alison was saying.

'What with the problems in your business and looking after Tara, Carol didn't want to burden you further, so she leaned on me.' Alison touched his shoulder. 'I do hope you're not offended?'

Stan reflected for a moment. So, his wife had known the whole time about the closure of the factory. How foolish it had been, he saw now, not to confide in her, deluding himself that she wouldn't find out.

'No, of course not,' he replied, still distracted. 'But where was Ben today? Surely he would have wanted to be involved in the funeral arrangements?'

'Not at all. I spoke to him when I managed to track him down at the cottage in Broadstairs,' Alison said.

'How did you know that he'd be there? Ben never even gave us the number.'

Alison shrugged. 'Ben was devastated. Nothing I said to him seemed to register. Now that he had lost his Carol, he didn't want to have anything to do with the funeral, which was why he couldn't bring himself to attend it today.'

Stan became pensive, only now appreciating the older man's grief.

'I know it's early to be thinking about these things,' Alison said tentatively, 'but have you considered what you're going to do about the property company?'

'No, why? What's it got to do with me?' Stan responded, thinking it an odd question.

'Stan, even I know that Carol owned part of her father's property interests, which I assume will now have passed to you?'

'But Ben doesn't want me anywhere near his business!'

'All I'm saying is that neither he nor you may have a choice, especially as Tara will end up inheriting the lot one day. It's just something for you to think about in due course.'

But Stan was in no fit state to think about the future. He had more important things on his mind, like how he was going to be both father and mother to his daughter and at the same time ensure that they could still afford to stay in the house.

'Right, I'll be going,' Alison announced, opening the front door. 'Let me know if you need anything, or if you just want to talk. I've already arranged with Tara that I'll do the shopping until you get settled, and don't argue, you can pay me back at the end of the week. Oh, and think about what I said earlier – about organising some form of counselling for your daughter. In fact, it might do you both some good.' She then went off to sit in her car, where she stopped pretending to cope and let go of her self-control, weeping for her lost friend until she could hardly see out of her swollen eyes.

At approximately the same time, a man dressed in a smart camel-coloured overcoat was climbing out of a taxi at London's Heathrow airport. He felt desperately sorry for Stanley to have lost his wife at such a young age, and also to have lost the business. Life could be tough, but that was the nature of business. Anyway, to help him out he had coughed up £50,000 – no small sum.

What's more, hadn't he taken the boy on the payroll in the first place, when anyone with an ounce of nous could see he wouldn't make a businessman in a month of Sundays? Stanley certainly resembled Arnold in that respect, at least. And was it *his* fault they were stuck in the middle of another recession? Such was the nature of manufacturing; you took a few knocks but then you picked yourself up again and got on with it.

On reflection, Harry had nothing to reproach himself with.

The man brushed a speck from the lapel of his coat. Just as well he'd had the foresight to purchase the freehold of the factory himself when he'd had the chance. That way, the receivers hadn't been able to get their thieving hands on it, he thought smugly as he approached the departure gate.

3

The 9 a.m. train from London's Euston station had just pulled into Birmingham's National Exhibition Centre. Stan collected his things, psyching himself up for the ordeal ahead. It was going to be hard to put on a confident face and pretend all was well, when in fact he was still unemployed and had only come here to sound out former colleagues about job opportunities in the trade.

Fortunately, unlike the main January exhibition, when trying to cover all eight halls in one day was next to impossible, furniture in the Spring Fair was confined to a much smaller area. Just as well, since Stan suspected that Tara would create a fuss if he stayed overnight. Understandable, since it was only three weeks since her mother passed away.

After the funeral, the girl had become uncharacteristically clingy as if she was expecting something terrible to happen to him next. Thank goodness he had Alison to rely upon. Inge was often out in the evenings, but Alison always made time to drive over to the house after her work as an estate agent and sit with Tara, so his daughter wouldn't be alone. It was a mixed blessing though, since even when he got home early, he never got a look in, Stan thought a little resentfully. The two of them would be having dinner together, after which they would spend hours talking about

Carol. Tara wanted to know everything about her mother and had started her own photo album from the stacks of photographs that were kept, meticulously labelled, in boxes.

Alison told him afterwards that it was his daughter's way of keeping Carol's memory alive – although he suspected that it also provided consolation for Alison herself.

Stan took the escalator up from the platform and followed the directions to the Exhibition. After registering and receiving his personalised badge, he made his way into the first hall, when he spotted the familiar face of Laurie Silver, his old Sales Director. Dapper as ever in his hallmark dog-tooth sports jacket and with the usual cigarette drooping from his mouth, Laurie and another man were deep in conversation with a former customer of theirs, whom Stan recognised as Toby Evans from the Co-op.

'Hello there, Stan,' Laurie called across. 'Didn't expect to bump into you here. You remember Toby?' He jerked a thumb at the sprightly individual wearing a very bad toupée.

'Yes, yes, of course. It's good to see you,' Stan replied, extending his hand to the man who, in the past, had been a frequent visitor to lunch in their showrooms.

'So, what brings you to Birmingham?' Laurie asked.

'Just looking around,' Stan replied guardedly. He had no intention of telling the world that he was unemployed and on the verge of losing his home.

'Great. Well, we're in Hall Four; you're welcome to come and have a look around. Quite a few of the lads are working at Ferndale's – they'd love to see you again,' Laurie said, striding away to continue his perusal of the competition.

'I might just do that,' Stan called back, keen to find out what had attracted his old employees to the lower-grade firm.

It was a few hours later when Stan, weighed down with two large carrier bags filled with catalogues, came across a closed-in stand which, with its pitched tent ceiling and muslin-draped walls, resembled a Sultan's palace. There was a buzz about the place. Eager salesmen stood frantically writing up their orders while others were using the phones in the small office booth, calling the factory in North Wales to ascertain the latest delivery information, leaving their customers to take advantage of the complimentary food and beverages.

Stan looked around and, to his horror, he saw that several of the displays attracting the most interest were identical to the former bestselling H. & A. Rose designs. Experiencing a rush of blood to the head, he marched onto the stand, determined to check on their sales prices and to find out who had been responsible for ripping him off.

'Can I help you, sir?' enquired a young woman in a tight mini-skirt whose job it was to make sure that no potential customer slipped through the net.

'I would like some information on the new ranges, if that's possible,' Stan replied, gritting his teeth.

'Certainly. If you can tell me what part of the country you are from, I will get hold of the representative who covers your area,' the woman said, repeating by rote the script she had been given.

Just then, David Morgan, the bloated owner of the business, strutted over. Stan had always tried to avoid crossing paths with the obnoxious individual, whom he regarded as arrogant and not a real furniture man. But for some unknown reason, his face seemed to fit. Stan knew all about the boozy junkets that Dave organised on his gin palace yacht moored in the South of France and also knew that he was on personal terms with many of his largest customers. But as far as Stan was concerned, he had just got lucky.

'Come to spy on the competition, have you?' the fat man jibed in his sing-song Welsh accent.

'See it didn't take you long to copy our stuff,' Stan said coolly, pointing to the mahogany and yew dining sets that had caused him to get so upset.

'I don't know what you mean,' the Welshman retorted, bristling at the insinuation that he had done something wrong.

Stan now knew it was no coincidence that his management team had left Rose's so abruptly. It was clear that they had been poached – and the first thing they had done was to undermine their previous employers by pinching their most popular ranges.

'Let me guess, you're selling the mahogany group over there for £499 and the yew for £549?' Stan speculated.

'You're way off the mark,' the fat man said, not prepared to disclose his prices. Then, condescendingly, 'Don't take it personally, Stanley. The multiples knew you were struggling to keep to the price points but they had winners on their hands, see – so they came to us for replacements.'

'You're even using the same drop handles on the units! The only difference is the chair covers!' Stan blurted out.

'That brown tweed of yours was a real dog's dinner; the velvet is a much better seller,' David Morgan revealed, impervious to the damage he had done. He went on: 'Your boyos didn't need much persuasion to come and work for me, I can tell you. See, we're a firm that's going places. We'll do twenty million turnover this year, now the new factory's up and running. State of the art place it is too – everything computerised. No other manufacturer can get near us. Not bad for a boy from the Valleys,' he gloated.

And that wasn't the end of it. 'Come and have a look at what else we're doing,' the Welshman said.

But Stan had seen enough. He hated to admit it, but the fat man was right: technically they were miles ahead of everyone else. And if survival was the name of the game, there was no question that Daffyd Morgan was a winner.

'Got to be going, thanks for showing me around.' Stan was worn out and his feet were killing him. He just wanted to get back to the comforts of home.

Leaving the exhibition, he checked his mobile phone. There were no missed calls from Tara – he breathed a sigh of relief. If he got the six o'clock train he'd be back before nine and could spend some time with his daughter before she went to bed.

Stan let himself into his house and found Tara curled up on the sofa, engrossed in a horror film on television, her homework books stacked neatly beside her.

'Hello, Daddy, had a good day?' she asked cheerfully. 'I'm watching *The Woman in Black*. It's nearly finished, then I'll make you something to eat if you want?'

'That's all right, I had something on the train,' her father replied. 'Where's Inge, by the way? She's supposed to be here.'

'I said she could go out.'

'But what did you do about supper? Did Alison come over?'

'She telephoned to say that she had a late showing at a property and couldn't get away. Don't worry, Daddy, it's not that difficult to make a plate of pasta! Anyway, Inge's got boyfriend problems. The last thing we need is *her* moping around the house.'

Stan felt terrible. He had tried calling home from the train but couldn't get a signal. And to think his daughter had been left on her own. It just wasn't right.

'I'll talk to Inge in the morning,' he said sternly.

'Don't, Daddy. You'll be wasting your time. She'll only walk out and move in with Marlon.'

'You know his name?' Stan asked, sounding surprised.

'Marlon has a black belt in karate,' Tara said admiringly.

'That's as may be, but you still shouldn't be here by yourself. Next time, I'll have to arrange a babysitter.'

'Daddy, don't be so silly! I'm quite capable of looking after myself.' Tara wasn't going to mention the trauma at school today when she had broken down in tears during a biology lesson and had had to spend the rest of the morning under the care of the school nurse; nor did she tell him that she had cried herself to sleep practically every night ever since her mother died. What was the point? He wouldn't understand. Her mother had warned her that she would have to be the strong one, because he was likely to fall to pieces.

'We'll talk about it tomorrow,' Stan said, yawning.

His last thoughts before falling asleep were not of his daughter sitting downstairs all alone, but of the uncomfortable revelations he had received that day.

4

It was a few days after Easter, which had come early this year at the end of March, and Stan was starting to feel more settled. This morning, he'd walked up Hampstead High Street to catch up with his old schoolfriend Howard Barnet in the Coffee Cup, a much-loved local meeting place dating from the 1950s.

'So – what do you think of the idea?' Howard Barnet asked, stretching his powerful legs out under the cramped Formica tables. With his long hair and sharp suit, he was conspicuously out of place in the quaint old café. Stan grinned to himself. If he himself was said to resemble Omar Sharif on a good day then Howard was more like a beefier Rod Stewart – with the same sex appeal.

'Sounds great,' Stan said aloud, finishing his orange juice.

'It'd sharpen you up a bit, Stan. I reckon you might even make a half decent salesman,' Howard chuckled.

'Bit premature to be talking about a promotion, isn't it?'

'Can't stand still, matey, you know me. Right,' said Howard, glancing at his watch. 'It's nearly eleven and the pubs will be open. Come on, let's go and have a couple of Scotches to celebrate properly.'

Things were definitely picking up, Stan thought to himself as they made their way up to the Holly Bush.

Knowing of Stan's background in accountancy, Howard had offered him a job looking after the books at his luxury car showroom in the West End. After all, they'd been at school together and had remained friends for a long time afterwards. It was only a temporary arrangement while the permanent position remained unfilled, but Stan felt encouraged. Being involved in the business would give him a motive to get up and out of the house every day.

Carol had never liked Howard, he recalled, and would have disliked the thought of them working together. She said that Howard was a bad influence and that her group of friends were far more *their type of people*. Perhaps, Stan pondered, she had secretly felt threatened by the suave manner of his good-looking long-haired pal. And although she always rigorously denied it, something told him that she didn't altogether trust herself with the brash car salesman.

The other reason for Stan's change of mood was the fifty thousand pounds that he had unexpectedly received from his mother. Elaine had merely said it was family money that had been earmarked for him, and that it was appropriate he should now benefit from it.

The pressure to sell the home in Hampstead was off, at least for the moment. This was just as well since his daughter hadn't spoken to him for two days after she accidentally overheard his conversation with a local estate agent. She had flown into a tearful rage, accusing him of trying to obliterate her mother's memory. She then ran upstairs and sobbed in her bedroom while he paced downstairs, at a complete loss, not knowing how to comfort her or how to explain their situation.

Fortunately, his father-in-law had finally resurfaced.

Stan knew that it was just what Tara needed, to have her grandfather back in her life. The phone call two days before, saying that Ben wanted to have a chat and would be around on Sunday, had caught Stan by surprise. He assumed that Miller Investments would be the subject under discussion as he had come to accept the fact that he was now the owner of 25 per cent of the shares which he'd inherited from his late wife. Admittedly, he didn't know much about property but anything had to be easier than the furniture business. And as Alison had intimated after the funeral, it was only right that he should have some involvement in the company.

When Stan got home late afternoon, he found Tara sat next to an unsmiling Alison at the kitchen table.

'What's going on?' he asked, noticing that his daughter was dressed in jeans rather than her normal school uniform, and that she appeared to be wearing make-up.

'You'd better tell him,' Alison said, turning to the stony-faced girl.

'So I haven't been to school – big deal!' she answered with a note of defiance.

'Inge gave the school secretary my number when the woman rang,' Alison explained to Stan. 'The secretary said she had no choice but to inform the Headmistress that Tara has been bunking off school again. That's where we've just come from.' Alison sighed. 'Fortunately, Mrs Bellman was prepared to make allowances for everything that Tara has been through and, on this occasion, she got off with a warning. However, if it happens again, Mrs Bellman will have no choice but to expel her. As she said, the school does have to safeguard its reputation.'

'But where have you been, dressed like that?' Stan asked, aghast at what he had just heard.

When there was no reply, only a sulky glare, Alison took charge. 'Your daughter appears to have been helping herself to the loose change that you've left around the house, and she's used it to go to Brent Cross and have a look at clothes,' she disclosed. The big shopping centre was on the local bus route and was a magnet for teens.

'Yes, and all I could afford was my bus fares and to get a coffee! I need that loose change because he's so mean with my pocket money. Fifty pence a week's pathetic!' the girl shouted and stormed out of the room, leaving her father in shock. He put the shopping down on the table and looked helplessly at their friend.

'Alison, I'm really sorry to involve you in all this,' he said, feeling out of his depth and with no idea of how to cope with the unpredictable teenager.

'Don't worry, I was fifteen once – it's really not that unusual. If it's any consolation, she's angry at the world, not just with you.'

'But what can I do? It's not possible to keep an eye on her all day and I can't expect you to rush round here every time something goes wrong.'

'I've got a suggestion,' Alison said a little tentatively. 'I don't suppose you would consider making me a guardian – jointly with you, I mean. It might actually solve quite a lot of problems.'

'I think that would be a fantastic idea.' Stan felt hugely relieved. 'Carol would definitely have been in favour,' he decided, taking up the chair his daughter had vacated. 'Actually, I was going to suggest we should consider boarding school.'

'Getting rid of a problem by sending Tara away? That's not the answer.' Alison shook her head, sending her red hair flying. 'Of course, it's your decision but I'm pretty sure that her mother would turn in her grave if you went that far.'

'But you've no idea quite how difficult she's become. I asked her what she wanted for her birthday but it didn't make any difference.'

'She told me that she wants a pet for her birthday. A dog to love could be a real benefit to her.'

Stan pulled a face.

'You don't seem over-keen on the idea?' Alison noted.

'You know how Carol would never have an animal in the house. Anyway, who would look after the bloody thing? I don't even know where I am with *her* from one day to the next.'

'That, my dear Stan, is because if you had taken the trouble to read that book I left you weeks ago on parental bereavement, you'd know what your daughter's been going through. At least the school has been supportive in that regard. Apparently, that chap Felix Elias who was brought in to talk to Tara, has been really helpful.'

'I never knew anything about that,' Stan said, peeved that as usual he'd been kept in the dark. 'At least the school should have let me know in case I wanted to be there.'

'Stan, you're too close. It's best that these things are kept at arms' length.'

'But *you* seem to be aware of exactly what's going on,' he said petulantly.

'It's important that Tara knows she can trust me,' Alison countered.

'I suppose so,' he conceded.

'It seems to me that she's getting more assertive, more like Carol every day,' Alison commented.

Stan looked defeated, realising it was true.

'Anyway, a man like you needs an assertive woman,' Alison said, only half-joking.

'That's not very flattering,' he retorted.

'The reason the two of you got on so well together was because you were opposites.'

'Is there anything you don't know about our family?'

'No, not much,' Alison laughed. 'So, you can rest assured I'll take my new responsibility seriously, as far as that daughter of yours is concerned.'

'Well, if you're sure, I'll get the solicitors to draw up the papers. Right, I'm going to find Tara,' Stan said, getting up from the table.

'It's best to leave her alone for a while,' Alison advised. 'She's just had an earful at school and I've also given her a piece of my mind. She'll get over it, you'll see.' Alison stretched. 'I don't know about you, Stan, but I could do with a stiff drink.'

'Good idea,' he agreed. 'I'll go out and get some wine.'

'There's some vodka in the freezer, if I remember correctly – assuming Tara hasn't drunk all of it.'

'*What!*' Stan exclaimed. The blood had rushed from his face and he looked a deathly pale.

'I'm only teasing. You really are so wonderfully naïve,' Alison said, touching his hand. 'I don't suppose you fancy a Chinese takeaway?' she said impulsively. 'My treat.'

'Great idea. Chinese is Tara's favourite. But wouldn't that be sending out mixed messages?' Stan asked. 'Getting rewarded for bad behaviour?'

'Under normal circumstances you'd be right but she's an adolescent and, apart from everything else, her hormones are probably playing havoc. It may not appear so, but she really needs a lot of TLC. Take it from one who knows, it can be a very difficult time.'

'I've obviously not been paying her enough attention. I had no idea . . .'

'You're a man and, if you don't mind me saying so, never particularly observant of the female species.'

'That sounds like a dig, if I didn't know you better.'

'It's just that because she's an only child and has had to fend for herself, your daughter has developed a tough outer skin.'

Stan said quietly, 'We would have liked a brother or sister for her, but we left it a while and then it just didn't happen.'

'Yes, that must have been a great disappointment to Tara. Although being one of five kids in a deprived part of Glasgow, I have to tell you, my life wasn't exactly a bowl of cherries either.'

Stan didn't really want to know. 'Right,' he said, suddenly feeling hungry, 'tell me what you'd like and I'll go and pick it up.'

Alison handed him some notes, saying, 'Tara likes spring rolls and chilli beef. Get a couple of chicken dishes, some Special Fried Rice and some mixed vegetables and we can share.'

'Are you certain I can't contribute?' Stan asked.

'I'm an independent woman,' Alison stressed.

'I had noticed,' Stan replied, giving her a lingering look.

An hour and a half later, the empty cartons, piled up neatly on the coffee table in the middle of the living room, were all that remained of the meal, which had been devoured to the last grain of rice. Tara was all smiles and laughter, the incident earlier in the day having been completely forgotten.

'Would anyone like some more tea?' the teenager offered, grabbing the empty pot.

'It's all right, I'll go,' Alison said, getting unsteadily to her feet.

'Looks like she had too much to drink,' Tara giggled when Alison was out of earshot.

'I think you're right,' Stan answered, feeling mellow himself from the half-carafe of sake he had consumed. 'To save her driving home, perhaps she should stay over in the spare room tonight,' he proposed.

'That would be great. We can have breakfast together tomorrow. I'll make scrambled eggs!' Tara was excited. 'It's a shame Alison is going away this weekend, or she could stay here with us. And with Grandpa coming on Sunday, we could be a family again,' she said wistfully, for a moment reverting to the childlike state she had been fighting so hard against.

Just then, Alison arrived with the tea.

'What have you two been speaking about when I was out of the room?'

'Nothing much, just that Daddy suggested you should stay here tonight,' Tara said. 'Right, I've got some homework to catch up on. See you in the morning.' Kissing her father and then throwing her arms around Alison, the girl who overnight had become a young woman, trotted upstairs to her bedroom.

'So, what do you say?' Stan said, inviting Alison to join him on the settee.

'If I didn't know you better, I would take it as some sort of a proposal,' Alison remarked, now fully alert.

'Well, maybe we should give it a try?' Stan replied.

'Stan, you know as well as I do that it wouldn't work.'

'Why's that?' he asked, sounding disappointed.

'I was the one who met you first, if you remember, but you only had eyes for Carol. She was going out with that chap, what's his name? You know, the one whose father owned a dog stadium in East London.'

'Charles Fisher,' Stan replied.

'He's the one. A real rough diamond – and there were quite a few others like that. Carol always had a lot of admirers but she wanted someone more refined. So the fact that I might have been available at that time didn't matter. You didn't take the bait.' Alison looked mock-reproachful.

'I don't suppose I can use not being properly adept at reading the signs as an excuse in my favour?'

Alison laughed. 'Thanks for the offer, but I think I'm safe to drive home,' she said, and went to get her coat. 'I'll call you tomorrow. Just keep a close eye on Tara. She really does need you.'

Stan tried to analyse his feelings towards the woman who had just left. It wasn't that he found her unattractive, although she had always been a bit too boyish for his liking. And it was perfectly understandable for his daughter to look on her as a ready-made replacement for her mother; for all intents and purposes, that was exactly what Alison had become since Carol died. But Stan knew, deep down, it was not a good idea. What was also clear, however, was that he was ready for a new woman in his life.

5

At midday on the following Sunday, there was a ring on the doorbell. Seeing the Rolls-Royce enter the drive, Tara had leaped downstairs to open the door to her grandfather.

'Hello, my little princess!' the man bellowed, striding into the house that he hadn't entered for over three months. 'I've brought you a present. If you don't like it, I'll change it for another one. Plenty more where they came from.'

'What is it?' the girl asked expectantly.

'Better open it and you'll find out.'

Her hands working feverishly, Tara tore open the bright red wrapping and took out an expensive leather handbag. Her eyes lit up.

'Chanel!' she cried. 'That was Mummy's favourite.'

'Glad you like it. It's the real thing, you know, not one of those Petticoat Lane knock-offs.'

'I love it. Thank you, Grandpa,' she beamed, giving him a hug.

'Now then, young lady, why don't you go and make me a cup of coffee while I have a word with your father. I take it he is here and not out playing golf with those posh mates of his?'

Tara let out a giggle as she looked around and saw her father walking down the stairs.

'Morning, Ben,' Stan called across to his father-in-law, who seemed to have aged considerably since the last time they had seen each other. The bags under Ben's eyes had become more pronounced and his face had taken on a sickly grey colour. Despite his upbeat demeanour, Stan suspected that it was purely a front to disguise his inner turmoil.

He had heard the old man arrive but thought it best to allow his daughter a few moments alone with her grandfather.

'You wanted to talk to me,' Stan said, taking Ben into the lounge.

Just as they were about to start their meeting, Tara arrived with a steaming cup of black coffee and a plate of biscuits. Slung across her shoulder was the handbag that had just been given to her.

'Look, Daddy, see what Grandpa has brought me,' she said, thrilled with her gift.

'You just need a pair of high-heeled shoes to match and you'll have all the boys chasing after you,' Ben remarked.

Stan forced a smile, attempting to hide his disapproval of the encouragement given to his daughter to grow up so quickly.

'Young Tara here's going to be a real beauty, you mark my words, just like her moth . . .' Ben stopped himself as the image of his daughter flashed through his mind. The profound sadness in his eyes was pitiful to behold. Then, almost as quickly, he snapped out of it. The colour returned to his face as he commenced on the main reason for his visit.

'Right, let's get down to business. So, how much do you want for them?' he said, leaning forward in a negotiation-like pose.

'Sorry, I'm not with you,' Stan replied.

'The shares in my company – how much?' There was a note of aggression in his voice which Stan found disconcerting.

'I really don't know. I mean, I didn't expect . . .'

'That I would want to buy them back? Look at this way, son: what good is your twenty-five per cent to you? No one wants a minority share in a private company. You've got no control, no entitlement to be a director, nothing else that could possibly be of use to you. It's not as if you couldn't do with the money, so I'd be doing you a favour by taking them off you.'

Seeing any prospect of joining the business vanish, Stan pondered for a moment on what to do next.

'Ben, I'll have to think about it,' he replied finally, wondering who he should go to for advice.

'Sure. Take as long as you like. As I said, they're no use to anyone apart from me. Oh, and by the way, I'm going to sue the specialists who treated Carol. I trust I can count on you for support?' The old man got up, a look of satisfaction on his round face, confident that he had got his own way.

'Right, I'm off. Give that granddaughter of mine a big kiss. I'll be in touch about the other thing,' he said, plucking his coat off the banister in the hall. 'I'm not going to let those bastards get away with it. I've already got the best counsel in medical negligence looking into it,' he said sternly, letting himself out of the house.

Now that Carol had died, Stan thought, it was as if Ben wanted nothing more to do with him. It was also clear that he felt deeply aggrieved that her shares in the company had passed to him. No wonder he felt that he should claim any rights attached to them. Their relationship, tenuous at the best of times, had only kept going because Stan was the father of Ben's sole grandchild.

No doubt the old man wanted to buy him out at a cheap price, but Stan had no intention of being dispensed with that easily. He had already decided: even if Ben Miller didn't want him involved, he was just going to have to put up with Stanley Rose's name remaining on a quarter of his company's share certificates.

As for taking legal action against the doctors, Stan found the whole matter absurd. Nothing the hard-working and dedicated medics might or might not have done would bring Carol back. Furthermore, the prospect of a lengthy legal battle to establish liability was not something Stan wanted any part in.

It was time for him to move forward and get on with his life, both for his and for Tara's sake. He was certain that Carol would have wanted it so.

6

The weather at the beginning of June had turned warmer after a very wet spring. Stan was in good spirits, getting dressed to go out. Tara said she was quite happy to be at home with Inge and had invited a friend from school to sleep over. So his conscience was clear.

It was his second date of the week. Not sufficiently put off by the first – with Eva, a waitress at the local pub that he always thought he fancied until he discovered she smoked like a trooper and couldn't put a sentence together – he had asked Dina out on a date. She was the petite blonde divorcée who ran the beauty parlour that Carol used to frequent and with whom he had always enjoyed a flirtatious relationship.

It was 11 p.m. by the time Stan and his date walked out of the renowned Bell restaurant in Aylesbury and got back to their car, a little worse for wear thanks to the bottle of Pouilly-Fuissé they had drunk during dinner.

'Are you sure you're all right to drive?' Dina asked.

'I'm fine. Don't worry, I'll get you home in one piece.'

'Shame,' the woman replied, smiling seductively. Then, leaning towards him, revealing her ample cleavage, she whispered in his ear, 'Do you think they might have a room?'

Needing no further encouragement, Stan kissed Dina

passionately on the lips, while he began moving a hand deftly up her leg. Feeling her warm breath on the back of his neck, inviting him to go further, he knew this was what he had been waiting for, all this long time. Under the cover of darkness, in a quiet country lane, the couple began frantically removing their clothes, their bodies aching for each other, when suddenly a mobile phone rang.

'Sod it!' Stan swore under his breath, seeing his home number on the screen. 'What is it, Tara?' he said, annoyed at being interrupted.

'It is not Tara, it is Inge,' the au pair replied, sounding stressed.

'Yes, Inge, what's the matter?'

'I was in my room and when I went downstairs to see if Tara wanted to have some supper, she wasn't there. Please, it's not my fault!'

'I thought she said Emma was staying the night?'

There was no response.

Stan pondered for a moment. It was obvious that his daughter had fabricated the entire story about her friend sleeping over and like a fool, he'd fallen for it.

'I'm on my way home,' he announced. The moment lost, he pulled up his trousers and started the car. 'Dina, I'm sorry about that,' he said, turning to his date, but it was to no avail. She had fallen fast asleep in the seat next to him. Stan accelerated away, feeling disgruntled that an evening that was showing so much promise had been put an end to so abruptly.

Despite his best efforts, trying to find the way back to London on unlit country roads meant they were reduced to a crawl. So completely focused on his daughter were his thoughts that he failed to see the blue flashing lights of a police car in his driver's mirror; it had been following him for the last five miles.

Stan pulled into a lay-by and wound down his window.

'Evening, sir,' a fresh-faced policeman said, peering into the car. 'Were you aware that you were driving at twenty miles an hour in the middle of a dual carriageway?'

'No, I'm sorry I wasn't. It was dark and . . .' Stan stuttered.

'Been on a night out, have we, sir?'

'Yes,' Stan replied nervously.

'Had a few drinks as well, I suspect?' the officer remarked.

'A glass or so at dinner, that's all,' Stan lied.

'Surprised if it was only a few, by the look of the young lady,' the young man commented, leering at the half-naked woman in the passenger seat who was still fast asleep. 'What do you reckon, Kev?' he said, addressing an older colleague who had remained behind.

'It's up to you, Rob. But if it was me, I'd breathalyse him.'

'Sir, please would you get out of the car,' the younger one said.

Now Stan was really worried. Obediently, he opened the door and followed the policeman over to a clearing.

'Read that number-plate for us,' the officer said, pointing to the stationary police car, twenty feet away.

'PLN 560 L,' Stan read out without any trouble.

'And show me your licence.'

Stan reached into his jacket pocket for his wallet and passed the document to the policeman, who shone his torch on it and then swiftly returned it.

'All right, sir, we'll let you off this time,' the older officer called Kev said, 'but make sure you keep to the proper speed next time. Slow driving on a major road is an offence.'

Just then, Stan's mobile rang again.

'Sorry, I must go, Officer, my car's in the phone!' he blabbered, striding back to his vehicle, but sufficiently out of earshot from the policeman, who hadn't noticed his faux pas.

Ignoring the last call, he jumped in the car next to his snoozing passenger and set off at a decent speed. Forty-five minutes later, he dropped Dina at her door in Stanmore, by which time she was wide awake but unsurprisingly non-committal as to whether they could see each other again. He then drove the five miles back to Hampstead, wondering what he was going to be confronted with next, before the night was over.

He certainly didn't expect to find Brian from next door parading up and down in the front garden in his pyjamas.

'Is anything wrong?' Stan asked, approaching his neighbour.

'Just those youngsters making a bit of a racket,' the other man replied, but without any animosity. 'I came outside for a bit of peace and quiet.'

'I'm really sorry for the disturbance,' Stan said, peering through his window at the large gathering that appeared to have taken over the house.

Once inside, he found the whole of the ground floor occupied by a number of young girls and boys whom he'd never seen before, some lolling around on chairs drinking cans of beer while others sat cross-legged on the carpet, passing around a cigarette with a suspiciously pungent aroma. Where the bloody hell was Inge?

'Tara, a word, please,' he said, addressing his daughter, who was lying on her back, a half-discarded bottle of vodka by her side.

'Yeah, what is it?' she mumbled, looking up at her father with a glazed expression.

Stan felt himself lose control. 'Pull yourself together,' he shouted, 'and get these friends of yours out of here!'

Gradually, the group of young people, showing the same lack of urgency as being moved down the carriage on a crowded tube train, gathered up their things and shuffled out of the house.

'Tara, what's going on? Where is Inge? I need an explanation,' Stan demanded, slamming the front door behind the last of the visitors.

'She's left for good,' the teenager replied, not the least fazed by her father. She was now sitting on a chair with her arms folded. 'When I got back tonight, I found her packing to leave. Marlon came to get her in the car. She said to tell you that I don't need a babysitter any more and that she's bored as there's nothing for her to do these days. So she's going to live with Marlon.'

'I see.' Stan should have seen this coming – but how irresponsible of the young woman, to leave Tara in this situation. 'But how about the fact that you lied, letting me believe you were with Emma, when you were gallivanting around heaven knows where with that rabble you invited into *my* house without permission!'

'It's not just yours – Mummy owned half. And anyway, she told me Grandpa paid for most of it,' his daughter sneered.

Stan realised that he had a fight on his hands. But if this was a test of wills, then his daughter needed to be told once and for all that she couldn't do what she liked and that, while they were living under the same roof, she would have to obey certain rules. Or, irrespective of what Alison had said, perhaps he would have no choice but to send her away to school.

'You're not even eighteen yet,' he ranted. 'I had no idea you'd already started drinking and smoking.'

'Didn't know you cared,' the teenager answered insolently. Then: 'I'm going to bed,' she said, and turned her back on her father.

'Hold on. What's *that* supposed to mean – that I don't care?' her father called after her.

'Seems you're only interested in meeting other women,' the girl said bitterly. 'How many times has it been this week?'

'Tara, that's not fair,' Stan said, following her out into the hall.

'Losing the most important person in my life – that's what's not fair!' the teenager screamed, tears running down her face.

Stan felt terrible. He went over to his daughter and took her in his arms.

'I'm sorry, you're right. I have been extremely selfish. But I genuinely thought things were getting better. Alison told me that you were feeling more settled at school and that your end-of-term grades were much improved.'

'I hate that place! You don't know what it's like hearing the other girls spouting off about how wonderful their mothers are and what new clothes they've bought them. Would *you* like to go to a school like that?'

'I had no idea it was that bad.' Stan backtracked. 'Perhaps I could get you in somewhere else?'

'They're all going to be the bloody same!' Tara cried out. 'I can't wait to leave and go out to work.'

'There'll be plenty of time for that after university. It is what Mummy would have wanted,' Stan stressed, attempting to impose his authority.

'Why, when she didn't go to uni herself?' the girl protested.

'Which is exactly the reason why she made me promise to send you,' Stan countered, having the feeling that he was at the beginning of a lengthy negotiation.

'I'll think about it, so long as I can study journalism,' Tara responded, sounding more conciliatory.

'We'll see, but this hasn't got anything to do with what happened tonight,' Stan reminded his daughter.

'I am so sorry that I ruined your evening,' Tara said sarcastically. 'Anyway, I tried calling you to tell you not to bother to come back, but there was no answer.'

So intent had he been on getting home, Stan now realised that the evening with Dina might have been salvaged, after all. Still, it was too late to make amends. He sighed, suddenly feeling disenchanted with the whole dating process.

'Who was it this time anyway?' his daughter enquired.

'I'll tell you if you tell me what you were doing with those people you invited over here.'

'Sounds like a reasonable deal, but I need to eat something first. Drinking on an empty stomach is not a great idea,' Tara said, heading into the kitchen.

It was two in the morning by the time they had finished talking. In the past, a reprimand followed by an avowal of *I promise not to do it again* had been the normal course of events. This was a completely different state of affairs, taking the form of a discussion between two adults – two equals. In the six months since her mother had died, Tara Rose had grown up.

Stan knew he'd probably overreacted, but the incident had jolted him into action. He didn't want to risk Tara going further off the rails. With the end of the school term in a few weeks' time, perhaps going on a summer holiday together would help cement the relationship with his daughter?

Her reaction to his dating Dina, however, wasn't at all what he had anticipated; it turned out that she had known the whole time that Dina had been Carol's beautician. What's more, one of the young fellows at the party was Dina's son Ollie – a fact that both youngsters found highly amusing.

Surprisingly, Tara hadn't mentioned Alison in weeks. Although the Scotswoman ensured that the Roses' home continued to run smoothly and still kept in regular contact by telephone, Alison had no wish to smother her ward and began keeping more of a distance, whilst not disappearing from their lives altogether.

The other matter that had cooled his relationship with his wife's best friend was because Alison had sided with Ben over taking action against the specialists. Stan's refusal to co-operate had put an end to any rapprochement with his father-in-law. What was worse, Ben had stopped his Sunday visits, effectively punishing his granddaughter, as if Tara were a party to thwarting him over his private obsession.

Stan could see now, that to both Alison and Ben, Carol was still at the forefront of their minds, and taking legal action was a last attempt at keeping her memory alive.

7

Stan lay back on his hard mattress, while a mosquito buzzed annoyingly above his head. It was his birthday today and he was feeling irritable. The prickly heat that had plagued him from the very first day of the holiday had got worse in the August humidity and was troubling him badly this evening.

Tara had heard about Clique 21 from some of her friends. With resorts scattered over southern Europe, she and Stan had selected one in Sardinia that catered for families.

Lugging their own suitcases to what was described in the brochure as 'a comfortable chalet', they found themselves instead in a basic hut with a stone floor for their two-week stay. Equipped with an ineffectual shower that dribbled water and a toilet that needed flushing half a dozen times after use, it certainly wasn't the Milano Marittima of his childhood. Not that the food was at all bad. It was just that you all sat at long refectory tables, placed next to a different person at each meal, and were expected to make conversation with them. It wasn't his kind of thing.

Stan had to keep reminding himself that they weren't here for his benefit. However, the bonding that he had anticipated with his daughter hadn't materialised. On the contrary, apart from breakfast they only saw each other fleetingly during the rest of the day. But then, Tara had always managed to make friends easily and she loved all the water sports that were laid on free of charge.

The sun had begun to go down over the Mediterranean. Stan looked at the two greetings cards on the dressing table from Alison and his daughter, and was suddenly filled with sadness. He couldn't remember the last birthday when he hadn't been with Carol. It still seemed such a blur.

Pulling himself together, he took a fresh change of clothes out of his suitcase, stood under the spurting shower and prepared for dinner. Tara had reluctantly agreed to eat with him, so long as she could go off afterwards. Of course, he didn't object, even if it meant sitting on his own at the bar as he had done every evening for the last week.

The dining area, lit up with Roman torches, was already packed with people tucking into huge piles of food. Being fully inclusive in the price of their holiday, they were determined to take full advantage of whatever was on offer. Stan spotted his daughter, in conversation with an athletically built youth with short curly hair.

'Oh, hello!' Tara called out, obviously embarrassed at seeing her father. 'This is François – he's from Paris.'

Stan smiled, taking his place opposite the boy who appeared to have captured his daughter's attention.

'François teaches water skiing,' Tara announced proudly. 'He said that I'm ready to try mono tomorrow.'

'Tara, she is a natural, n'est-ce pas?' the instructor confirmed, his mouth full of barbecue chicken. 'She must continue to practise and next, who knows – maybe the Olympics! It is not impossible.'

'François! You're making fun of me,' his protégée protested.

'I had no idea,' Stan intervened. 'She's never tried it before.'

'That's because we only ever went to Jersey and the sea was always too rough,' Tara reminded him.

'You've not been to Italy or the Cote d'Azur, Tara? This is your first time? Ah, it cannot be true,' François tutted, refilling all three wine glasses from the terracotta jug in the middle of the table.

'I'm going to get some food,' Stan said, and left them to it. He went over to the buffet tables that had been laid out in a large U shape and joined the hungry throng, many of whom were queuing for a second time. Looking across at his daughter, at ease in the company she fitted into so effortlessly, he had mixed emotions. Naturally, he should have been happy that she was enjoying herself. She was obviously more resilient than he had imagined and, in truth, far more so than himself. But then he recalled that he was always miserable on his birthday.

He began to think about what he was going to do when he returned to London, but therein lay the problem. The stint doing the books for Howard had come to an end and now Stan had too much time on his hands – time in which to wallow in self-pity. Perhaps he should go back and gain his accountancy qualification, he mused. At least it would provide the financial security that he badly needed. The other thing he was going to do, he decided, was to get back in touch with Dina. He had only tried to contact her once after the fiasco of their first date, but she was in Dorset to attend her father's funeral.

His appetite restored, Stan went back to the table, more optimistic over his prospects. Tara had already finished her meal and appeared impatient to go off and find François.

Stan had spotted the boy slope away earlier, presumably to rejoin his colleagues at the water-ski school.

'You don't mind if I leave, do you, Daddy?'

'No, of course not. Go and enjoy yourself – but don't be too late,' he added automatically, starting on his dish of scampi Provençale.

'Happy Birthday – and don't *you* get too drunk!' Tara yelled, running off to find her instructor.

The brief exchange attracted the attention of a sun-tanned couple a few places away, who raised their glasses in his direction.

'We wish you Many Happy Returns,' a rotund man called out in a discernible German accent. His shirt was opened to the waist, revealing a hairy chest and heavy gold jewelry. 'Come and join us,' he beckoned.

Grateful for the offer, Stan moved down the wooden table.

'I'm Wolfgang and this is my wife Gretchen,' the fellow said, pointing to the flaxen-haired woman sitting opposite him and wearing a low-cut dress to display her full breasts.

'Stanley, pleased to meet you,' he said, shaking hands.

'You are from the UK?' Gretchen asked.

'From London,' Stan replied. 'And you?'

'We come from Munich. Do you know it?'

'No, I'm afraid not.'

'That's a pity. It's a fine city with the prettiest Frauleins in the whole of Germany,' Wolfgang declared, giving Stan a wink and openly eyeing up a curvaceous female a few feet away. 'And that was your daughter?' he went on to enquire.

'Yes, Tara,' Stan replied.

'She's young to have a boyfriend, *nein*?'

'He's just her water-ski instructor,' Stan answered defensively.

'Wolfgang!' his wife remonstrated. 'You must excuse my husband, Stanley. He becomes too familiar when he has had a few drinks. So, it's just the two of you here?' she asked, taking over the conversation.

'Yes, for two weeks,' Stan replied.

'And it's your first time at Clique 21?'

'We thought we'd give it a try.'

'This is the best village,' Wolfgang beamed. 'It's our fifth time.'

'I didn't know what to expect but Tara appears to be enjoying it,' Stan replied.

'And you, I suspect, not so much?' Gretchen pried.

'We came mainly for my daughter,' Stan said.

'It's important to join in,' the woman said kindly. 'Wolfgang and I are, how you say, adventurous? We'll try anything. But for someone who is shy, yes, I can see that it can be quite difficult.'

She smiled warmly at him, then announced: 'So, now you will spend the evening with us. Have you been to the discotheque? The music's *wunderbar*!' She began humming an Elton John song that Stan vaguely recognised but couldn't name.

'That's very kind, but I'm a little tired, probably from too much sun, and dancing's not really my forte,' Stan said, trying to extricate himself.

'Nonsense, you'll come with me,' Gretchen insisted. Whereupon she seized Stanley by the arm, leaving her husband in deep conversation with an attractive young Dutch woman.

As Stan followed her down a steep path that led to the

sea, he could hear the sound of loud music and laughter in the distance. The bar, which during the day was no more than a kiosk with a thatched roof, providing refreshments for the numerous activities along the two-mile beach, now looked completely different. With its low-level seating and candle-lit tables, the place had been miraculously transformed into a nightclub. A bare-chested young man wearing headphones sat perched on a raised platform, busily organising the evening's play-lists.

Praying that he wouldn't run into his daughter, Stan and the woman who had befriended him blended in with the mostly young people on the makeshift dance floor, gyrating to the Rolling Stones' 'Brown Sugar'. After another couple of similarly highly charged Gloria Gaynor and Donna Summer tunes, Stan and Gretchen joined the crowds of revellers at the bar.

'You just need to relax,' Gretchen said, sipping her vodka and orange.

Stan was drinking from a cold bottle of Peroni beer – a welcome relief on a particularly sticky evening. He couldn't remember the last time he had been to a club in London. It was probably Tramps in the West End when he had started going out with Carol. Although it was always a good place to impress young women, in truth, like now he felt awkward and couldn't wait to leave.

'You know, you remind me of someone,' his companion remarked. 'An actor.'

'I have been told there is a similarity with Omar Sharif,' Stan said casually, just wanting to finish his drink so he could go to bed.

'*Nein!* Another, also with your hair and a moustache . . .' pausing while she tried to remember. Then after a few seconds, a broad smile breaking on her face, she exclaimed, 'I know, it's Tom Selleck! Have you seen him in *Magnum*? He was very good.' She lowered her voice. 'But you are far more handsome.'

'No, I can't say I have, but thank you for the compliment,' Stan replied, feeling uneasy at the intense way the woman was looking at him.

'Stanley, do you not like me?' Gretchen said suddenly, brushing her thigh against his.

'Yes, yes, of course,' he stuttered, moving his leg away, wondering again why it was taking so long for her husband to appear. It was obvious that the woman had had far too much to drink, which explained her coming on to him.

'You know Wolfgang doesn't mind,' she said, placing his hand on her large breasts. 'Sometimes he likes to join in also. We have – how do you say – a very modern outlook on marriage.'

Stan froze. The innocent drink that he had imagined had turned out to be nothing of the sort. He'd been set up! Suddenly he had visions of Wolfgang waiting in the nude for his wife to return with her 'catch' for the night. He needed to get away.

'Gretchen, thank you for your company, but I really need to go and find my daughter,' Stan said firmly, separating himself from the woman. As he hurried off, his last glimpse was of her chatting undeterred to another couple who had just arrived at the bar.

Out of breath from the steep incline, he eventually arrived back at their cabin. Not expecting his daughter to be back, he let himself in and switched on the light.

'Daddy,' a voice whimpered, 'I want to go home.' Tara was already in bed and her eyes were bloodshot from crying.

'Whatever's the matter, sweetheart? You seemed to be having such a good time,' Stan said, going over to his daughter.

'François is a pig! I waited for him for over an hour and then I saw him with that girl from the ski school. They were kissing and he'd forgotten all about me.' She burst into tears.

Stan sighed. 'I'm sure he's a nice young man but remember, it's just a job as far as he's concerned. Next week, there will be another group of new arrivals – that's just how it is in a place like this. And he is probably quite a bit older than you.'

'He told me that he'd just broken up with his girlfriend. He said that he really liked me. Anyway, nineteen's not too old. There were six years between Mummy and you.'

Even though they had only known each other a brief time, it was clear that the instructor had broken her heart. Stan sat down on the bed and put his arms around his daughter to comfort her. It was then he recalled the crush he had had on Judy, the American girl who had taught him to water-ski in the South of France, when he was a young boy. The difference then was that he was ten and she was twenty-three!

Tara sat up and blew her nose. She was already looking better. 'And did you have a nice birthday, Daddy?' she asked.

'You know me, I never worry too much about these things.'

'That German couple at dinner did seem very friendly.'

'Yes, they were,' Stan replied carefully, wanting to forget all about the bizarre episode.

'I ran into the man on the way back and he asked me to mention to you that he was having a party. Theirs is the chalet right at the end. You should have gone, Daddy.'

No way! Stan thought. Aloud he said, 'I'm glad I came back here,' grateful that he'd been there for his daughter in her hour of need and also for his own lucky escape.

Tara placed the last layer of tissue paper on top of the neatly folded clothes and zipped up the case. She had insisted on doing the packing for both of them, carrying on the practice from her late mother.

Stan settled the modest extras bill and boarded the coach with Tara back to the airport, completely unaware of the message for him to call home urgently, pinned on the communal noticeboard outside the office.

The holiday had eventually achieved what he had intended, a closer relationship with his daughter. For their last week, they had been inseparable. Stan was always there on the back of the boat when she finally mastered the art of balancing on one ski. Meals were taken together until the last couple of days, when an Italian boy befriended her. François had been all but forgotten, her affections now bestowed upon Luigi, a serious-looking young man from a Catholic family outside Rome, who had given Tara a present of a Latin Bible.

Tara knew she was Jewish, but up until that moment, it had never been a point of discussion. Now, all of a sudden – and in a move which Stan suspected was purely for the benefit of her latest beau – she wanted to know more about the other religions, about faith, and whether Carol, from whom her Jewishness was inherited, held any such beliefs.

It was almost as if the girl needed to strike some kind of a deal with the Almighty, Stan thought sadly, implying that if she became a better person, it might somehow bring her mother back.

8

Three days earlier

The ambulance, its siren screaming, sped away from the quiet West London street, heading to the Hammersmith Hospital. Inside, two male paramedics were trying to revive their patient, a man in his early seventies who had suffered a major heart attack.

A neighbour had happened to pass on her way to the shops and spotted him slumped against the steering-wheel of his Rolls-Royce, parked in his driveway. After dialling 999 for an ambulance, she had identified the man as Benjamin Miller, and was also able to provide the contact details Ben had once given her, of his next of kin, his friend Alison in London and his companion in Broadstairs.

The two paramedics did what they could for the dangerously ill man.

'He's not responding,' said the older one. 'We got to him too late. I daresay he had a history of heart disease.'

'Thank God the car was stationary,' the younger one commented, 'or it could have been a lot worse.' He hated it when they lost someone and the ambulance became a hearse.

'We'll have our break when we get there, son,' his colleague said to cheer him up. 'If you're lucky, I'll treat you to a Kit-Kat.'

Richard Jeffrey returned to his office from lunch and cast his eye down the afternoon's appointments. A heavily lined face and pebble-lensed glasses made him look a good deal older than his forty-one years, and the mild disposition he displayed in public concealed an utterly ruthless streak towards anybody who crossed him.

Even trying to get emotional about Ben Miller didn't come easy. The funeral that morning had gone off smoothly enough. Since the old man had no family apart from his granddaughter and useless son-in-law, who had conveniently shied away from the responsibility of organising the event, it was left to Richard to make all the arrangements. Richard had known Ben Miller for well over twenty years and Ben, more than anyone else, had helped to get the firm Richard had co-founded with a friend, Nigel Lowndes, off the ground, explaining that he was looking for a firm of solicitors who wouldn't cheat him.

The three of them hit it off immediately and before long, Lowndes Jeffrey were handling all of Miller Investments' business, which enabled them to move to new premises more in keeping with their growing reputation as a specialist property firm.

Their relationship with Ben was close, and Richard was confident it was only a matter of time before Ben suggested that he got to know his daughter, Carol, with a view to becoming the man's son-in-law and heir. He couldn't have been more wrong. When he threw out hints in that direction they were met with a comprehensive rebuff, with

Ben making it crystal clear that Carol was completely out of bounds.

The fact that the beautiful Miss Miller was beyond his reach was galling enough, but for Ben to have preferred that idiot Stanley Rose over him was something that Richard Jeffrey would neither forgive nor forget. True, Rose was a good-looking fellow from an established family, Richard couldn't dispute that – but Stan had been born into money, whereas he and Nigel, two working-class lads from a housing estate in Erith, South London, had had to work their way up from the bottom with a modest loan of £1000 from the NatWest Bank.

The injustice rankled. Nevertheless, in his professional life Richard Jeffrey had learned to be patient. When the time was right, the Millers and the Roses would pay dearly for the way he had been discarded.

Now, not a year later, the father had gone the same way as the daughter before him. As Richard pondered on this, the phone rang on his desk, informing him that his three o'clock appointment had arrived. There was no point dwelling on it any further, he decided. Probate had to be obtained, and as executors to Ben Miller's estate, an orderly disposal of assets would need to be conducted for the substantial amount of inheritance tax that would have to be paid. Lowndes Jeffrey would then take advantage of the 'instalment option', ensuring that the firm would carry on charging fees for the next ten years.

Stanley Rose was shown into the plush boardroom on the first floor of the opulent Mayfair premises.

'Stanley, it's always a pleasure,' Richard greeted him smoothly. 'I'm sorry for your loss – I gather it came as quite a shock. Please make yourself comfortable. Would you like some tea or coffee?' he offered, trying not to show the secret contempt he felt for the visitor.

'No, I'm fine, thanks,' Stan replied, just wanting to get on with the meeting to which he'd been so abruptly summoned. Although the two had only met sporadically over the years, his impressions of Richard Jeffrey were not favourable. The fellow had the supercilious attitude typical of so many other professionals. But as his late father-in-law's closest adviser, and now that they were going to be running the property company together, of necessity they would have to establish a good working relationship.

A tearful Alison had been waiting at their home to break the news when Stan and Tara arrived back from Sardinia. She and Ben had seen a lot of each other since Carol passed away, she told them, and she had actually been at his house having dinner the night before he died. Ben had apparently spent the whole evening talking about his daughter in the present tense as if Carol were there next to him.

'How's young Tara taking it?' Jeffrey enquired now. 'I know how fond she was of her grandfather.'

'It's been a tough couple of days,' Stan allowed, choosing not to go into details. Seeing those she loved being taken away one by one, he'd expected Tara to be devastated, or at least angry. Instead, the self-control she exercised left him feeling thoroughly ashamed of his own emotional reaction to the loss of the last remaining connection to his late wife. Stranger still was her not putting up a fight, when he suggested that going to another funeral might prove too traumatic. She had willingly gone over to stay with Grandma Elaine, since there was never any question, even in death, of his mother deviating from her principles and burying the hatchet so far as Ben Miller was concerned.

'Very well. I suppose we should get on with it,' the solicitor said, giving a cursory look at the documents in front of him. 'The will is quite straightforward. Since Carol predeceased her father, the major part of the estate has been left in trust for Tara until she reaches the age of eighteen. Then there's the house in Warwick Avenue Maida Vale, a fairly large portfolio of stocks and shares, and the cottage in Kent. I imagine you're looking at a value of around ten million. Although the shares in the company will have to be agreed.'

'By whom?' Stan wanted to know.

'The District Valuer, regarding the properties. Then it will be a long-drawn-out discussion with the Capital Taxes offices, I'm afraid.'

'Sounds expensive,' Stan remarked.

'Can't be helped. These things just have to take their course,' Jeffrey said and shrugged dismissively.

'What can I do in the meantime?' Stan asked.

'Well, it wouldn't do any harm to have another trustee on board. As you'll appreciate, although I was very fond of your father-in-law, I can only devote so much of the firm's time to the estate.'

'Yes, I understand, which is why I . . .' Stan began.

'So why don't you familiarise yourself with the portfolio,' the solicitor butted in. 'I'm sure you'll soon find your way around. Obviously, we'll have to keep the chauffeur and a few of the maintenance chaps on for the time being. Oh, and here is the last set of figures,' he added, handing over a bound copy of the company accounts. 'You already know Stephen Fink from Kramers the Accountants, I believe. That should be enough to get on with.' He then stood up, indicating that the meeting was over.

'I'll let you know when we receive probate,' he said briskly. 'In the meantime, look after that daughter of yours. She's going to be an extremely wealthy young lady one day.' There was more than a hint of resentment in his words.

'Yes, yes, I will,' the visitor answered, dazed by the huge numbers involved and trying to absorb the revelation that his 25 per cent holding was worth a staggering £2.5million.

Stan was feeling ebullient as he stepped out of the building into the late-August sunshine. The meeting had gone well – very well indeed, he decided. Even though Richard Jeffrey had carved out the prime position for himself, there was no disputing that the company belonged to *his* family – the Roses – and in the not too distant future he, Stanley Rose, would be in full control of it.

9

Stan walked around the West London showroom a second time, waiting for Howard Barnet to finish with his customer, a stunning-looking woman with long black hair who, unless he was imagining it, kept looking in his direction.

After the meeting with Richard Jeffrey a couple of weeks ago, he felt sufficiently buoyant to ditch the Renault and purchase a new car, a model that would reflect his newfound wealth. He also knew that there was no better place to come than the swish West End showroom of his friend Howard Barnet. Looking admiringly at the classic Aston Martin DB6 and Ferrari Daytona, Stan noticed that the remainder of the cars on show were predominantly German. There was no question that Howard had balls. The value of the stock alone, Stan estimated, must have been in the region of a million pounds.

'Stan, won't be a minute, chummy,' Howard called across, placing the customer's cheque in his pocket as a man in overalls drove up and parked outside in a gleaming white Mercedes coupé.

'Thanks, Jackie,' Howard told the dark-haired woman. 'I'm sure you'll be happy with her – you've got yourself a great deal.' Relieved at the first bit of business he'd been able to conclude for a month, he then handed the customer a large envelope, saying, 'Your receipt, service book and spare set of keys are in there.' After which, he escorted the attractive female to her new vehicle.

'That's what I call a classy bird,' he said with a smirk on his face, returning to Stan.

'Who is she?' Stan asked, watching the woman drive confidently away.

'Forget it, mate, you couldn't afford her – not unless you've suddenly come into some money.'

'That's the reason I'm here,' Stan said smugly.

'Really?' The car dealer cocked an eyebrow in disbelief.

'Don't sound so surprised. Things have just taken a turn for the better,' Stan revealed, glancing again at a sleek two-door *coupé* with pop-up headlights.

'Well, that's different,' Howard allowed, smelling another sale. 'Lovely, isn't she?' he remarked. 'Doesn't come much better than the BMW 8 series.' He looked over Stan's shoulder. 'That baby has got the lot – V12 engine, leather upholstery. It's the best ride I've ever had and that's saying something.'

'I assume you're talking about the car?' Stan jested.

'No, your old woman,' the car salesman came back, quick as a flash. Then, realising what he'd said, 'Stan, I'm sorry,' he gabbled. 'I didn't mean . . .'

'That's OK,' Stan replied, not taking offence. 'So how much do you want for it? I'm prepared to throw in the Renault if it helps.'

'Not if you don't want me to charge you more,' Howard said jovially, quickly recovering from his tactless remark. 'Cash or are you going for finance?'

'Say, half and half?' Stan answered.

'The list price on that beauty is . . .' Howard murmured,

running his eye down the folded piece of paper he had just retrieved from the inside pocket of his jacket.

'Howard, cut the crap. What's the best deal you can do on it?'

'Twenty-five grand down and the balance over four years.'

'That sounds reasonable.' Stan put out his hand.

'Aren't you going to want to test-drive it first?'

'Yes, of course, so long as I can be away by three. I want it in the drive by the time Tara comes back from school. Hopefully it might cheer her up a bit.'

'Ryan says she's taking her grandfather's loss really badly,' the man in the shiny suit sighed. 'You're aware our kids are quite friendly? Only, when I mentioned you were coming in, he wanted me to find out if she's all right because he hasn't seen her around for a few weeks.'

'Tara has been quite withdrawn lately,' Stan explained casually. 'But you know what teenagers are like; can never understand what's going on inside their heads. Tell Ryan I'm sure she'll be in contact soon,' was all he said, the subject dismissed without further thought or discussion before turning his attention again to the BMW.

Later, the paperwork completed, Stan drove off in the luxurious new sports car he had just purchased. Stopping at the traffic lights at Hanger Lane, he felt in his pocket for the business card Howard had given him with the telephone number of the woman in the showroom. He should have been feeling upbeat, but all that was going through his mind were Howard's last words: *You do know I was only joking about Carol, don't you?*

*

Richard Jeffrey glanced at his gold Rolex watch and started to dress. With a bit of luck, he could still make it back in time for his conference call at four. That was one of the perks of being senior partner at a West End firm of solicitors. No one dared object if you left the office for a couple of hours.

Just then, the woman with whom he had just finished making love sat up in the king-sized bed.

'I do hope your wife knows what you get up to in your lunch-hour,' she said.

'Why, does your girlfriend?' Jeffrey countered immediately.

There was a pause. 'How did you know?' Alison asked.

'What, that you liked women?'

'Well, I don't actually go around broadcasting it.'

'Let's just say I like to find out everything about those I get into bed with,' he divulged.

'And I believe in taking advantage of love wherever you can find it. Anyway, my girlfriend and I have an open relationship,' Alison replied candidly.

'That's not much of a compliment,' Jeffrey remarked, putting on his jacket.

'There's plenty more where that came from, if . . .' Alison teased, throwing back the covers and parting her long legs.

'Sounds like there's an implied condition somewhere?'

'Spoken like a true lawyer,' she sighed.

'All right, you'll get the instruction for the properties. I assume that *is* what you're after?'

'That's not very nice! Please don't make me out to be a cheap whore, and in any case, hadn't you better clear it with Stanley Rose now he's involved?'

'Firstly, my dear Alison, no one ever said you were

cheap and secondly, our boy Stanley is going to do exactly as he's told.'

'Richard, you're a right bastard, do you know that?'

'And an extremely clever one at that,' the solicitor added glibly, leaving the suite he'd hired for the afternoon and which had cost him next to nothing. The Gulf War, together with the spate of social unrest caused by the government's unpopular Poll Tax measures had put the dampeners on the tourist trade, and he didn't see any reason why he shouldn't take full advantage of the situation. The fact that it had got rid of Margaret Thatcher in the process was a definite plus since he couldn't stand the woman, but even that wasn't sufficient to lift the feeling of gloom that had descended on the capital. He actually had a great deal of sympathy with the protest marchers and, if things hadn't turned out differently, he might well have enjoyed looting those Oxford Street stores. But having worked his way out of the same shit-hole of a life, unlike those other poor bastards without a penny to rub together between them, he could afford to think that way.

Passing through Berkeley Square, Richard Jeffrey had good reason to feel pleased with himself. Having secured the services of the best estate agent in town – even if the means were slightly unconventional – he had guaranteed his firm the conveyancing work, the fees for which would pay for his holiday to the Caribbean to celebrate his fifteenth wedding anniversary. The other, more important part of his plan, was strictly private, but with the dirt he had already gathered on Alison Brown, it was only a matter of time before she helped him to secure what should already have become his.

10

Stan arrived home to find his daughter up in her room with the door closed and the curtains drawn.

'Sweetheart, it's the middle of the afternoon. Aren't you feeling well? Do you want me to call the doctor?' he asked, concerned.

'Leave me alone!' came the muffled response from under the covers.

'OK. Look, if you need anything, just let me know,' Stan replied, moving away, presuming that she'd soon be able to sleep off whatever was wrong.

Completely forgetting what Howard had said about his daughter's state of mind, he went along the hallway to his office, to look again at the list that he already knew by heart of the fifty freeholds that made up the company's £10 million portfolio. Never having ventured to that part of West London, his only previous exposure to the area was gained from the Notting Hill Carnival, held every August Bank Holiday. He still remembered his father, Arnold, sitting in front of the television, captivated by the costumes of the local West Indian community and particularly by their brand of jazz.

All but a handful of the properties were situated in the less salubrious part of Ladbroke Grove that ran north from the Westway flyover to the canal at Kensal Green – a multicultural area typified by street markets and small family businesses not dissimilar to New York's Lower East Side at the turn of the twentieth century. Living accommodation consisted predominantly of Victorian houses in various state of disrepair that had been converted into self-contained one- and two-bedroom flats. Over 50 per cent were occupied by rent-controlled tenants, some paying as little as £30 a week, which explained the relatively modest annual rent roll of £150,000.

Now he had been given the keys to the ground-floor office next to the tube station, and his hand was firmly on the pulse of the business, Stan intended to show Richard Jeffrey that he was fully up to the task of running his late father-in-law's company.

Going downstairs to the kitchen to get something to eat, Stan suddenly decided he'd go out for a pizza instead and bring something back for Tara for when she woke up. It was still light and would be an opportunity to take the BMW out for a spin to the High Street.

Getting behind the wheel of so much power, he found it exhilarating and worth every penny of the £50,000 price tag. He was lucky to find a parking space outside the restaurant but, seeing that there was a queue for tables, he ordered two medium-sized pizzas to take home. He was just about to place his order in the car, when he noticed that the rear offside wing had been badly scraped with green paint.

His heart sank. A brand new car, fresh out of the showroom, he couldn't believe it.

Stan hadn't noticed a group of yobs who had gathered menacingly on the pavement, talking loudly amongst themselves.

'Musta bin that plumber's van what parked behind you!' a young lad called over.

'No, it weren't. It were that bloke on the bike what went past,' another joined in, guffawing.

'Nah, I reckon that bit of fluff wiv the pushchair dunnit; saw her wiv me own eyes,' the smallest of them sniggered.

The raucous bunch then drifted slowly away. Suddenly, one of them turned around and gave Stan a V sign.

'Flash git!' he yelled. 'Next time, mate, you should be more careful where you park, c--t!'

Appalled that an act of vandalism should have occurred so near to where he lived, Stanley got back into the damaged vehicle. It was still only six o'clock. With a bit of luck he might be able to find a body-shop in the area that was still open. He'd go home and look in the *Yellow Pages*.

On parking outside the house, Stan discovered an agitated young man in a T-shirt and jeans standing on the front step. It was Ryan Barnet, Howard's sixteen-year-old son. He assumed the boy had come over to see his daughter, and Tara hadn't heard the bell.

'Hello, Ryan, I saw your dad earlier,' Stan said, opening the front door. 'Come in. You must excuse me, I've got to make an urgent call.' And he dashed past the lad into the house. 'Tara's in her bedroom – go up if you like.'

'Actually, Mr Rose, it was you I wanted to see,' the young man replied – to thin air.

Then: 'Damn! They're closed!' a voice cursed. And Stan reappeared clutching the *Yellow Pages* directory. 'Sorry, Ryan, what were you saying?'

'Tara's really not well,' the boy announced, seeming genuinely concerned, but Stan was oblivious, his mind on the damaged vehicle.

'I looked in at her before. She seemed all right – just said she wanted to sleep,' he told Ryan, hoping that another garage might still be open.

'I think something terrible is going to happen if she loses any more weight,' the young man fretted.

'Oh, I'm sure it's nothing serious. I've just been out to get her some dinner,' Stan replied casually.

'She hides it by wearing layers,' Ryan divulged. 'You see, she doesn't want anyone to know what she's up to.'

'We have supper together a few evenings a week. Admittedly she never eats that much,' Stan said more attentively, 'but there is always food in the house.' An awful thought crossed his mind. What if the money he gave to Mrs Gordon, their elderly cleaner, to do the shopping ended up in her pocket instead of their fridge? He now regretted that he had been so quick to take the chore away from Alison.

'For some reason she's got it into her head that she's fat.' Ryan looked imploringly at Stan. 'Tara needs help, Mr Rose, otherwise she could well end up like my Cousin Jules.'

'Why, what happened?' Stan enquired apprehensively, finally realising that he hadn't taken the situation seriously enough.

'I don't know exactly. She spent a week on a drip in hospital and nearly died. She'd been starving herself, you see – just like Tara. It's anorexia, and it can be fatal.'

'My God! Thank you, Ryan.' Stan went into a panic. He threw down the directory and rushed upstairs. Suddenly he had visions of how he used to get up in the middle of the night when Tara was a baby, to check that she was still breathing. He opened the door and ventured inside, relieved to see that his daughter was breathing peacefully and was deeply asleep.

He sat on her bed, cradling the sleeping girl in his arms, wondering how he could have been so stupid as to neglect the most important thing in his life.

By the time he emerged from his daughter's room, Ryan Barnet had already gone.

The next morning, Stan rose early after a restless night, the events of the previous evening churning over in his mind. When his daughter came out of her bedroom, he was surprised to discover her dressed and ready for school.

'How are you feeling?' he asked.

'Fine – why?' she replied, not bothering to look up.

'I was really worried about you. Howard's son dropped by, claiming that you've not been eating properly, and I just assumed . . .'

'I'm not anorexic, if that's what you are worried about,' Tara said, cutting Stan short. 'You don't want to listen to Ryan, he's an old woman.'

'He really does care about you.'

'Nice to know someone does.'

'What's that supposed to mean?'

'Put it this way, you haven't exactly been the paragon of concern. I mean, it doesn't put you in a particularly good light for my boyfriend to have to come over and tell my father that he should take notice because his daughter's fucking fading away!'

'Tara, let's not go into this again. You know I do everything I can. But you *are* looking too thin,' Stan stressed. 'I was going to take you to see Dr Josephs first thing,' wondering why Alison hadn't mentioned anything to him.

'What – and take a day off work?' the girl said sarcastically. 'You *must* have been worried! On second thoughts, I could do with an appointment with the quack.'

'But you said that you were feeling better?' Stan was becoming confused.

'I'm going to ask to be put on the pill.'

Stan stood in shock, wondering whether he had heard correctly. 'I didn't know that . . .'

'What – that I was sexually active?' Tara butted in, enjoying seeing her father squirm. 'Mummy was right. You really don't know much about women, do you?'

'So you mean you're not?' Stan said, wanting reassurance.

'No. I'm still a virgin, unfortunately. The pill's just to help make my horrible period pain less unbearable. Still, it is comforting to know that your father thinks his daughter puts it about.'

'I didn't say that,' Stan retorted, riled at being made fun of. He sighed. 'Look, go and have your breakfast, and then I'll take you to school.'

'You don't have to. I really don't mind taking the bus.'

'Have you got money for lunch?' Stan asked, taking out his wallet.

'I've got some left over from last week, but I could always do with some more, if you're offering?'

Knowing again that he was beaten, Stan handed her a crisp five-pound note.

'I'll see you outside,' he said, leaving the room.

Tara smiled at the three diet pills she had concealed in her hand. The money would come in useful, but not for the purpose her father intended. She felt a sudden, momentary pang of guilt. Of course, Alison had noticed the signs straight away and had taken her to see Lola Shapiro, a psychotherapist who specialised in teenage eating disorders. Tara had managed to talk her guardian out of mentioning anything to her father, provided she agreed to carry on with her treatment, which she had done for a few weeks, but it was her life and she could do with it as she pleased.

Tara cocked back her head and swallowed her last three tablets. It felt good to be in control.

'Wow! Whose car is that?' Stan heard his daughter call out.

'It belongs to a friend,' he lied, afraid of what she would say if she knew the truth.

'Why can't we have something cool like that rather than the clapped-out thing you drive around in all day?'

Again, Stan had been caught off-balance. He would have put money on the fact his daughter would have criticised him for splashing out on such an extravagance. Plus the fact was, he had already made up his mind to ring Howard to tell him that he had made a terrible mistake, and to ask him to take the BMW back. On reflection, maybe he was being too hasty. Since he had worried unnecessarily, perhaps he would get the work done and keep the vehicle, after all.

'Apparently, he talked about selling it,' Stan said, reverting to the ruse as Tara came through the door. 'I'll make an offer if you want me to?'

'It's your money, although it doesn't quite go with your image,' she said cheekily.

'I thought you just said you liked it?'

'Don't you think that someone aged forty is a bit too old to cruise around town in something like that?'

'So you've changed your mind?' Once again, Stan was confused.

'We need to get going if you're taking me,' Tara said, having already lost all interest in the subject.

Behind the wheel of his less than pristine sports car Stan left, utterly bemused by his teenage daughter. They travelled in silence to King Edward's private school in Hampstead, to which Tara had moved at the beginning of the new school year.

'Did you notice the invitation that came?' Stan asked eventually.

'You mean did I see that Grandma is getting married?'

'It is good news for once, don't you think?'

'In whose opinion?'

Stan sighed. Could he get nothing right? 'I thought you'd be pleased.'

'What – someone else who I won't be seeing any more? Soon you'll be the only one left,' Tara retorted.

'That's ridiculous – of course you'll still see each other. You're her only grandchild.'

'That won't stop her from moving in with what's his name.'

'Tara, it is normal for couples to live together once they're married.'

'Not miles away in bloody Hyde Park,' she answered back sulkily.

'I'm sure nothing's been decided yet,' Stan said, trying to calm the situation.

'Are you completely deluded?' Tara was enjoying giving her father a hard time. 'She's been with the same bloke for years and you're telling me they haven't decided where their love nest is going to be?' She paused. 'Do you think they still do it?' she asked with a straight face.

Stan tried to stop himself smiling. Not half an hour ago, he was accusing his daughter of being sexually active, now the same thought flashed through his mind concerning his elderly mother and her even more elderly fiancé.

'Why don't you ask her?' was all he said.

'Don't think I won't, the next time I see her – which probably won't be until the bloody ceremony.'

The car pulled up at the bus top outside the school gates.

'What time will you be home?' Stan asked.

'Normal time, about six. p.m. Alison's coming over. She asked if you'd be there.' Tara then got out and slammed the door.

'When was that arranged?' Stan called to her, surprised that he hadn't been informed earlier. But it was too late. The girl, thinking that she was out of view, was flirting with one of her male teachers, who seemed to be doing nothing to discourage her.

Just as he was about to pull away, a boy whom he didn't recognise shouted after him, 'Nice motor, Mr Rose, though I don't think the go-faster stripe down the side does a lot for it!'

11

The mild autumn lasted through the November of 1991 but brought a much colder December. In the meantime, there was no let-up in the activity of the Provisional IRA, seeking to end British rule in Northern Ireland. Their terrorist attacks brought havoc and fear to the streets of London, almost on a daily basis. The most prominent so far had been the launching of mortar shells at 10 Downing Street back in February.

Stanley stood with his hands in his overcoat pockets by the *For Sale* notice outside the double-fronted building in South Kensington, waiting for the estate agent to arrive. It hadn't taken long to get to grips with the property business. He had already sold a couple of one-bedroom flats above a pub, making a handy twenty grand profit along the way. Taking into account the sharp downturn in the market it was, he considered, quite an achievement.

The first thing he had done was to put himself about in the area and let it be known that he was now running Miller Investments. News of Ben's untimely passing had got around, and people were genuinely sad. Lives were all the poorer, now the eccentric man with the loud voice could no longer be seen with his small entourage parading down Ladbroke Grove. Quite how highly he was thought of was typified by the large turnout of estate agents at his funeral, the men and women with whom he had forged solid relationships over the years. It was spelled out to Stanley Rose in no uncertain terms that *he* couldn't expect to find deals unless he was prepared to offer sweeteners – something that went completely against the grain as far as he was concerned. Knowing Ben, he would have been surprised if his late father-in-law had ever resorted to this.

The purchase of a whole house in the more exclusive area of South Kensington was an ambitious proposition. The house would be the jewel in the portfolio, and the first move in Stan's master-plan to reposition the properties from shabby West London to a much classier part of the capital.

Stan believed that his fortunes had truly turned around. Seeing how indispensable he had become to the company it was now surely only a question of time before Richard Jeffrey formalised his position as Managing Director.

The other reason for his high spirits was the new woman in his life. He'd fallen for Jackie Harris after that first time in the car showroom. Eventually drumming up the courage to call her, he couldn't have hoped for a more enthusiastic response. That was ten weeks ago and the couple had become inseparable ever since. Stan was looking forward to spending their first Christmas together with their two lots of children and intended to take her away for a romantic weekend in Paris over the New Year.

Just then, he spotted an harassed Alison Brown walking at high speed towards him.

'Stanley, I'm so sorry to be late,' she said, giving him a kiss. 'The Edgware Road was closed because of another bloody terror alert. The whole of the West End is in turmoil. Anyway, how have you been?'

'All good. So, what's the SP on the place?' Stan asked, impatient to get on with the viewing.

'I'm told it can be bought for just under half a million for a quick deal before it goes to auction.'

'With vacant possession?'

'Yes, apart from the protected tenants in the basement, which you already know about,' she confirmed. 'You can inspect the rest of it,' she went on, taking the steps up to the front door.

'Doesn't sound too bad,' Stan replied, following behind.

'The property hasn't been touched for years, so as you can see it's a complete gut job.' Alison had opened the door and was now standing on the exposed floorboards of what had once been the grand entrance hall. 'Just think what a great family home this must once have been,' she went on, taking the ornate iron staircase to the first floor.

'I reckon it's worth more as flats.' Stan had already done the calculations. 'With a decent architect you could be looking at eight units without the basement.'

'Sounds like you've developed a nose for the business,' Alison said admiringly. And then she added: 'The top two floors are slightly smaller and the ceiling height is not quite the same. We can go and have a look if you want to?'

'It's not necessary, I've seen enough.' Stan started to make his way back down to the ground floor. 'I've got an appointment with the bank this afternoon so I'll get back to you later, if that's OK? But you can take it that I'm interested.'

'Fine. It's not going anywhere,' the agent said, trying to catch up with her client, who had already exited the property. 'And congratulations, by the way. I heard from Tara that your mum's getting married,' she added, hoping to delay his departure a little longer.

'Yes, thanks,' Stan replied, more interested in taking another look at the premises from the outside.

'Have you got time for a coffee?' Alison asked, her teeth chattering in the cold.

'Not really.'

It was clear to Stan that Alison was in no hurry to get to her next appointment – that's if she had one at all, since business was so slow – but with just a few working days left before the holiday period set in, he himself had things to get on with. On the other hand, they hadn't seen each other for a long time and he didn't want to seem unfriendly after everything she had done for Carol, and for him and Tara.

'OK – look, I've got half an hour,' he said, changing his mind. 'Danté's is at the end of the street. We can grab something there.'

They hurried down the pavement and entered the smoke-filled establishment, occupied at present by groups of students from the French Lycée and Imperial College, sat at round aluminium tables with their cappuccinos and freshly baked croissants.

'Ben used to take me here,' Alison said, glad to be out of the cold.

'Really?' Stan was surprised that his father-in-law would have ventured out of his North Kensington domain.

'Apparently, this is where he used to do most of his deals – so Theresa told me.' Alison glanced at the proprietor's wife, who had just come out of the kitchen with another order of cooked breakfasts.

'Right, what would you like?' Stan asked, passing the menu across the table. He was a little put out, thinking the diner was his own discovery.

'Those bacon and eggs smell great and I'd like a black coffee,' she replied. 'And you?'

'I'll have my usual – poached egg on brown toast, and tea.'

'That sounds depressingly healthy.'

'I need to lose a few pounds,' Stan replied, attempting to attract the attention of the owner's daughter to take their order.

'Whoever she is must be making you happy, because you're looking good on it,' Alison remarked, trying to lighten the atmosphere.

'I can't grumble,' Stan said, oblivious to the compliment. It felt so awkward that he was striving to make conversation with someone he had known for twenty years but with whom he no longer had much in common.

'Tara seems happy at her new school,' Alison said, tucking into her meal when it arrived.

'You probably know more than me,' Stan said, adding sauce to his plate. 'She never tells me anything – not that we see each other that often. Either I'm working or else she's gone off to a friend's place.'

'Even at weekends?' Alison wiped her mouth on the paper napkin.

'It seems that way,' Stan replied, showing no pangs of conscience.

Alison sat, trying her utmost to control her feelings of outrage. Maybe if she divulged that Tara was suffering from bulimia, it might infuse some sense of responsibility into the man who, now a new woman had come into his life, was content to leave his daughter marginalised. But Alison had given her word to Tara that she would not say anything to Stan, and she wouldn't risk damaging her relationship with her ward by breaking her promise.

The first anniversary of Carol's death, in a few weeks' time had, of course, been playing on both of their minds. Alison had accompanied Tara to the cemetery to visit her mother's grave, as she had done almost every week for the last year, after which the two of them spent hours on the phone, trying to console one another. Alison couldn't help wondering whether Stan, since he had made no reference to it, had already forgotten the date when he had lost the woman who had shared his life for so many years. Part of her was relieved that Carol wasn't alive to witness how things had turned out in her absence.

They finished eating in silence then, after Stan paid the bill, the former close friends went their separate ways, now mere acquaintances kept together by nothing more than the prospect of concluding a business transaction.

'Thanks for breakfast,' Alison said, stopping at her car. 'Send my love to Tara and tell her I'll be in touch before Christmas.'

To her disgust, all he said was: 'I will – and let me know when I can get into the basement flat,' indicating that that was the only thing on his mind.

Despite being caught up in the middle of a snowstorm, he then went back to have a last look at the property, confident that if he could secure the finance it would add a significant amount to the value of the company. His fortune would soon be made.

He was just about to drive away when he noticed a message on his mobile phone from Richard Jeffrey, asking Stan to call him back urgently.

12

The next day at 9 a.m. Stanley entered the offices of Lowndes Jeffrey and took the lift to the first floor. A sense of foreboding had gripped him ever since he received the bombshell informing him that his father-in-law's will was being contested. How was it possible that from feeling so upbeat, everything had changed radically in the space of twenty-four hours?

Jackie and he had had their first row because she had accused him of moping over dinner. Then Tara was getting into trouble again due to her lackadaisical attitude at school. What really annoyed him was the accusation from her Head of Year, an arrogant young man whom he had met for the first time yesterday, insinuating that with his daughter's GCSEs less than a year away, Stan needed to show a better example at home. With the considerable fees he was shelling out each term, the last thing Stan needed was a lecture from a scruffy individual about his parental responsibilities.

'Good morning, Mr Rose. Take a seat and I'll tell Richard you're here,' said the pretty young receptionist.

Stan positioned himself in a soft leather armchair opposite a pleasant-looking grey-haired lady in a well-cut brown tweed suit, who sat flipping casually through a set of papers.

Having failed to glean any further information other than the sparse details Richard Jeffrey had given him, Stan had gone over every possible scenario in his mind. Was he saying, for example, that for some reason the will wasn't valid? That surely couldn't be the case. Hadn't the same set of solicitors also drafted his and Carol's wills without any problem? Or was it perhaps that there was another one in existence that had suddenly turned up? Whatever the situation, it had left him with an unwelcome feeling of uncertainty.

He looked up from his brooding as a stern-faced little woman walked briskly towards them.

'I'm Roz Wilson, Richard Jeffrey's secretary,' she said curtly. 'Mrs Cunningham and Mr Rose, please follow me.'

Stanley assumed that the older lady was some sort of professional adviser, as they were shown into the boardroom to await the arrival of the senior partner.

'You must be Stanley,' his companion announced out of the blue, sitting down beside him. 'I've heard so much about you. And how is Tara? She must be quite a big girl now.'

'Yes, she is,' Stan replied cagily, wondering who she could be, and how she seemed to know all about him.

'The last time I saw her, she could only have been about nine or ten. Ben brought her to the cottage. We had a lovely picnic on the lawn.' Tears formed in the woman's eyes. 'You must excuse me,' she said, taking out a handkerchief to blow her nose. 'These past months since his death have been extremely hard.'

'Would you like a glass of water?' Stan offered, showing his concern.

'You're most kind. I'll be fine. Ben always said that he

couldn't have asked for a more decent son-in-law for his Carol.'

'He did?' Stan was surprised. He assumed that this Mrs Cunningham must be a distant relative of the Millers, since he hadn't encountered her before.

'That's what finished him off. He died of a broken heart after he lost his daughter.' The woman's voice shook. 'Carol meant the absolute world to him.'

Just then, Richard Jeffrey hurried in, looking rushed. 'Ah good, I see you two are getting acquainted,' he said. 'Better for everyone concerned if things can be settled amicably.'

'Except for him – I shouldn't trust him an inch if I were you,' the woman muttered as an aside as Jeffrey took a seat opposite them at the boardroom table. Stan found himself chuckling inwardly at the caustic comment that fortunately only he had heard.

'So, let's make a start, shall we?' the solicitor said, giving Stan a sharp look and untying the ribbon on the client folder. 'Coffee should be on its way.'

'Don't suppose you could make it a cup of tea?' Mary Cunningham enquired. 'Coffee gives me indigestion. And perhaps you could ask that secretary – you know, the one who doesn't smile much – for a plate of biscuits. I haven't had a thing since I came up on the train this morning.'

'I'm sure that can be arranged.' Jeffrey picked up the phone next to him.

'So what I was thinking,' the woman said, suddenly taking charge of the meeting, 'is that the document which you claim is the Last Will and Testament of Benjamin Louis Miller should be torn up, since it's not worth the paper it's written on, and that we should start again.'

'But surely that can't be right?' Stan butted in, panicking.

'Leave this to me, Stanley love,' Mary said, patting his hand.

'For your information, I think you'll find that the will in question, dated 30 July 1987, is perfectly valid and had been filed correctly,' Jeffrey snapped. 'You might not have noticed that it does make provision for various legacies, one of which – for £10,000 – is to yourself, Mary Cunningham.'

The solicitor then proceeded to push a copy of the will up the table towards her.

'I'm quite aware of what it says, dearie,' she responded tranquilly, unwilling to be patronised. 'The fact is, that as a common-law wife, which for *your* information is what I've been for the last thirty years, I'm not going to be got rid of with a pittance, just so that you can get your hands on my Ben's business!'

Stan gasped. He couldn't believe what he was hearing. Obviously, he knew that his father-in-law had lady friends, but Carol had never mentioned that there was anyone special in his life – unless it had been going on while Carol's mother was still alive and Carol had known all along?

'So, what exactly are you looking for?' Jeffrey asked, sounding more conciliatory.

There was a pause while the woman at the other end of the table appeared to be collecting her thoughts. She then gave her considered response.

'You may remain executor, Mr Jeffrey, but you must resign from the board. Then I will work out a suitable remuneration package with young Stanley here,' she said confidently.

'You mean you want to run Miller Investments?' Stan asked incredulously.

'Don't sound so surprised. Ben wouldn't have bought a lease on a sweetie shop without consulting me first. I was always the one with the nose for a deal. So long as we were together, he couldn't put a foot wrong which, I think you'll agree, gives me a moral right to be involved in the business I helped build up.'

Richard Jeffrey was the first to break the silence that had enveloped the room.

'Mrs Cunningham,' he said, clearing his throat, 'whilst I have some sympathy for your position, there's no possibility of agreeing to your request.'

'Then you'll hear from my lawyers,' Mary said firmly, whereupon she gathered up her things and rose from the table.

Relegated to the status of spectator at what should have been no contest, Stan found himself full of admiration for this audacious stranger.

'There's not a court in the land that would uphold what is, at best, a spurious claim,' the solicitor huffed, trying to regain the upper hand.

'Is that so?' the visitor replied, undeterred. 'You're obviously unaware of the records of the fees you've been charging – or should I say *over*charging – since you moved into these extravagant premises. I'm sure the Law Society would find that they make interesting reading. Would you like to see a copy?'

'I never received any indication that Ben was unhappy with our advice,' the solicitor responded stiffly, all of a sudden less sure of himself.

'Ben passed all your invoices, not thinking for a

moment that you would possibly cheat him. But I knew different.' Her voice hardened. 'Three hundred thousand pounds over the last twenty years, verified by two other firms of solicitors. Both highly respected names – perhaps you know them?'

Mary Cunningham held up the same papers that she had been looking at earlier.

'And I take it that you would be prepared to make this information public?' Richard Jeffrey responded, the careless arrogance of only fifteen minutes ago now replaced by an unlikely subservience.

Mary Cunningham remained impassive. She had chosen her moment and had timed it impeccably.

'Good. I am so pleased we've reached an agreement. It's so much better when things can be settled *amicably*,' she said, repeating the words that Jeffrey had used earlier. 'Oh, and I shall expect the Director's forms, naming Stanley and me in your place,' she went on.

'And the details of our charges?' the solicitor asked.

'Unlike you, Mr Jeffrey, I'm a person of my word. You've no need to concern yourself.' Then, addressing the man with whom she had just gone into business, she said, 'Come on, Stanley love. We've a very great deal to talk about.'

With that, the two new associates walked out of the room, leaving Richard Jeffery with a long face; he wanted to give the impression that Mary Cunningham had outsmarted him. The reality was that agreeing to the woman's demands had suited him perfectly. Now, having nothing to do with the company, he could concentrate solely on the considerably more lucrative role of Executor of the Miller Estate.

And as far as a record of his professional fees was concerned, he'd put money on the fact that the Cunningham woman was bluffing.

13

Another Christmas had arrived. Another year nearly gone. Stan sat fidgeting in his office in the house, waiting anxiously for his daughter to get a move on. Faced with the prospect of sharing the decision-making process in Miller Investments with Mary Cunningham, he was glad for the ten-day respite. Although she said that they would work well together, if her performance at Lowndes Jeffrey was anything to go by, she was obviously used to getting her own way.

It still seemed odd to Stan that Mary had only surfaced after Ben's funeral. She explained it away by saying that they had been on one of their frequent breaks and she had confined herself to the cottage in Kent. Then, when she heard the news of Ben's demise, she had been far too upset to say goodbye to the man whose life she had apparently shared for the last thirty years.

What to do about Tara was another issue. His daughter had recently immersed herself in a new pop subculture and had become obsessed with the Black Sabbath rock band. In any other circumstances, Stan would have understood that it was a difficult anniversary for the fifteen-year-old, but Tara had become so obstreperous that it was simpler to avoid another argument and let her do her own thing. However, father and daughter had been invited to a family lunch at his girlfriend Jackie's house, and now that things had got back to the way they were, he wasn't about to let Jackie down.

Stan looked anxiously at his watch. It was already one o'clock and there was still no sign of his daughter. What was he supposed to do? Being banned from the bedroom filled with macabre images of skulls and bones and posters of bloodthirsty vampires that resembled a set from a Dracula horror film, he picked up his mobile and sent her a text message. A few seconds later, a reply came back. *I'm not going.*

In a fit of temper, Stan marched up and banged furiously on her door. 'Tara, let me in!' he screamed.

There was no reply.

'Did you hear me?' He tried a second time.

Suddenly, there was the sound of voices, then of the door being unlocked, and out came a bleary-eyed young fellow with nothing on his feet who walked past him without any form of acknowledgement.

'Who the hell was that! And what was he doing in your room?' Stan shrieked at the girl, invisible in a sea of black.

'Just a friend,' she replied, yawning.

'Who spent the night in your room?'

'Didn't think you cared. Anyway, don't go all moral on *me*,' she said insolently. 'When was the last time *you* slept in your own bed?'

'That's different. I'm not fifteen.'

'At least with Jezz, I'm keeping it in the family.'

'What's that supposed to mean?' Stan said angrily.

'You know his father Charles.'

'Charles Fisher?'

'That's the one.'

'What happened to Ryan?'

'He's still around,' Tara responded indifferently.

'And that's Charles's son? He wasn't very polite,' her father grumped.

'What do you expect? We were just about to go at it again, and you put the poor bloke off his stride.'

'I *beg* your pardon?' Stan said in disbelief at what he'd just heard.

'Well, Mummy would have approved, even if you don't,' Tara retaliated. 'You know she and his dad were an item?'

'Actually, I didn't,' Stan replied, at a loss.

'He was mad about Mum, so Jezz tells me. Charles says he can't believe how much like her I am.'

'What else did he say?'

'Grandpa didn't think he was good enough. He wanted someone from a posh family. So you could say that you got her on the rebound.'

Stan stood motionless, wondering what other aspects of her past his late wife had withheld from him.

'Don't look so shocked. That's mild in comparison to all the other things I could tell you.'

'Like what?' Stan replied, trying to draw more information out of his daughter.

'Never you mind. I'll write it down one day,' Tara announced provocatively. 'I reckon it'll make a great story.'

'There's no time for any more of this. Are you coming or not?' Stan ground out.

'Why? Because you want to introduce me to whoever you've been having it off with?'

'How dare you talk about Jackie like that! I'll have you know she's a respectable woman and one on whom I happen to be extremely keen.'

'You've fallen right in, haven't you? Mummy was right – you really are a soft touch,' the girl mocked.

'I don't know what you're talking about,' Stan spluttered.

'On second thoughts, it might be quite a laugh, seeing who you've lined up to take Mummy's place.'

Tara pushed back the bedcovers, revealing her scrawny frame. 'Give me five minutes.' She then disappeared into the bathroom.

It was past two in the afternoon by the time they turned into a characterless close of modern houses.

'Christ! It's just like *Brookside* on TV. They all look the bloody same!' Tara said snidely. 'What's the betting it's the one over there with the flash car in the drive?'

Refusing to rise to the bait, Stan parked behind the white Mercedes convertible. Then, taking the Harrods champagne hamper he'd purchased especially for the occasion, he hurried up to the house and, grabbing hold of the oversized lion-faced knocker, banged resolutely on the door.

'See if you can be pleasant for once,' he pleaded to the Goth girl with a large silver cross around her neck, chewing gum beside him.

'Don't worry, Stanley, I won't embarrass you,' Tara answered sarkily.

Just then, a heavily scented woman in a revealing silk shirt and tight leather trousers came to the door. She was holding a drink in her hand and appeared slightly unsteady on her feet.

'Didn't think you were going to make it,' she said in her unmistakable Essex accent.

'I'm really sorry, Jackie,' Stan replied, kissing his girlfriend on the lips. 'Something came up at home, it couldn't be helped,' he gabbled. 'This is for you,' handing her the festive basket.

'He means me. I'm Tara, by the way,' the chalk-faced girl said.

'Yes, of course you are. Your father has told me ever such a lot about you,' the hostess replied, looking her up and down disapprovingly. 'I think we should go straight in, though the dinner's probably already done to death.'

Leading the way through the hall, garishly decorated with red flock wallpaper and heavy brass light fittings, they entered a bright double-aspect living room. At one end of it was an extended dining table, covered with a crisp linen tablecloth on which stood a pair of silver candelabra, producing an overpowering aroma from their fragrant-smelling candles. In each of the five place settings was a glass bowl of prawn cocktail, next to which was a solitary Christmas cracker.

'I'll go and call the boys,' Jackie announced. 'Must be starving, poor things.'

'Sounds like the perfect family,' Tara muttered, a little too loudly.

'I'll come and give you a hand,' Stan said, giving his daughter a dirty look before joining his girlfriend in the kitchen.

At that moment, two lanky youths with deadpan expressions came in and took their places at the lunch table.

'Hello, I'm Tom,' the older one announced in a monotone, avoiding looking at their female guest.

'And who's he?' Tara asked, glancing at the spotty brother.

'Matthew,' the younger one answered more softly.

'Seems like you want to be here as much as I do,' Tara remarked.

'We were supposed to be with our dad in Majorca,' Tom said resentfully.

'At least there is more to do over there,' the younger brother added.

'So why didn't you go then?' Tara asked.

'Dad got arrested last week and is on his way back to England,' Tom said, speaking freely.

'Why, what did he do?'

'Something about dodgy invoices, so Mum says. He imports all sorts of gear and the tax authorities got suspicious of how he could afford such an extravagant lifestyle when his business kept losing money.'

'That's why he took off abroad, when they were after him?' Tara's interest was suddenly whetted.

'No, not really. Dad claimed he'd not done anything wrong or illegal. As far as he was concerned, everyone in his line is at it,' Matthew explained.

'Though it didn't help when he tried to bribe that bloke from the Revenue,' Tom disclosed. 'He's facing up to five years in prison, according to his solicitor. Anyway, after he and Mum split up, he moved to a villa in Magaluf.'

'And you live here with your mother?' Tara asked.

'Yes, worst luck,' Matthew moaned, scooping up some more of the starter with his spoon. 'We go to school in Elstree so we're stuck. At least Tom's only got another year left to go.'

'Surely it can't be as bad as all that,' Tara sympathised.

'Our mother's selfish – she's interested in no one but herself,' Tom said flatly. 'We're only with her so she has an excuse to squeeze every penny she can out of our old man.'

'And how about the fact she's out with a different bloke every night?' his younger brother said, giving his two-pennorth.

'I thought . . .' Tara began, the comment catching her by surprise.

'What – that your dad was the only one?' Tom sniggered.

Just then, Jackie came to the table with a gravy boat, followed by Stan carrying a large platter of roast lamb, surrounded with burnt roast potatoes and overcooked Brussels sprouts.

'Stanley, give me that and go and open the champers,' she instructed. 'I'm gasping for another drink – and bring the Cokes while you're at it; they're in the fridge.'

Leaving the main course in the charge of his girlfriend, who began carving the meat onto the plates stacked up in front of her, Stan disappeared back into the kitchen

'You can see she's got him well trained,' Tom sneered.

Tara, still picking at her first course, couldn't believe what she was witnessing. How on earth had her father allowed himself to be blinded by this awful woman? She might have her own differences with him, but that was her right – she was his daughter. Seeing him return a few minutes later, awkwardly balancing the bottles under each arm, there was no way she was going to just stand by and watch him be humiliated.

'Tara, you must be taking your GCSEs. What school are you at again?' Jackie enquired.

'King Edward's in Hampstead,' the girl replied, anticipating trouble.

'I can't say I've heard of it,' the older woman said dismissively. 'My boys are at Haberdasher's. Habs costs a bomb but my ex, Jason, says that it pays dividends to have a *private* education. Although I went to a state school, and I did all right.'

'That's a matter of opinion,' her eldest son muttered under his breath.

'Sorry, Tom, were you saying something?' She looked daggers at her elder son.

'No, Mother, I was just wondering if there's any more lamb?'

'Actually, Jackie, King Edward's *is* private. A lot of famous people in the arts send their children there,' Stan stepped in, feeling the need to defend himself.

'I would have thought boarding school would be more suitable than one of those free-thinking places,' the hostess said condescendingly, only thinking of how it would make her life easier if this stroppy girl were out of sight and out of mind.

'Sorry, what makes you qualified to make a judgement like that?' Tara came back, trying to keep her temper.

Stan cringed, fearing what was coming next.

'Only what your father already told me – that you're a bit of a handful. That is what you said, Stan, isn't it?' Jackie replied, taking another large gulp of champagne.

'Did he really?' Tara snapped. 'And did he tell you why I am the *handful* as you so tactfully put it? Did he mention that this time last year my mother was dying? Or were you too busy running around him like a blue-arsed fly?'

The comment produced muffled sounds of laughter from the two boys sitting opposite each other.

'I'll have you know, young lady, I've never had to chase after a man in my life!' Jackie said, drawing herself up.

'No, you probably didn't have to. Tell me, how many expensive restaurants did it take before you let my dad go to bed with you? Or did you do it on the first night?'

'Stanley, don't just sit there and let her talk to me that way!' the hostess yelled, spilling her drink.

'Tara, please apologise to Jackie,' Stan said half-heartedly, his expression showing his total bewilderment at the situation that had got totally out of hand.

'I should have known that you'd take her side!' the teenage girl cried, scowling at her father. 'Mummy was right. She knew you had no balls!' With that, she got up abruptly from the table, throwing the cracker at the lamb.

'Tara, please!' Stan called after her, only just getting to his feet.

But it was too late. She had stormed out of the house and was halfway up the street before her father caught up with her.

14

Mary Cunningham was already sat at a table with her mug of tea when Stan entered Dante's, where they'd arranged to meet. The last ten days of 1991 had been a disaster and he was glad it was over. Firstly, Jackie had refused to go with him to Paris. She had explained that, although they had a lot of fun together and the sex was great, she was looking for a relationship without complications, and having Tara in the background meant they would never have their lives to themselves. She had conveniently forgotten that she had two children of her own, neither of whom had had to suffer the same trauma as his fifteen-year-old daughter.

At Jackie's suggestion, they had agreed to cool things for a few weeks, although Stan suspected that was the end of it. Not that it made the situation any easier with Tara who, after the debacle on Christmas Day, wasn't talking to him again. They had had a blazing row about her claim that Jackie had a string of other boyfriends. The fact that she said she just didn't want to see him make a fool of himself, he put down purely to his daughter's spitefulness. He didn't believe a word of it. To add to the difficulties between them, it was made abundantly clear that she had no intention of staying on at school after her GCSEs. Tara was entitled to the major part of her grandfather's company, so she knew that she would never be short of money.

'Good morning, dear,' Mary called out from behind the *Daily Mail* newspaper. Today she was wearing a smart grey suit, was fully made up and looked very different from the first time he had seen her at the offices of Lowndes Jeffrey. 'Had a peaceful break with young Tara, I trust? Mine was pretty awful. I went to stay with my older sister, Celia. She's as deaf as a doorpost and now her knees have given up on her, she's confined to the house, poor old thing. Not much of a way to spend the festive period. Still, it took my mind off Ben.' Then she perked up, saying, 'Come and sit down. I've got a proposal for you.'

Stanley took off his coat and ordered a coffee.

'Right, going forward,' Mary said, coming straight to the point, 'I reckon it's better all round if you run things on your own.'

Stan was taken aback, wondering what had brought about this sudden change of plan.

'I can tell that it's come as a bit of a surprise,' she noted.

'You could say that,' Stan replied, clearly unprepared.

'You see, I'm getting on a bit,' Mary explained, 'and the last thing I want to do is to get in your way. So, what I was thinking is a one-off settlement and then you can run the company without any interference.'

Stan pondered for a moment, asking himself again what had made Mary change her mind and why she hadn't reached the same conclusion at the meeting in Richard Jeffrey's office. Something didn't add up. Then it came to him. The woman had shrewdly managed to get the solicitor out of the way first, thinking that she would be able to secure a far more lucrative deal from Stanley.

Mrs Cunningham had obviously deduced that he was a soft touch.

'How much are you thinking of?' he asked, following the woman's direct approach.

'That's the question I've been mulling over these last few weeks,' she replied. 'The properties are worth about ten million, so that fellow Jeffrey estimated, and who am I to disagree with him? You do understand that being greedy is not in my nature, so I was thinking, two hundred thousand pounds would seem about fair, don't you agree?'

Stan remained impassive, hoping that his expression didn't portray what he was really thinking. He was tempted to call the woman's bluff; after all, there was no dirt that she had on *him*. So what was there to lose?

'A bit of a jump from the ten grand you were offered, isn't it?' he said flippantly.

Mary Cunningham laughed. 'Yes, it is. But you know that was hardly realistic.'

'I had in mind more in the region of twenty-five thousand,' Stan countered, sensing there was a deal to be done.

The woman opposite paused while she finished her tea. 'It feels strange being in this place without Ben,' she said. 'I do miss him terribly.' Taking out a handkerchief, she blew her nose. 'You know he saw you as the son he never had,' she revealed.

'He certainly never gave me that impression,' Stan replied resentfully. 'In fact, he made it especially difficult.'

'Ben was old school,' Mary said gently. 'I knew him when he had nothing. It was just after the war ended. My fiancé had got killed in action and I met this handsome chap at a dance at the Café Royal in Regent Street. In those days, Ben was busy buying up bombsites in the East End – that's where he started.'

She was silent for a moment, absorbed in her memories of happier times. Then she suddenly recovered her poise and told Stan: 'He knew you had it in you. There was no better judge of character than Benjamin Miller. Why do you think he allowed you to marry his Carol? You've no idea how many young men she had to turn away because he didn't think they were good enough for her. He worshipped that girl of his.'

Stan's thoughts turned to Tara. Could he truthfully say he felt the same way about his own daughter? he wondered. Or more likely, was their strained relationship the result of her being deprived of the love and affection that he had failed to give her? As always, whenever there was something unpalatable about himself that needed to be addressed, he put the matter firmly out of his mind.

'I asked him more than once whether he'd let me join him in the business but he didn't want to know,' he said instead.

'Ben knew you were going through a hard time. He wasn't heartless; he just wanted you to fight for it, that's all.' Mary finished her tea and gave a sigh. 'So, where were we?' she said, returning to the matter in hand. 'Look, make it seventy-five thousand and let that be the end of it.'

'Fifty thousand and that's as far as I'm prepared to go to,' Stan responded.

The grey-haired lady extended her hand across the table. 'We have a deal,' she beamed. 'Ben would have been proud of you.' She opened her handbag and took out a crumpled envelope. 'This is for you,' she said, passing it to Stan. 'Don't look so worried – it's not a summons. Just put your signature at the bottom and I'll be on my way.'

Stan cast his eye down the single sheet of paper stating the precise amount of the settlement that had just been agreed.

'Don't suppose you brought the chequebook with you, by any chance? Only I don't trust bank transfers,' the woman said, seeming eager now to get away.

'Sorry, I didn't,' Stan replied. Taking out his pen from his jacket, he was still trying to get to grips with the fact that Mary had anticipated the exact amount of her settlement beforehand.

'Not to worry, the post is just as good. The address is on your copy,' she said, handing him the duplicate letter. Tucking the signed document away in her bag, Mary then got up from the table, bade him goodbye and headed off for Gloucester Road tube station.

Stan sat reflecting on the bizarre encounter that had just ended. It suddenly occurred to him that the meeting in Richard Jeffrey's office and the contesting of the will had been nothing more than a charade, most probably instigated by his late father-in-law as a test of Stan's ingenuity.

It was still light when Stan arrived home later that afternoon. Most of the agents were on holiday until the second week in January and so he decided to leave the office early. Perhaps he would give Jackie a call and see if she was free and they could have dinner together. Now that he was his own boss and there was no one breathing down his neck, he could start seriously planning for the future.

Going downstairs, he passed Tara. She was sitting, writing furiously at the kitchen table, and he was relieved to see a discarded Kit-Kat biscuit wrapper in front of her.

'Back from school early?' he enquired, looking over his daughter's shoulder.

'I'm writing letters to newspapers to try and get them to give me work experience during the holidays. I thought you'd be pleased.'

'I think that's great,' Stan answered, wondering why the child was all of a sudden seeking his approval.

'You know that's what I've always wanted to do, and it's where a lot of writers start,' the girl explained. There was a vibrancy about her again that lit up the room. 'I intend to become a journalist.'

Suddenly, Stan saw Carol sitting in his daughter's place. The hours his wife would spend writing to people all over the world, people whom she might have met just once – he never could quite comprehend it. That, and the fact that both mother and daughter shared the same love of English literature explained why his wife had been adamant that Tara should be encouraged to go to university. It was the least he could do, to comply with her wishes.

'If you want, we could have supper or get a takeaway and I can tell you what my form teacher, Mr Stevens, said to me,' Tara said, looking up.

Without thinking, Stan said: 'I'd love to, but Jackie . . .'

His daughter's face fell. 'Yes of course, sorry, I forgot she is your number one,' she replied bitterly and returned to her writing.

'That's not fair,' Stan argued. 'Can't we do it tomorrow evening instead? I'm told there's a great new Indian in the High Street.'

But there was no response. The precious opportunity to bond with his daughter had been thrown away and wasted.

15

Richard Jeffrey was the last one in the office that January evening. He was only just back after the Christmas break, and several new clients' files had accumulated on his desk. The ten-day holiday in Antigua was already a distant memory and there was something far more important on his mind – namely, his last appointment of the day.

The call from the commissioner on the ground floor informed him that a Miss Alison Brown had arrived. Richard was perusing a deposition that needed to be filed with the court in the morning, when he noticed the familiar figure of the estate agent standing uncertainly outside his open door.

'Alison, do come in. I hope that I haven't made you alter your arrangements but this is the only time when we can be certain to have the place to ourselves. It'll be more comfortable if we sit over there,' he said, beckoning her to join him at the seating area at the other end of the office.

'Richard, you mentioned on the phone that it was important,' the visitor reminded him, sinking back into a winged leather armchair.

'Yes, and needless to say, it is strictly confidential.'

'I assume it concerns Stanley Rose or Miller Investments?' Alison said perceptively.

'His daughter, actually,' the solicitor confirmed.

'Tara? But she's only just sixteen; she's got nothing to do with the company.'

'Not directly, but she is the beneficial owner of 75 per cent of the shares.'

'Yes, that's what her grandfather left to her in his will.'

'And therein lies the problem. You may not be aware, but under Trust Law, the beneficiary must be deemed competent to look after his or her property. Now, I have good grounds to believe, through no fault of her own, you understand, that Tara . . . how I can put this delicately . . . is somewhat of a wayward child and one, at present, not responsible enough to take possession of a holding valued at several million pounds.'

'And what evidence do you have on which to base such a preposterous allegation?' Alison was shaken.

'Let's say I've made certain enquiries. Her teachers, especially at the last school, where she was asked to leave, were surprisingly forthcoming.'

'That was because Southbridge was too structured. Tara needs an environment where she can express herself more easily. That place stifled her individuality,' the agent responded firmly.

'Alison, I can appreciate that you want to defend the child. After all, she was the daughter of your *dearest* friend – but it doesn't explain away the truancies from school, the smoking and bullying. Do I need to go on?'

The visitor was shocked at how Richard Jeffrey had managed to lay his hands on what should have been confidential information between the parent and the school. A shiver ran down her spine as she intuited what was coming next.

'So what are you suggesting?' she asked.

'Taking account of your special relationship with the family,' Richard began, 'and the fact that you are already her legal guardian, you'll just need to keep a close eye on young Tara to ensure that she stays on the straight and narrow. She will need to be responsible enough to take possession of her inheritance.'

'I think I should be able to deal with that,' Alison replied. Feeling relieved that there was nothing more onerous expected of her, she got up to go.

'I haven't quite finished,' the solicitor announced, gesturing to her to sit down again. 'Under the terms of the trust, the property passes to the beneficiary on him or her reaching the age of eighteen, which in Tara's case is in just under two years' time. Part of your duties will be to see that she signs certain important papers.'

'What type of papers?' Alison queried.

'Let's just say that on a transfer of this magnitude, it's in the interests of all concerned to mitigate the tax liability which, thanks to her father's recent successes in the property market, would in normal circumstances put a heavy strain on the company's cash-flow. My advice, as main trustee, is to transfer the holding to an offshore company which has been set up especially for the purpose.'

'Until when?' Alison quizzed, unaware that she was raising her voice.

'There's no need to be alarmed. It's all above board and when, in the future, it's deemed appropriate for Tara to have some or all of the shares, they would be returned to her,' was the lawyer's glib response.

'I think I should talk to Stanley first and tell him what you are suggesting,' Alison said.

'On the contrary, it would be best to keep him out of

it,' the man asserted. 'Anyway, from what my sources tell me, he is far too wrapped up in his personal life to have the child's best interests at heart. I doubt that he would raise an objection. But to protect yourself, you will need to ensure that Tara takes independent advice before she signs. I will arrange for one of the other partners to provide the comfort required.'

Seeing that there was no end to his resourcefulness in order to get what he wanted – even employing the services of a private detective to check on Stanley Rose wouldn't have surprised her – Alison knew she would have to tread carefully.

'And what if I refuse?' she asked, suddenly emboldened.

'Alison, think twice. It really would be most foolish of you,' the solicitor replied.

'Richard, that sounds very much like a threat, which I don't appreciate.' For a second time, she got up from her chair.

'My dear,' he said silkily, 'I don't think it would do you any good for Tara to find out just how friendly you were with her mother.'

The colour drained from Alison's face as she understood that she was being blackmailed.

'What exactly are you insinuating?' she said, trembling.

'Made quite interesting reading, those letters we found when we cleared out the house in Maida Vale . . .'

'They were private. You had no right to look at them!'

' . . . saying how much in love you were with poor Carol.'

'It was a crush, nothing more,' the visitor protested.

'One that went on for ten years, I believe. I'm sure you would agree with me that it was a bit more serious than a mere crush?'

'Carol was never that way inclined. So you've got nothing on me,' Alison shouted.

The lawyer just sat back and smiled.

Alison knew she was facing the most awful dilemma. If she went to Stan, telling him how she had felt about Carol, with the far-fetched story that Richard Jeffrey was holding a gun to her head, he probably wouldn't believe her; and if she didn't go along with the solicitor's deceit, Tara would get to hear all the lurid details that he would no doubt embellish, driving a permanent wedge between them. Either way, she knew that she had no choice but to accept what was being proposed.

Stan sat cooped up in his Ladbroke Grove office, as he had done every day for the last few months, arranging the sale of properties in order to start paying off the several million pounds of inheritance tax due from the Miller estate. Still, having settled the latter with the Revenue at a value of just under eight million pounds, it was a damn good start. Fortunately, now Ben Miller's house had been sold, there was more than enough money to pay the first instalment to the Capital Taxes Office and to settle Mary Cunningham's fifty thousand 'legacy'.

Naturally, he had informed Richard Jeffrey of what had been decided. To his credit, the solicitor didn't harbour any ill feeling that he'd been done out of his directorship of the company; in fact, only then did he admit that it had been a cause for concern because of a possible conflict of interest. Now probate had been granted at the lower end of expectations, the fellow seemed satisfied to have retained the trustee work for the estate and grateful for the opportunity to quote for the conveyancing of the properties, which he assured Stan would be competitive. Richard Jeffrey, Stan thought, appeared to have learned his lesson.

Stan put down his pen and looked at his watch. It was nearly time to leave. The viewing of the basement flat he'd been unable to get into before Christmas couldn't come quickly enough. A problem that had been discovered in the title of the freehold had worked in his favour and prevented the building from going to auction. Alison, sounding unusually distant on the phone, said she was unable to attend with him today, but had cleared it with the tenants for him to go there in her absence.

Enjoying the warm May sunshine through the open roof of his BMW, Stan turned off Gloucester Road into Cornwall Gardens, the garden square that had brightened considerably with flowers and green leafy trees since his last visit, four months previously. He entered the shabby, stucco-fronted property through a wrought-iron gate and took the staircase to the lower-ground floor. Receiving no response to his ringing, Stan was just about to go, when a dignified lady opened the door.

'Sorry, I was at the other end of the flat and I couldn't hear the bell,' she said, slightly out of breath.

'Mrs Isaacs, I'm Stanley Rose. Alison Brown said it would be all right if I came and had quick look around?'

'Yes, yes, of course – please come in,' the woman said pleasantly. 'You'll have to excuse my husband. His leg has been playing him up and he's in bed.'

'That's perfectly OK,' Stan replied, entering into the immaculately presented home.

'Can I get you a cup of coffee?' she asked.

'That's very considerate, but I'll only be a few minutes,' Stan replied, eager to get started.

'The living accommodation is all on this side,' Audrey Isaacs told him, passing the eat-in kitchen. 'And this is our living room,' she said, standing at the entrance of a long rectangular room with sash windows, in the centre of which was an elegant marble fireplace. 'Originally, it was two separate flats that were subsequently put together.'

'Must have been some time ago?' Stan commented.

'You are right. Edward and I have been here for twenty years.'

'I must say, you've kept the place beautifully.'

'Thank you. Even though we are only tenants, it is our home.' The elderly lady paused, before saying anxiously, 'Mr Rose, may I ask if you are intending on purchasing the property?'

'I'm seriously considering it,' Stan replied.

'I suppose that you would want us to vacate our flat, then?' Her lips quivered.

'It's far too soon to be thinking about that,' Stan hedged, 'but I'd like to see the rest of the apartment if it's not inconvenient.'

Following the quarry-tiled corridor around to the other side of the U-shaped property, they arrived at the door of the main bedroom. Mrs Isaacs tapped quietly.

'It's all right, you can come in,' a man's voice called out.

'Edward, this is Mr Rose,' she said, introducing Stan to her husband.

'Pleased to meet you, come right in. I'm not usually laid up like this,' the husband said. 'A few days' rest and I'd be right as rain, so the doctor told me. That was two weeks ago. Shows you how much they know.' He recollected himself. 'Anyway, you don't want to hear my complaints. Audrey tells me that you are interested in buying the place?'

'Yes, that's correct,' Stan answered, gazing around at the cosily decorated and spotless room.

'I expect it'll cost you a few quid to get hold of all this lot. Quite a few have tried over the years, but I think the sums involved put them off; then there was the cost of moving us out. The figures probably didn't stack up. I'm no property man, of course. Men's clothing was my game.'

'Teddy – I mean Edward,' his wife corrected herself, 'made bespoke woollen overcoats.'

'Everybody in the East End knew Isaacs of Hanbury Street,' her husband reminisced. 'I knew a Rose – in the furniture business,' he said, scratching his head. 'That's right . . . there were two brothers, Harry and Arnold. That wardrobe over there is one of theirs. Still going strong after more than thirty-five years.'

'Harry's my uncle,' Stan said, surprised by the coincidence.

'So whose boy are you?' asked Teddy Isaacs.

'Arnold's, his older brother, but my father died a long time ago.'

'And Harry's son – what happened to him? He always spoke a lot about the lad.'

'I think you've made a mistake. Harry never married.'

'That's more than likely; my memory does like to play tricks.'

'Don't worry, thank you for showing me around,' Stan replied, thinking nothing of it.

'But you haven't seen the other two bedrooms,' the wife pointed out.

'I don't want to take up any more of your time,' Stan said. 'I'll need to think about it, but I promise I won't do anything without informing you first.'

'Spoken like a true gentleman,' Teddy Isaacs nodded. 'Not many like you in the property business.'

'Thanks again, I can see myself out,' Stan said.

'And if you see your uncle, tell him you ran into Teddy Isaacs and send him my best,' the invalid called after him.

The visit had left Stan feeling excited by the enormous potential of the place. He knew now that he had to have the property. Instead of returning to the office, he decided on a brisk walk, attempting to put his thoughts into some semblance of order. Without a particular destination in mind, he strode along the Cromwell Road, past the vast Natural History Museum with its ornate terracotta façade and then the Science Museum, and before too long he reached the Serpentine lake in the middle of Hyde Park.

Buying lunch from a water-front cafeteria, Stan spent the afternoon in these beautiful surroundings, working out schemes of how to maximise the value of the property he'd just seen. As others before him had already ascertained, all of these schemes depended on obtaining vacant possession of the Isaacs' flat. Being able to place them in alternative accommodation might have helped, but he had nothing remotely comparable to offer them. Also, he suspected that Teddy Isaacs was a wily old fox who would demand top dollar before he agreed to move. Nevertheless, there was no way Stan was going to let the opportunity pass.

Taking out his mobile phone, he tapped in his agent's number.

'Hello, Alison, I thought I should give you a call.'

'I was just on my way out,' the woman replied. 'How did the viewing go?'

'Pretty well what I expected. Needs a lot of work but I think one could make something out of it,' Stan said, underplaying his hand.

'Are you going to make an offer, because I'm showing it again tomorrow and I wouldn't want you to miss out,' Alison pressed.

'Sounds like you're trying to talk the price up – and I thought you were supposed to be representing me,' Stan said, sounding put out.

'I am, but I have to cover myself. I can't afford for the vendor to dis-instruct us, especially the way the market is.'

'All right, I'll pay the asking price, subject to contract, but I want a twenty-one-day lock-out period to get the deal done. You can give Lowndes Jeffrey as solicitors.'

The line went dead for a few seconds.

'Alison, are you still there?'

'Yes, I'm just writing it down.'

'Thought that would make your day,' Stan said happily.

'I'll put the offer up and get back to you before close of business,' Alison responded without emotion.

'One more thing,' he added. 'I'll need access at least a couple more times – you know, for the bank and for my surveyor.'

'Once the deal has been agreed, I can't see that being a problem,' she said tersely.

'Thanks, Alison,' but the line had already gone dead. Stan sat holding his phone, wondering why she had sounded so unfriendly. Assuming that it was purely the strain of a tough market getting to her, he quickly put it out of his mind.

Confident that he was about to secure his first major purchase, Stan walked briskly out of the park and hailed a taxi to where he'd parked his car. By the time he got back to the office, there was a fax from Alison informing him that the deal had been agreed.

The next thing was to share his good news with Jackie. They had been seeing each other again on a more regular basis, and if he could get a reservation, he would surprise her with supper at La Famiglia, her favourite Italian restaurant in World's End, Chelsea. Hopefully, they would then spend the night together. Jackie had said that she felt less inhibited in Hampstead than at her own place.

At first, Stan was reticent, fearing a backlash from Tara. But that was her problem. If, as he hoped, Jackie would sooner or later become the next Mrs Stanley Rose, his daughter would have to get used to her being around.

The evening turned out differently than he had expected. Jackie had developed a migraine over dinner and he had to take her home early. On the plus side, Tara and he had a chat that didn't result in another argument. She was feeling buoyant because of the offer of work she had just received from the *Sunday Times* during the summer holidays. Things, she assured him, were also going well at school. There was, he suspected, an ulterior motive for her abnormally friendly disposition. She wanted to be allowed to go on holiday to Greece with Ryan – they too were back together. The fact that Stan didn't dismiss her request out of hand, Tara took as his acquiescence and went off to bed happy.

Stan slept fitfully. He dreamed he was at work in the

furniture factory. It was a bitterly cold morning and the heating had broken down. His gloved hands moving feverishly, Stan was feeding panels into a veneer press, trying to keep warm. Suddenly, Harry walked past, in jovial conversation with a smartly dressed young man whom Stan had never seen before. His uncle paused briefly for a glimpse at the latest pin-ups of big-breasted women plastered over every spare space of the pitted concrete walls.

Then the young man stopped abruptly and turning to him, said, 'How many sets have *you* done this morning?'

'Twenty so far, sir,' Stan heard himself say, in a voice that didn't belong to him.

'Better get a move on, then. That batch has to be completed by lunchtime,' the fellow said sternly, before joining Harry's inspection of the slimline gate-leg tables that were coming off the production line.

'But I'm the Governor! I shouldn't be behind a machine!' Stan called across the factory floor.

The young man just stood and stared at him with a scornful expression.

'Stanley, you had your chance, my boy, but you threw it away.' This time it was Harry talking.

'It wasn't my fault. You must believe me!' Stanley wailed.

'A son takes over the business from the father, that's just the way it is,' Harry said, putting his arm affectionately around the young man who'd accompanied him.

Stan woke up feeling unsettled. What did it all mean? Who was that unpleasant individual, the same age as himself – and what was he doing with Harry?

Dismissing the dream as an absurd fantasy, Stan knew he needed to pull himself together. He had a busy day ahead with the Cornwall Gardens deal and he couldn't afford to be distracted. Yet however hard he tried to concentrate on work, for the rest of the day the faces from the night before remained in his head.

A seed of doubt had been sown. There were only two people to whom he could turn for reassurance, his mother and his uncle in Spain. Fortunately, his mother's engagement party was on Saturday night. The only question was, could he wait three whole days to regain his peace of mind?

16

Trying to avoid the sudden downpour, Stan, accompanied by Tara and her boyfriend Ryan, moved swiftly to the entrance of the austere residential building and took the lift up to the third floor. Even though Elaine Rose hadn't made an official announcement that she was moving in with Paul, she was already spending all of her time in the vast mansion flat on the Bayswater Road. The house in Hampstead Garden Suburb had gone on the market and been sold almost immediately to a young South African dentist whose family was expanding.

Looking over at his daughter, Stan was relieved at the effort she had made for the occasion. With her neatly combed hair and tight-fitting black taffeta cocktail dress that showed off a pert figure, apart from the piercing in her nose, there were few traces of the previous macabre look that had been adopted to shock. Stan had very much wanted to bring Jackie, but she said it would be 'making a statement', so he reluctantly came without a partner.

They entered a drawing room already packed with guests sipping on their glasses of champagne. Stan eventually caught sight of his mother with her fiancé, Paul, at her side. Even at a distance, he had to admit they made a handsome couple.

'Stanley, darling, I'm so glad you were able to make it,'

Elaine said, going up to her son and kissing him.

'Paul, how are you?' Stan said, and shook hands with his soon-to-be stepfather.

'Couldn't be better,' the silver-haired man replied, beaming. 'You know Sara,' gesturing at the slim woman all in green, a few feet away. There was no mistaking the host's eldest daughter, who shared the same angular features as her father. She and Stan had only met on a few previous occasions but there was a serene quality about her and he had to admit that he had rarely encountered a woman who exuded such class.

'It's good to see you again,' Stan said to her, keeping one eye out for his Uncle Harry, who had grudgingly agreed to come over to London from Spain for the occasion.

'You can come closer,' Sara said, smiling, 'since it seems we're going to be related.'

Not wishing to offend, Stanley went over and kissed the woman tentatively on the cheek.

'There, that wasn't so hard, was it?' she laughed.

A waiter appeared with a tray of drinks and Stan helped himself to a glass of champagne.

'Not for me, thank you,' Sara said. 'I'm driving as my husband couldn't make it. David is entertaining business people from abroad – or so he told me.'

'What, on a Saturday night?' Stan asked casually, before mentally berating himself.

The comment had obviously hit a nerve, resulting in a few seconds of embarrassing silence.

'Is your daughter with you?' Sara asked, changing the subject.

'Tara's over there,' Stan said, pointing to where she was happily holding court with a group of other young people.

'Doesn't look as if she suffers from being shy,' Sara commented.

'Tara' s very much like her mother in that respect,' Stan revealed.

'It must have been very hard after your wife died, bringing up a teenage daughter alone. I've got two boys of my own, and I don't think there's any truth in the notion that sons are much easier.'

Stan, who was eager to get away, nodded politely and then said, 'Would you excuse me? I need to go and have a word with my mother.'

'Yes, of course,' Sara replied, in turn going off to find her children.

Elaine Rose was gossiping away animatedly in the other corner of the room with her two closest friends, Stella Stone and Regine Marchant when they saw Stan coming towards them,

Stella, the overweight red-head in a sequinned dress that resembled a coat of chainmail armour, sighed and said, 'What a good-looking fellow that son of yours is.'

'I'm not sure your Monty would have been too happy to hear you say that,' the more petite Regine giggled.

'I don't know, younger men are all the rage these days,' Elaine interjected, already a little tipsy after too much champagne.

'From my experience, that's not entirely accurate when it comes to North-West London,' Regine joked.

'And she should know,' Stella quipped. 'By the way, how *is* the match-making business these days?'

'That's what I'm trying to tell you,' Regine reiterated. 'Because we only specialise in second marriages, we don't tend to get too many gigolos in our part of the world.'

'Oh Reggie, it's such a shame you never found anyone that lasted after Bernard died,' Elaine lamented.

'That's the very reason why I set up the Temple of Fortune Agency,' Regine explained. 'When it didn't work out with Albert, the Moroccan, I was beginning to lose hope of ever finding anyone. Then the same thing happened with Morris. It wasn't me – I could cope with the unsociable hours of a kosher butcher – but it turned out that I wasn't religious enough for the rest of his family, would you believe it? So at the age of sixty-one, I found myself on my own again.'

She turned to their hostess and said warmly, 'But Elaine, you've done really well for yourself. Paul is an absolute gem – if you'll excuse the expression.' A comment that caused the small group to break out into titters.

'I've always maintained *that's* the quality of man that we need on our books,' Regine went on. 'But with so many unattached women, we'd probably need about a hundred and fifty Pauls to go around.' At that, the three women tittered again. They were enjoying themselves.

Stan went up and taking his mother by the arm, said, 'Ladies, you don't mind if I drag her away for a few minutes?'

'Of course not. After all, we can't expect to have the bride-to-be *all* to ourselves,' Stella replied archly, the sequins of her dress dazzling Stan as they caught the light.

'Did you know Elaine's first husband?' Regine murmured, when their friend and her son were safely out of sight.

'Yes. Poor Arnold – he was a smashing chap, as good-looking as they come,' the red-headed woman imparted. 'But she was never happy with him.' She shrugged and emptied her glass.

'Why was that? He sounded like a real catch.'

'Regine, can't you stop thinking about your business just for two minutes?'

'All I'm saying is that there was something that didn't quite add up, why she ended up with Arnold – but I could never find out what it was.'

'And I'm sure it wasn't for want of trying,' Stella said.

'You know me,' the other one chuckled. 'Come on, we're not paying – let's go and get another drink. And I could eat a little something.' The two women sailed off towards the buffet and the bar.

Meanwhile Stan and his mother had found a quiet corner and were engaged in conversation.

'And who is that boy Tara has brought with her?' Elaine enquired, looking disapprovingly over at her granddaughter.

'You remember my friend Howard in the car business? That's his son, Ryan. Nice lad.'

'Is she serious about him?'

'Mother, Tara's only sixteen!'

'I was only a few years older than that when I got married to your father.'

'Things are different today – and besides, Tara wants a career.'

'Yes, she told me something about wanting to be a journalist.'

'That's right, and you know how strong-willed she is.'

'And I also know who she takes after – and it's not her father.' Elaine helped herself to a mini-smoked-salmon blinis offered by a waiter carrying a silver tray. Stan followed suit, taking two.

'Mother, that wasn't necessary,' he said, putting them both in his mouth.

'You're right, I'm sorry,' Elaine said, tasting the caterer's offering cautiously. 'Now, I don't want to pry but are *you* seeing anyone?' she asked, dabbing her lips.

Stan hesitated for a moment, surprised that Tara hadn't mentioned Jackie, in derogatory terms, to her grandmother.

'There is a woman who I like a lot, but she couldn't make it this evening.'

'You mean you thought it was too soon to introduce her to the family,' Elaine said perceptively.

'Something like that,' Stan replied, unwilling to elaborate. Then: 'I can't see Harry here. Don't tell me you forgot to invite him?'

'I'm not with you. Of course we did,' Elaine replied, her suspicions suddenly raised.

'We haven't offended him, have we?' Stan asked.

'Not that I can think of. He wasn't able to make it . . . That's right,' she fumbled, 'he mentioned something about a bridge tournament he was organising. Why the sudden interest in your uncle?'

'Just that I met someone a few days ago who said he used to be a friend of his, back in the East End days, and he wanted me to remember him to Harry.'

'Did he say anything else?' Elaine asked, trying not to let her concern show.

'Only some tall story – and you're not going to believe this – that Harry had a son. I told him he must have got Harry muddled up with someone else because he never married. I just thought if he'd been here, he might have been able to throw some light on the subject.'

'Surely you're not taking what that man said seriously?'

'Well, apparently Harry was a bit of a lady's man in his time. It wouldn't be such a surprise if a child or two of his suddenly crawled out of the woodwork, would it?' Stan smirked.

Elaine hid behind her glass of champagne. 'No, I suppose not, although it probably would have happened by now. Anyway, I should be getting back to Paul or he'll think I've abandoned him.' She moved away to find her future husband, leaving Stan no closer to resolving the mystery of an unknown cousin.

All of a sudden, his attention was drawn to a kerfuffle taking place in the middle of the room. As he went over to see what it was all about, an incensed Ryan Barnet brushed past him.

'Ryan, what's the matter?' Stan called out after him.

'You'd better ask your daughter that,' was all the youth said before marching out of the party without even saying goodbye to his hosts.

Stan looked at his watch – eleven thirty. If he left soon, he'd drop his daughter home and go over to Jackie's. She had mentioned that she wasn't going out. However, seeing that Tara was still having such a good time, he had no choice but to wait. In fact, as it turned out, they were the last ones to go.

His mother seemed to have got her second wind and insisted that they stay to the end. This suited her granddaughter, since Tara was still enjoying being the centre of attention with her crowd.

It was well past 1 a.m. by the time they got home.

'What happened with Ryan?' Stan asked the girl, who had dozed off on the way home.

'He kept saying I was ignoring him. He'll get over it – or he won't,' Tara said coolly.

'I thought you were going to Greece together?'

'That's off. It was a bad idea anyway,' she said, getting out of the car. 'I've got my keys. I assume you're going on somewhere?'

'I didn't say anything about that,' Stan replied sheepishly.

Tara's expression said it all. She then made her way down the path to the house alone.

Stan sped off and half an hour later, taking advantage of the empty roads, he pulled up outside Jackie's house. To his surprise, a Porsche was in the drive, parked tightly against his girlfriend's Mercedes. At that very moment, a broad man in an open-necked sports shirt appeared at the front door – with Jackie. Stan looked on while the two kissed passionately on the step before the man made his way around to his vehicle.

He knew then that it was over between them.

Overcome with tiredness, Elaine kissed Paul goodnight. There was plenty of time for them to be together after they married. In the meantime, she felt more comfortable in the guest suite at the end of the hall. She should have been exuberant. After all, she was with a wonderful man who worshipped her and would go to the ends of the earth to make her happy. However, that talk with Stanley had left her feeling unsettled. Of course, she had suspected that her affair might rear its head one day, but it was such a long time ago she had almost forgotten all about it – that was, until her daughter-in-law's funeral when Harry had all but avoided talking to her. Now her son was in possession of a version of what had happened forty-odd years ago, she was worried that it was only a question of time before the truth came out.

As she removed her make-up and dropped her silk nightie over her head, Elaine's main concern was not her son, however, but whether she should say anything to Paul or allow him to continue believing that she was the virtuous woman he assumed her to be.

17

The black cab pulled up outside the premises of the Pretoria Bank in Moorgate in the City of London. Stan got out and paid the driver, then entered the granite building. After registering at reception, he was directed to the banqueting suite on the fifth floor. Only having been to the bank once before, and only recently having established a facility with them, he was surprised to have received the invitation to their Midsummer Day's cocktail party.

Feeling slightly apprehensive, he entered the opulent offices where, in true City form, no expense had been spared – and was greeted by an attractive waitress wearing a man's dinner suit and carrying a tray of drinks. Stan took a glass of red wine and began to circulate amongst the small clusters of guests, hoping to find someone to talk to. When a short man with a round friendly face came up to him, Stan recognised him as Lucas Voss, his account manager.

'Stanley, good of you to come,' the fellow greeted him in his broad South African accent. 'There are a few people here that it would be worthwhile you meeting. By the way, I don't suppose there's a possibility of tickets for any of the Spurs matches next season?' he said as an aside.

'I've still got the feelers out,' Stan replied evasively. Finding out that they supported the same football team had done much to cement their relationship and he wasn't ready to spoil it by telling Voss that, even though the season hadn't started yet, most of the big games would probably be a sell-out.

At that point, a man in a perfectly tailored dark grey suit and blue tinted glasses approached them.

'Hello there, Brendan,' the manager said, going up to shake the hand of the bank's most important client. 'Stan, this is Brendan Cole. And Brendan, meet Stanley Rose, a new client. How are you?'

'In the pink, old boy,' the cultured fellow replied. 'Though I'd be even better if you hadn't stung me with that exorbitant commitment fee on the Harrow Road deal. You have got to watch these chappies like a hawk,' he said, addressing his comments to Stan. 'It's not by accident that they can afford buildings like this, you know, when the rest of us poor blighters are operating out of any old back-street office. Bankers like Lucas here are the ones who make the real money, while chumps like us take all the risks.'

'Don't listen to Brendan, he gives us bankers a bad name,' Lucas chuckled.

'*Bankers* being the appropriate term,' the tall man joked. 'So, Stanley, what brings you here?' he asked, peering down at the nametag pinned on Stan's lapel. 'Miller Investments . . . that name rings a bell.'

'Stanley has recently completed on a property in Cornwall Gardens,' Lucas divulged.

'My old stomping ground!' Brendan exclaimed. 'Had a hell of a lot of fun in that neck of the woods, a few years ago.' It was clear by his expression that he was referring to more than bricks and mortar.

'I was lucky to get hold of it,' Stan said. 'Though I had to get the basement tenants out.' He didn't recount the difficult experience he'd had when he revisited the premises after completion. Mrs Isaacs, so different from the proud woman he'd encountered on his first meeting, was completely dejected, informing him that her husband Teddy had suffered an embolism and lay seriously ill in hospital. Expecting the worst, she had already made plans to move in with her son in North London and put up no resistance to the offer of twenty-five thousand pounds to vacate her flat; in fact, she considered it more than generous. Feeling that he should have done more for the couple, Stan also offered to pay her moving costs and solicitor's fees, effecting the transfer of the property to his company.

'I remember now – Benny Miller, that old scoundrel,' the tall man blurted out with genuine affection.

'He was my father-in-law,' Stan revealed.

'Well, let me tell you, Stanley, they didn't come any more honourable than Ben. We did quite a few deals together over the years. His word was his bond, which is more than I can say of that shyster firm of lawyers he used. His loyalty to them was typical, but misplaced. A nastier bunch of chancers I've ever come across – and I wouldn't trust them with a fiver of my own money!'

Stan recalled the same sentiments being expressed by Mary Cunningham in Richard Jeffrey's office. It might have been coincidental, but he vowed to himself to keep a close eye on them in future.

'It's good to meet you, Stanley,' Brendan Cole said cordially. 'Here's my card. If you're anything like Ben, perhaps we can do business together – assuming that Lucas and his credit committee here cough up the money. It just so happens that I've become involved in a development in Southern Spain that might be of interest. I'll send you a brochure – why not. Cheerio!' he said, striding away.

'He seems a nice fellow,' Stan commented.

'Very much so, and Brendan also happens to be one of our largest developers,' the banker disclosed. 'You could do a lot worse than piggyback on his shoulders.' Voss took Stan's empty glass of wine and helped him to another from a tray. 'Now, don't think I'm being rude,' he went on, 'but I need a few words with Gérard Le Saux over there,' and Stan saw a serious-looking individual with a nervous tic. 'Don't be fooled by appearances,' Voss advised in a low voice. 'If you want to get into commercial property, he's the guy you'll need to know. Go and help yourself to some food and I'll introduce you later. Oh, and regarding the three million revolving facility, off the record, the sentiment seems to be favourable.' The man winked before joining his other guests.

Stan left the cocktail party feeling upbeat about his prospects. The bank obviously had confidence in him, which was a major plus. He had learned that the only way to get on in the property world was with other people's money – and he intended to utilise every penny of it. His other cause for optimism was meeting Brendan Cole. The man was a fantastic contact; his experience in the property world could prove invaluable.

When he got home, he saw that his daughter had invited Ryan over. Apparently, the pair had made up their differences and were sat at the dining-room table revising intently for their GCSE exams in two weeks' time.

'Before you ask, I have eaten,' Tara said, looking up from the Emily Brontë set book in which she had been immersed.

'We brought in some Indian from that new place,' Ryan added. 'You should try it – it's really good.'

Typical, Stan thought, recalling that he hadn't been able to get his daughter to go there with him when he had suggested it. But at least she was eating properly again, which was the main thing.

'By the way, Grandma called, wanting to know where you were. She sounded upset,' Tara mumbled from behind the text into which she'd once more buried her nose.

'It's already after ten. I'll call her in the morning,' Stan replied. 'Ryan, how are you getting home? I can take you. Or if you prefer a minicab, Tara's got a number. Though it won't be long before you'll both be starting driving lessons.'

'Thanks for the offer,' the boy said politely, 'but my dad promised he'd come and pick me up when I'm ready.'

'Send him my best, will you? Right, I'll see you in the morning, Tara,' Stan said, eager to get away. He knew it was futile, but he was tempted to give Jackie another go. Thinking better of it, he decided to go instead for a drink at Morton's, the private members' club in Mayfair. Perhaps his luck would be in and he'd meet some female company at the bar. He didn't want to be around when Ryan's father turned up.

Like Alison, Howard Barnet was part of a past that he'd left a long way behind.

18

Summer 1994

Stan reclined in his expensive office chair, sipping on his midday scotch and soda, wondering where the time had gone. Roscole, the company he had set up jointly with Brendan Cole eighteen months previously, had produced dividends beyond his wildest dreams, prompting the move to prestigious West End premises. He had readily forfeited the cosmopolitan cafés on Gloucester Road for the more refined French patisseries of Marylebone High Street.

Seeing the huge amounts of money to be made in commercial rather than residential property, he and Brendan had both put in two million pounds and leveraged themselves up to the hilt. Their first deal was an office block in Fitzrovia which was bought at auction and sold on to a pension fund, making a healthy profit. Then they purchased a building off Chancery Lane, occupied by lawyers, whose lease agreements were soon due to expire. Brendan knew the freeholder, who had overstretched himself, enabling the courtyard-Listed building to be picked up for a song. The creation of twenty-five new leases at increased rents put the value up by a cool three million. A stream of other transactions followed and the pair suddenly found themselves with a net worth of just shy of £7 million.

Brendan had made it clear that because of the twenty-year disparity in their ages, Stan as the younger man would be the one expected to find the deals to take their company to the next level. This, he thought, was fair enough, taking into account that he had the benefit of the older man's knowledge gained from thirty years in the business, plus the introduction to all his contacts. Having no children interested in following in his footsteps, it gave Brendan great pleasure to be able to channel his energies through his protégé.

Gazing across Manchester Square at the Georgian building which housed the Wallace Collection of fine art, and thinking how much he had achieved in just a few years, Stan wondered what his father-in-law would have said if he could see him now. Not only had he managed to pay off the remaining inheritance tax liability early, but the proceeds from additional sales of the company's properties had been invested in his new venture with Brendan. If past achievements were anything to go by, his daughter's 75 per cent stake would treble in value by the time she was twenty-one!

Stan sat down at his desk and rang through to his secretary. A waif-like girl in a navy-blue frock that looked like a gymslip appeared magically in front of him, holding a wallet in her tiny hand.

'Good, Laura, you've got my itinerary to Spain.'

'You're booked on tomorrow morning's eight o'clock Iberia flight from Heathrow and returning on the five past nine the same evening,' she said, passing the tickets to her employer. 'Mr Cole has arranged for a car to pick you up at Malaga and take you to the development. Then you'll have lunch and the rest of the afternoon free before having to be back at the airport at seven. And finally, don't forget that you have an appointment at one today at the Institute of Directors,' she reminded him, striding away at a pace.

'No, I won't, thank you,' Stan called after the efficient young woman.

He couldn't really afford the time away from the office, but since La Quinta was Brendan's baby, he wanted to appear supportive. In any event, he had arranged to go over to see Victoria, the new woman in his life, late tomorrow evening, after he got back. The firm of Rider & Company, which she ran with her less able brother Ned, had established them as the most aggressive commercial agents in what was otherwise an exclusively male-dominated sector. What's more, Victoria had put a number of deals their way that hadn't yet hit the market. It helped that with a model's figure and emerald-green eyes, she was also extremely beautiful – and independent, living in her own house in a smart street behind Kensington Church Street. If his flight home tomorrow wasn't delayed, he hoped to be with her before midnight.

Damn! He'd just remembered that it was Tara's school leaving party the next night. She had especially asked him to make a note of the date and he'd failed her and forgotten all about it. Now there was nothing he could do, unless he could think of someone to take his place. His mother would have been ideal, except she hadn't been the same since the break-up with Paul Klein.

Convinced that it was a minor storm in a teacup that would swiftly blow over, Stan soon found he was wrong. Citing irreconcilable differences as the reason for calling off the wedding, Elaine had moved back into her old house in Hampstead Garden Suburb, the sale of which had fallen through with the South African couple who had expressed such strong interest. Convinced that there must be something more serious behind the issue with Paul, Stan had offered to play go-between but it was to no avail. Elaine had made up her mind and, as she said, there was no going back.

Stan went to the contacts list on his mobile phone, searching for Alison Brown. Tapping in the number that used to be lodged firmly in his memory, he was put through to her voicemail. Deciding against leaving a message, he realised he had run out of options. It was a pity because relations with his daughter had got so much better. She was happy enough with Ryan to repeat their two previous summer holidays to Greece. Now she'd decided to stay on in the sixth form after all, she was in strict competition with him over who would achieve the better grades in their A-levels. Stan didn't want to disappoint her by not turning up. Tara had calmed down a lot since her GCSEs and had seen the sense in staying on at school.

Suddenly he got an idea. Picking up his internal phone he said, 'Laura, I don't suppose you're free to attend Tara's school leaving party tonight? She really likes you and it would get me out of a hole. Naturally, I'll pay you overtime.'

The brisk young woman readily agreed and, relieved that he'd solved the problem, Stan left the office where his driver was waiting outside in the company Range Rover. Focusing on the scheme in Convent Garden that was being offered to him by Brendan's good friend Sammy Talachi, they proceeded to Pall Mall for his meeting with the Iranian billionaire.

*

As it sped away from Malaga's international airport, the temperature in the chauffeur-driven limousine registered 40 degrees. Stan, feeling sticky in his lightweight Armani suit, had forgotten quite how hot Spain got in the middle of July. Nevertheless, he was glad to be away.

Tara's hurt expression, after he'd told her that he wouldn't be at the school dinner, had been playing on his mind. It would have been better if they'd rowed; at least then she would have got it off her chest instead of remaining resolutely silent as always, holding back her tears.

The truth was that by putting business first again, he had let his daughter down on one of the most important occasions of her life. Picturing all the other students surrounded by parents proud of their children's achievements made him feel more guilty than ever. But his reaction was always the same: go after another deal, make more money, deluding himself that he could pay off his conscience that way.

Taking a sharp right turn, they began the gentle ascent and, passing a green landscape of olive trees and winding streams, soon arrived at the picturesque village of Benahavis. Brendan was standing by the roadside in an open-necked shirt, studying the plans he had been working on for the last two years. In front of him lay a vast mountain gorge scattered with dilapidated stone farmhouses and offering a distant view of the Mediterranean.

'Good trip?' he beamed, going up and putting his arm around his younger colleague when Stan climbed out of the car. 'Pretty spectacular eh?' he said, pointing out the panoramic view with his free hand.

Stan was left speechless. He had never seen a place of such natural beauty before. He could now understand why

Brendan had been so enthusiastic about the development. With a mixture of apartments and private villas and an exclusive eighteen-hole golf course, it had the potential to be the most exclusive resort on the Costa del Sol.

'Right, let's go. I'll drive and we can go through the numbers over lunch. Hope you like fish? The restaurants around here specialise in seafood.'

'Great, I'm starving,' Stan replied, only having managed to grab a quick coffee before his flight that morning.

A little further up the mountain, they stopped outside a small taverna. Passing through a pretty garden with an eating area shaded by large parasols, they entered the busy restaurant amidst the wafting aroma of Andalucían specialities and were ushered to a corner table past a big group of boisterous ex-pats with sunburned faces. A handful of local businessmen looked on, trying to hide their displeasure at being outnumbered.

'Do you want to leave the ordering to me?' Brendan asked, chewing on an olive.

'Fine, if I could just get something cold to drink. I'm really parched,' Stan said, helping himself to a crusty white roll from the breadbasket.

The waiter was called over and, without referring to the menu that he already knew by heart, Brendan gave their order.

'So, what's been going on since I've been away?' he asked.

'Sammy wants to do a deal,' Stan replied enthusiastically. 'You remember he mentioned the property he owns in Covent Garden? Well, I went to see it. He's got three buildings in Long Acre.'

'How much does he want for them?' Brendan quizzed.

'I think he can be knocked down to five million. They are all fully let to good covenants such as Next and Vodafone.'

'Stan, it's your call, but my experience of Sammy Talachi is that he doesn't give anything away that's any good, so just be careful.'

'Point taken. Actually, he did mention that there was another party interested.'

Brendan gave a knowing smile.

Just then, a waiter appeared with two plates of fried calamari on a bed of salad, while his colleague stood behind with an ice bucket containing a bottle of white Rioja wine.

It was past three o'clock by the time they reached dessert. Stan thought he would burst, if he ate another thing.

'Now you know why people need siestas,' Brendan joked, draining the remaining wine in his glass.

'That was fantastic,' Stan sighed, finishing his last mouthful of Crema Catalana and licking the spoon.

'I knew you'd like our project,' Brendan said, returning to the deal that had become his obsession. 'If you're interested, I'll cut you in for twenty per cent at the original buy-in price. It would have been more but, as you can appreciate, I've got other partners to take into consideration.'

'I understand,' Stan said blearily. He wasn't used to drinking at lunchtime and in the heat, the wine had gone to his head.

'So long as you tell me you're in, I'm prepared to stake your four mill and split the profit with you.'

'Why would you do that?' Stan asked, stunned by the other man's generosity.

'My dear boy, the scheme should sell out at around fifty million on which we should easily clear twenty per cent. I'm already a wealthy man. I just want to protect what I've got and I know I can trust you.'

'Yes, of course. I wouldn't do anything to jeopardise what we've built up,' Stan replied, filled with admiration for the father-like figure next to him.

'By the way,' Brendan went on, 'before you get completely carried away thinking that Christmas has come early, I've earmarked one of the larger villas for myself. Anne, my wife, loves it out here and quite apart from already being a proficient golfer, she's recently started taking Spanish lessons. But there's life left in the old sod yet, so don't think you'll be getting rid of me that quickly,' Brendan ended light-heartedly, summoning the waiter to bring the bill.

After leaving a generous tip, the two got up and made their way out through the restaurant, which showed no signs of a let-up in activity. Stan suddenly noticed an elderly man whom he thought looked familiar. He was the only one at his table talking, while the rest of the mixed company sat in respectful silence, listening intently.

It couldn't be . . . but it was! The man in question was Harry Rose. In two minds whether to go up and say something or join Brendan outside, Stan impulsively went over to where his uncle was seated.

'Hello, Harry,' Stan said, from no more than a foot away.

It only took a split second for the look of annoyance on the old man's face to change to one of surprise.

'I don't believe it!' he said, getting up and pinching Stan's cheek as he had done when he was a lad. 'This is Stanley, my nephew,' he announced proudly to the others present.

'Didn't expect you could afford to come on holiday to a place like this,' Harry then said condescendingly, getting up and moving away with Stan from the table.

'Actually, I'm on business for the day and returning to London this evening,' Stan clarified.

'Glad to see that you're doing all right for yourself,' Harry commented, 'especially after the hard time you've been through.' He turned back to his guests. 'Young Stan here worked for me in the business,' he told them. 'Our firm, H. & A. Rose, was the market leader in dining-room suites after the war,' he boasted. 'Then when I retired, the business went slowly downhill – not that I'm saying Stanley here was entirely to blame.'

Stan just stood there feeling foolish and saying nothing, regretting that he had made the effort to come over. For a moment he had forgotten that he was a millionaire in his own right, not a young man back at the factory in awe of the man who was now talking down to him.

'Anyway, son, it's really good to see you again,' Harry said after a short pause, indicating that the brief audience was over. 'I'm glad the fifty thousand I gave to your mother helped to get you back on your feet. Send her my best, will you – and tell her I'm sorry again about not making the engagement,' he added, unaware that the wedding had been called off.

'That Paul, he's a lucky fellow,' were Harry Rose's last words before returning to his party.

Brendan was sat outside enjoying the sun, when Stan appeared looking unsettled.

'Fancied another dessert or was it a piece of talent that

kept you back?' Brendan jested. 'Sorry, I forgot that you've only got eyes for Victoria Rider – not that I blame you with that fabulous ginger hair. But be careful, my boy. Women like that, used to getting their own way in business, can be a nightmare in their private lives.'

'It was an uncle of mine who lives out here. Imagine the coincidence of bumping into him today! I hadn't seen him in a while,' Stan said, justifying his absence.

'You should have introduced me,' Brendan said, only half-seriously.

'Sorry, it was a bit rude of me,' Stan acknowledged, still put out and wanting to forget about the unfortunate episode.

'Right-oh,' Brendan said good-naturedly, getting to his feet. 'So unless there's anything else we have to talk about I'll run you back to the Marbella Club where I'm staying, and if you don't mind, they'll arrange a car to the airport. I'd take you myself but that lunch has rather got the better of me and my air-conditioned bedroom beckons.'

The two men said their goodbyes outside the renowned beachfront hotel, arranging to meet back in their London office in ten days' time. While Stan sorted out his ride to the airport, Brendan took the lift up to his penthouse suite. Waiting for him stretched out naked on the king-sized double bed was Luisa, his twenty-seven-year-old mistress.

Stan stood outside Victoria's house in Kensington and rang the bell a second time. Again, there was no answer. There must be a logical explanation, he thought. Perhaps she was entertaining clients and was unable to get away. Just as he was getting into a taxi to take him home, he remembered what Brendan had said about females in business. Perhaps he had misjudged Victoria Rider, after all.

Tara's car was in the drive when he got back to the home he had grown out of. On the hall table, left open, was the English prize she had received for the most original essay; no doubt an unsubtle dig because he hadn't been there to see her receive it. In a few months, she'd be away at university – hopefully with more important things to worry about – and he could get on with making a new life for himself, starting with a move to a more up-market area to reflect his status.

Exhausted from all the travelling, Stan went upstairs and got ready for bed. Parading in front of the dressing-room mirror, it was clear he'd put a little weight on in the face and had filled out a bit around the waist, but it was nothing too drastic for a man of his age, he rationalised. On reflection, he couldn't have cared less that Victoria Rider might have had second thoughts. With the recent delivery of a new Ferrari, there would be no shortage of other women at his disposal.

Flopping on the bed, instead of being happy about all the positive things that had happened that day, like getting involved in the La Quinta project with Brendan or the fact that he had decided to go ahead on the deal with Sammy Talachi, something about the bizarre episode with his uncle had made him feel uneasy but he couldn't put his finger on exactly what it was.

Just as he was about to fall asleep, he remembered Harry saying that he had given his mother the fifty thousand pounds – which Stan had always assumed had come from her. This was something that he would certainly ask her about, he decided muzzily, the next time he saw her.

19

The next morning, Stan crept stealthily downstairs, hoping to avoid a confrontation with his daughter before he left for work. The last thing he expected, therefore, was to see her sitting at the table, typing away furiously on her laptop.

'Morning, Daddy, good trip to Spain?' Tara greeted him cheerfully.

'Yes, it was fine,' Stan stammered, wrong-footed again by the teenager. 'Congratulations on your prize, by the way,' he added, a little shame-facedly.

'Thanks. I gave it to Grandma but she left it behind when she brought me home.'

'I didn't think she was going to be able to come?' Stan said, pleased to hear the news. It made up for his absence.

'It only took a phone call – and guess what? She loved it, especially the after-dinner speeches. She said it reminded her of the school in Yorkshire where she got evacuated to during the war. Alison was there as well, although she left early, so there was really no need for you to have worried.'

'What happened with Laura?' Stan asked.

'Oh, I told her that she didn't have to stay – a bit of luck really, because there weren't any spare tickets.'

Stan looked at his daughter, feeling a strange mixture of resentment and admiration. She was obviously far more resilient than he had cared to admit; harder to accept was his impression that she really didn't need him.

'It was a bit strange though. Grandma kept going on about what you were doing in Spain,' Tara let slip. 'Why was she so interested?'

'I need to have a word with her about that,' her father said thoughtfully.

'She'll be here soon, so you can ask her yourself.'

Stan looked puzzled.

'Apparently, I'm in favour at the moment.' Tara grinned.

'What's that supposed to mean?'

'You obviously didn't notice the Rose expression of disapproval when it came to Ryan. Grandma and you have got one face!'

'That's not fair – I don't dislike him. Anyway, when you're away at university, there'll be plenty of opportunities to meet other young men.'

'That's the point: I've decided *not* to go to university,' Tara announced, peering up from her computer. 'I never wanted to carry on studying after A-levels.'

'But how about the offers from King's College and University College?' Stan was shocked. 'You did so well to get them. You can't just throw those chances away!'

'What, you want me to go just so you can brag to your friends about how well your daughter has done? And please – spare me the line about how Mummy would have wanted it. My mind is made up.'

Stan knew from experience that it was pointless arguing with his headstrong daughter, but he wasn't yet ready to concede.

'Won't you at least consider taking a gap year?' he said reasonably. 'That's what a lot of kids do, go travelling and see the world and start university afterwards. You won't have to work to pay your way. The trust money will be yours in a few months and . . .'

'I fully intend to pay my own way but without asking *you* for help,' Tara told him. 'That's why I've been short-listed for a job at *Cosmopolitan* magazine. If I get it, I'll be starting as soon as I get back from holiday, assuming my A-level grades meet the predictions.'

Stan was lost for words. He felt a twinge of envy, perhaps because he wished he had shown the same resolve when he wanted to pursue his music, instead of caving in and following the 'sensible' career in accountancy his mother had in mind for him.

'Don't look so glum,' his daughter said kindly. 'You'll still see quite a lot of me.'

'When's this going to happen?' Stan asked, somewhat subdued.

'Well, I shan't be able to move out straight away, you know, not on what they're paying me, unless I can find someone to share with me.'

'I can see that you've got it all worked out,' her father sighed, knowing when he was beaten.

Tara gave a smug smile. 'Oh, and Alison seems to have come around to the idea, in case you're thinking of asking her.'

Suddenly, there was a ring at the bell.

'It's Grandma. I'll go,' the girl said, getting up to answer the door.

A smiling Elaine Rose came in with her granddaughter by her side.

'I hope you told Tara how proud we all are of her?' she said, the rebuke clearly directed at her son.

'Mother, it couldn't be helped,' Stan replied, downplaying the fact that he hadn't been able to make the school event.

'Well, I hope your business trip was worth it,' came the curt response. Then his mother added in a lighter tone: 'Tara and I are going to Bond Street. I think a piece of jewelry would be an appropriate gift for working so hard, don't you?' she said, exchanging a knowing look with her granddaughter.

'Thank you, Grandma. I'll go and get ready. Won't be long,' Tara said, striding happily away.

'Stanley, you really do need to spend more time with her. You'll only regret it when she's away at university,' Elaine warned him, settling herself in one of a pair of matching armchairs.

Stan didn't respond, thinking it would be better for Tara herself to tell her grandmother that she had other ideas.

'You'll never guess who I bumped into yesterday,' he said instead, lolling against the fireplace.

Elaine remained impassive while she waited for confirmation of what she feared was coming. Stoically, she recalled their conversation at the party, the one which had precipitated her calling off the marriage to Paul.

'Harry was having lunch at the same restaurant – talk about coincidences,' Stan tutted. 'Hasn't changed a bit – still showing off in front of his bunch of cronies.'

'What did he say to you?' Elaine asked quietly, focusing her attention on her son.

'Only asked how I was doing. Actually, I think he was a bit peeved that I was there – as if I had entered his private domain without being invited. But he did mention that he was the one who gave me the fifty thousand pounds.'

'And did he tell you why?' Elaine looked wary.

'No, but it gave him great pleasure to let his friends know how generous he'd been.'

'Stanley dear, I'm afraid there's rather more to it than that,' his mother said. Her eyes had misted over, and she needed a moment to compose herself.

'I was only nineteen when I met your father. It was different in those days; girls of my age, from my background, were usually betrothed by then. Anyway, one day I accompanied my father on a journey to the East End. Being the eldest, I was his favourite and he wanted to show me the street where he grew up. My parents were redecorating their house and needed to buy some new dining-room furniture, so that after that, we drove over to H. & A. Rose to take a look. Even just after the war, your father's firm was the only place one went to. I'd never been into a factory before and had no idea what to expect.'

Stan sat back attentively.

'Although it was explained that they normally never dealt with the public, they were prepared to make an exception and we were permitted to look around. I can still remember that wonderful smell of varnish in the showroom. Then, we were joined by the most handsome man I had ever seen. He was the image of the film star Dick Powell. I'm talking about your father, Arnold. It was impossible for any girl not to fall madly in love with him. Anyway, as we were leaving, he came up to me and in front of my father asked whether he might see me again.'

'You always told me that Grandpa wasn't keen,' Stan said, still having no idea where all this was leading.

'That was an understatement. My parents had very definite ideas on the subject, and I'm afraid that as your father didn't fit the mould, they refused point blank.'

'But that obviously didn't stop you?'

'You know what happens when someone says no to me about something I've made up my mind about.'

Stan thought how ironic it was that he had experienced the exact same thing with his own daughter just moments before.

'So, you went ahead and married Dad anyway,' he concluded. 'I didn't know how dead set against it your parents were.'

'When they realised they had little chance of dissuading me and that I would go ahead, with or without their blessing, they softened to the idea – probably because they didn't want to lose me and any future grandchildren.'

'So, you got your own way and lived happily ever after. I know all this,' Stan remarked somewhat impatiently.

'That was just it.' Elaine sighed. 'It wasn't like that.'

'What do you mean? Dad adored you.'

'I'm afraid it was very one-sided. He was a lovely man, your father, but my parents were right: we were from different worlds.'

'But you were the perfect couple – everyone said so!' Stan felt alarmed. Having unearthed what was obviously a dark family secret, he sensed that there was more to come.

'It was merely a façade – put on mainly for your benefit,' his mother confessed.

'So why did you stay together?'

'I knew how much you idolised your father, and you were my paramount concern.'

'So, you lived unhappily together all those years – and I've only just found out about it?' Stan said, feeling aggrieved.

'I'm afraid divorce was out of the question and, in any case, your father would never have agreed.'

'So what did you do?'

The moment had finally come, the moment that Elaine Rose had always dreaded and hoped she could avoid. Hadn't she done her best to protect her son all his life, possibly to his detriment? Now he was about to hear the truth and she would have to bear the consequences.

'I had an affair,' she said. 'It wasn't something planned, nor that I was proud of, but it was a chance to escape the dull life that I had found myself trapped in and I grabbed it.'

'With whom?' Stan asked, astounded by this latest revelation.

His mother paused for a second, trying to find a way to soften the blow.

'Your Uncle Harry always liked me. At first, I thought it was just a petty rivalry with his older brother. But he had a way about him and I'm sorry to admit that I succumbed to his charm.' The woman took a deep breath and braced herself for her son's reaction.

'You're saying that you were carrying on with Harry behind Dad's back?' Seriously agitated, Stan began pacing the room.

'I knew it wasn't right but there were no children involved. I deluded myself into thinking that I might have a future with Harry. He said that he would be able to sort things out with Arnold – and foolishly I believed him.' Elaine paused before going on, 'The trouble was, Harry – the scoundrel that he is – had a few other women in tow and I didn't find out until it was too late that he had not the slightest intention of being with me.'

'What do you mean by "too late"?' Stan said, confronting his mother.

'I was pregnant.'

'*What?* What did you say?' Stan stammered, sure that he hadn't heard correctly.

'I was pregnant – with you, Stanley. Harry is your father,' she confirmed unequivocally.

'But that's impossible.' Stan took in a deep breath. He had come out in a cold sweat. Feeling light-headed, he just about managed to stagger over to the chair next to his mother.

'But surely Dad would have known?' he whimpered.

'Since having a child was not what Harry had in mind, we let Arnold believe that the baby was his,' Elaine continued unemotionally. She realised this was no time for half-truths.

Suddenly, Stan recalled what Teddy Isaacs, the basement tenant at Cornwall Gardens, had said about 'Harry's boy' that had seemed so far-fetched at the time.

Stan just sat there staring into space. He didn't notice Tara coming back into the room, her face a deathly pale. She had overheard her grandmother's words and could barely take in this revelation. She needed time to absorb it.

'Is Daddy all right?' she asked, feeling she had to say something. 'He looks as if he's just seen a ghost.'

'I'm afraid I've had to impart some rather upsetting news to your father,' was all Elaine was prepared to divulge. 'No doubt he'll tell you all about it when he's good and ready.'

Then, buttoning her coat and feeling as if the weight of the last forty-odd years had been lifted from her shoulders, Stanley's mother simply got up to take her granddaughter out shopping, leaving her shocked son to recover from the bombshell she had just dropped.

Paul Klein was working in his study when Elaine arrived at his flat later that afternoon.

'How did it go?' he said, getting up to greet the woman he loved unconditionally.

'Stanley took it very badly,' she replied, drained of all of her resolve. Then, unable to control herself any longer, she began weeping.

'Darling, please don't cry.' Taking out a handkerchief, Paul went up and gently dabbed her eyes.

'You are the most adorable man,' Elaine snivelled.

'Stanley had to know some time – and you *were* very young at the time,' he said soothingly.

'That's no excuse for what I put him through. You should have seen the look on his poor face. My son is going to end up hating me for the rest of my life!'

'He'll come around. It'll just take time. More of a problem is what we're going to do about Harry,' the silver-haired man remarked.

'What can we do? He abrogated any responsibility as soon as I became pregnant, so he's not likely to change now, is he?' Elaine said bitterly.

'And how about Stanley? Don't you think he'd be curious to hear his father's version of events?'

'Why would he? After all, there was nothing stopping Harry from coming clean after Arnold died. I suspect he thought he could get away with carrying the secret with him to his grave.'

'Then I suggest that you should be the one to break the

bad news to him,' Paul Klein said firmly.

Not certain that she had heard correctly, Elaine moved away.

'Let me think about it,' she muttered, following on a couple of minutes later with, 'Flying to Spain there and back in a day is going to be tiring,' as she became more receptive to the idea.

'Perhaps you should think about staying overnight?' Paul suggested.

'You wouldn't mind?' she responded, surprised by the comment.

'Darling, you had plenty of time to do something about *that* if you had wanted to before we got together – not that I would blame him for trying,' Paul teased, but secretly seeing it as a perfect opportunity to establish whether she still harboured feelings for the chap.

Harry Rose was waiting impatiently inside the air-conditioned airport terminal for the arrival of the British Airways late-afternoon flight from London. It was just like Elaine to make a drama, he thought to himself.

'I need to see you,' was the only reason she had given him on the phone for her trip.

Naturally it had to involve Stanley: why else would she have been prepared to make the 1400-mile journey to Spain in the height of summer? If it was more money she was after, now she was well ensconced with that wealthy diamond merchant, she should go and ask *him*. Harry had done his research on Paul Klein; the bloke was a multi-millionaire! That was typical of his former sister-in-law: always had her nose in the air, thinking she was better than everybody else.

From the first moment Harry laid eyes on her all those years ago, he knew she was way out of his league. The shameful affair that had been conducted at his instigation was only to prove to himself that the young lady from Knightsbridge was not beyond his reach. But then for years afterwards, flitting from one unsatisfactory relationship to another, never finding anyone to compare with her, happiness seemed destined to elude him. That was why he had resisted so vehemently when Elaine had said that Stanley wanted to come into the business. Looking so much like his mother, the boy reminded him of the only woman he had truly loved.

The hardest thing, denied to him by his treachery towards his brother Arnold, was the realisation that he could never have a relationship with his own son! That was the oath he had sworn to Elaine and was the reason that he remained aloof from the lad; the hard exterior, which he portrayed, was purely a façade to enable him to deal with the situation that was tearing him apart inside.

As he stood brooding, lost in thoughts of the past, a well-presented woman strode confidently through the automatic doors, pulling a small overnight case behind her.

'Hello, Harry,' she said with her usual panache. 'You needn't have bothered, I am quite capable of getting a taxi.'

'Let's just say my curiosity got the better of me,' he replied. 'Though you took a bit of a chance, didn't you, with those terrorist attacks?'

'Compared to the Blitz, a few bombs here or there were hardly going to put me off,' she replied disdainfully, referring to the IRA bombing at Heathrow airport a few months earlier.

The two former lovers strolled out into the warm night air. Harry helped his visitor into the Seat convertible and they drove away towards Puerto Banus, a fashionable marina just south of the holiday resort of Marbella.

'Where are we going?' Elaine asked.

'I assume you haven't eaten?' Harry shouted, trying to make himself heard above the noise of the on-coming traffic.

'I'm sure I can find something at the hotel,' she said, trying to hold back a yawn.

'No need, I've booked a restaurant at the port. I'll drop you back afterwards.'

'Doesn't sound much like the Harry I know. I thought you'd want to get this over and done with and put me on the first plane back to England,' Elaine jibed.

'Don't think very highly of me, do you?' Harry responded, heading towards Torremolinos, a route he knew with his eyes shut.

'You forget, I do know you rather well,' his passenger said more warmly.

Harry returned her smile. Drawing up at a tollbooth, he handed over a few pesetas to the attendant in his sentry box and continued in silence along the N340 coast road, arriving twenty minutes later at their destination.

As they entered the colourful water-front restaurant, two guitar players, in traditional costume, were moving through the tables serenading the diners with the Cuban hit song 'Guantanamera' – which Harry had always taken to be called 'One Calamari'.

'Is this the place where Stan ran into you?' Elaine asked casually.

'That was in the hills,' Harry replied, wondering if that brief encounter a few weeks ago was the reason for Elaine's impromptu visit. He went up and gave his name to the hostess, a voluptuous female with tightly pulled-back hair.

'I see you haven't changed much,' Elaine teased, catching him ogling the woman.

Harry grinned as they were shown to a front-row table overlooking the illuminated harbour packed with luxury cruisers.

'Stanley knows the truth about us,' Elaine announced forthrightly.

'I suppose it was bound to happen sometime,' Harry replied, not bothering to look up from the menu. 'Have you decided what you want?'

'I assume there was a reason why you mentioned that the fifty thousand came from you,' Elaine said, unable to think about food until she had had her say.

'Yes,' Harry confessed, reaching across the table for her hand. 'But to be quite honest, I didn't have the guts to tell him the rest.'

'But you assumed *I* would?'

Harry responded with his usual smirk.

Just then, a waiter came up to take their order.

'A seafood salad will be enough for me,' Elaine indicated.

'And for the *señor*?'

'The paella, please. I'm telling you, it's the best on the coast,' Harry enthused. When the waiter had gone, he said, 'Elaine, I'm not getting any younger and I want to try and make up for the wrong I've done, while I still have the chance.'

'And what exactly do you mean by that?'

'Well, you can hardly expect me to call the boy up after

all this time and say that his father would like to have a relationship with him, can I? I'm probably the last person he'd want to see.'

'So what do you propose?' Elaine didn't mention that her son had also wanted nothing to do with her too, since that day at his house. Perhaps it was too late for either of them to make amends.

'I can see that Stan's landed on his feet with Brendan Cole,' Harry said, suddenly changing tack.

'You know him?' she asked, only having heard of Stan's partner once before.

'Course I do! I was the one who set the bloke up on the Costa del Sol in the first place. *And* I found the site for that La Quinta project of his. In fact, I've got a tidy sum invested in it myself. Frankly, I was a bit put out that Brendan never came up and said hello at that place we were at for lunch,' Harry pondered, making space for the plate of food that had just arrived. 'Don't suppose he put two and two together that Stan and me were related. Still, so long as that son of ours is doing all right, that's all that matters,' he said, picking up his fork.

The remainder of the meal was taken up with trite conversation between two people well on in years, who in their own ways still had feelings for the other; each hoping the spark that was once between them could be re-ignited, but neither able to communicate what had been suppressed for too long.

Elaine spent the night alone in an unglamorous hotel room, less disappointed than she had envisaged by the absence of a romantic liaison. Feeling that she had failed to make any significant headway with regard to her son, she flew back to London early the next day, relieved that Paul was there to meet her, and that she had finally got Harry Rose out of her system.

At roughly the same time, a dapper elderly man entered his English lawyer's office in Malaga and handed him his instructions for his Last Will and Testament, nominating his son Stanley Rose as his sole beneficiary.

20

Alison refilled her tumbler with vodka for the umpteenth time that evening, attempting to anaesthetise herself against the guilt of her treacherous deed. The document that was causing her so much anguish stared accusingly up at her from the coffee table in the middle of the living room.

Three weeks earlier, she had gone around to the Roses' house after work, in time to take Tara to her end-of-year school dinner. It was to be Alison's farewell to her. Tara was no longer the withdrawn child she had comforted so many times after her mother and grandpa died. The girl whom Alison had looked upon as her own daughter was now an independent young woman who had managed to overcome everything the world had thrown at her and was now full of joie de vivre about starting her career as a journalist.

The spiel Alison had prepared proved unnecessary: Tara agreed to sign the papers without question. It was only at Alison's insistence that the eighteen-year-old girl heeded her advice to check with the solicitors first. Naturally, Tara assumed the paperwork was to do with her grandfather's company but, as in the past, she showed little interest in anything to do with business. As she saw things, it typified her father's continued obsession with money – a pursuit that only brought unhappiness.

Under the pretence of representing her ward's best interests, Alison had been party to depriving Tara of what was rightly hers. Thank God, she thought, that there was a way out of this so she wouldn't have to live with what she had done.

Alison looked over at the naked black woman, fast asleep on the sofa in the August heat. She and Syrenna had met in a gay bar in Camden three years previously. Syrenna had just finished work at the British Library and had gone to the pub for a few drinks before returning to her small flat in Tottenham, North London. Alison had been on her own since the break-up from her long-time girlfriend, Janine, and was just looking for company. The pair hit it off immediately. A short time afterwards, they moved in together to Alison's apartment.

Those were such happy memories . . . unlike the hell she was going through now. But it would all soon be over. Several days had gone by and she still hadn't returned the lawyer's calls. One ultimatum passed, and then another. Richard Jeffrey's patience was finally exhausted. His text made it clear that if he wasn't in possession of the document by the following day, Tara would be told about the letters to her mother.

Fortunately, thanks to Syrenna's promise to deliver the envelope by hand, it wouldn't come to that. By the time Richard Jeffrey arrived at the office in the morning, the signed paperwork would be on his desk and Alison herself would be in a better place.

Clutching the bottle of vodka, she staggered through to the bedroom, nearly waking her lover. She glanced at the packet of sleeping pills which lay on the dressing table;

she had changed her mind more than once about taking them. After one particularly light-hearted night out, when she and Syrenna had talked about emigrating to Australia, she actually thought it might be possible to start a new life. But deep down, Alison knew there was no escape from what she had done: it would haunt her for ever.

The distraught woman went over to the bed. Opening the first packet of capsules, she popped the contents into her mouth. She thought about the family that she'd lost contact with – the father, a shipbuilder on the Clyde who had hanged himself after being laid off – and her mother, who was only able to get through the day with a bottle of whisky to prop her up. No wonder all four children had issues. Her twin sisters Gail and Belinda, qualified kindergarten teachers, had become Buddhists and had gone off to Tibet, while their brother Gary had settled for a quiet life as a farm labourer in the Highlands. None of them would miss her.

Feeling no initial effect from the pills, Alison reached for the bottle and took another gulp. She had a sudden urge to retrieve the letter to Tara which she had crumpled up and discarded earlier on. Clumsily, she managed to get off the bed, crouching down to the waste-paper bin to rescue the note that had suddenly taken on such importance. As she attempted to straighten up again, she hit her head hard on the brass door handle and fell unconscious to the floor, clasping the letter.

My dear Tara,
 I am writing these words to you with tears in my eyes, begging for your forgiveness. Please believe that when I asked your father to accept me as your

guardian, I had only your best interests at heart. I had treasured you since you were a little girl and, as far as I was concerned, our relationship became even more precious and meaningful when your dear mother passed away.

Unfortunately, your father's lawyers, Lowndes Jeffrey, uncovered some aspects of my past that Richard Jeffrey threatened to use against me unless I cooperated in their deceit. You see, they had copies of certain intimate letters which they vowed to make public, thereby causing you to sever our friendship. That was something I couldn't bear, my darling. And that is what drove me to do what I did.

By asking you to sign those papers, I knowingly deprived you of your inheritance. It was such a cowardly act. I see now, far too late, that I was only thinking of myself, about losing you, not about you and your future. How I wish with all my heart that I had been brave enough to stand up and do the right thing! I deceived myself into believing that I could carry on living as if nothing had happened. But I know now that's not possible.

Forgive me, darling Tara. I pray that you will retain happy memories of the good times we had together and be strong for your father. He is a good man who loves you as much as he is able.

With all my love,
Alison

The next morning, a plain white envelope, marked for the personal attention of Richard Jeffrey, was delivered by hand to Lowndes Jeffrey Solicitors.

Syrenna Raphael was in a tearful state when she left the house early that day. She couldn't get the image of Alison's lifeless body out of her mind. After making the short diversion to Mayfair, she got on a tube at Green Park for the half-hour journey to work. Later that evening, as instructed by Richard Jeffrey, she reported the incident to the authorities. After what seemed like hours of questioning, and making a statement that was for the most part true, the police allowed the body to be taken away for examination.

There was, however, no trace of a letter in the dead woman's hand.

Richard Jeffrey locked the safe and returned to his desk. The document showing the transfer of shares, signed by Tara Rose, would remain in his possession for the time being. In the meantime, the bank account he had opened in the name of Alison Brown, containing funds of £20,000 and a first-class plane ticket to Panama would mysteriously turn up at Fitzcrombie Estate Agents where she held the position of senior sales negotiator. In the investigation that would inevitably follow, it would become quite clear that their employee had been involved in some surreptitious activity on the side. It was a small price to pay and would create the necessary distraction while he got everything in place with his offshore company.

Richard had been meticulous in every detail of the operation. Fortunately, the Miller Investments' Articles of Association had never been updated regarding directors' approval for share sales, and since its Registered Office had remained at Lowndes Jeffrey, Stanley Rose would be faced with the indignity of having to file his company's Annual Return showing a transfer of which he had no knowledge and could do nothing about. Once the banks were tipped off with regard to the change in shareholding – courtesy of an actor friend he'd paid to impersonate the new owners – Stanley would find himself out on his ear. Following this, Richard Jeffrey would bide his time before buying the minority shareholder out for a pittance, thus ridding himself of the Rose and Miller names for good.

Peering down at the crumpled letter, blood-stained from Alison's fall, he picked up his silver desk lighter and lit one end of the suicide note. It had been easier than he had imagined, obtaining Syrenna Raphael's cooperation. When she had telephoned him, in a panic about what her girlfriend kept threatening to do – and worried that she would lose the home that she had purchased jointly with Alison if the latter committed suicide, he assured her that in that unfortunate eventuality, he would arrange for their mortgage to be paid off.

There was a price for this. In return, he stipulated that, should the worst happen, Syrenna must remove any evidence that might implicate his firm in any wrongdoing. He didn't point out that the Mortgage Protection Policy, which his firm had put in place when the women bought the property, would have paid out, in any case, on the death of one of the owners – if it appeared to be a straightforward accident such as Alison's head wound resulting from a drunken fall and after mistaking her dose of sleeping tablets.

Richard Jeffrey was content. He had achieved his initial objective, albeit at the expense of the Scottish woman's life.

Sometimes the weaker ones went to the wall, he shrugged, and it was just unfortunate that Alison Brown happened to be perfectly placed to correct a gross injustice. Just as satisfying, Stanley Rose would eventually find himself with a useless 25 per cent holding, working for a company which was now under Richard's sole control. In the meantime, it was in his interests to use the fellow to carry on growing Miller Investments as if nothing had changed.

Three days later, the post mortem completed, the coroner was sufficiently satisfied with the pathologist's report to issue a temporary death certificate. Alison's body was released for burial, which in normal circumstances would have been to her family – but in this instance it was to Syrenna Raphael, conveniently nominated by Alison as her next-of-kin. Since her role in the cover-up placed her at the forefront of any wrongdoing, Syrenna needed little persuasion to remain silent and allow Richard Jeffrey to make the funeral arrangements for a woman whose death, at least to the outside world, seemed like a tragic accident.

21

Stan left the office early as he had every day that week. It was the beginning of October and notwithstanding the strong improvement in the economy since the beginning of the year, there had been no visible pick-up in the property market. Anything worth buying had already been snapped up by a few predatory developers, leaving a handful of overpriced deals that no one wanted.

Sunning himself in Spain, Brendan was the clever one. But with all the money he had in the bank, the Irishman could afford to take it easy. Apart from their joint holdings in Roscole, the major part of Stan's wealth was all tied up in Miller Investments. Granted, with the profits that were being made, he could still pay himself a six-figure salary – but that wasn't *real* money. Not that he regretted for one moment pulling out of the deal with the Singaporeans, who had approached him to purchase his company. Even though they'd been prepared to up their offer a couple of times, the £15 million didn't exactly fill him with excitement. If they wanted it that badly, they'd be back again, prepared to pay his asking price of £22.5 million – that was more like it!

Walking the length of Bond Street, he crossed Piccadilly and hurried down St James's Street into Pall Mall, arriving after a few minutes at a shabby-looking building, not at all in keeping with the grander premises on either side. Brendan, being on the selection committee of Burts, the exclusive private members' club, had been able to fast-track Stan's application – which was handy since there was a three-year waiting list, added to the fact they weren't overly keen on letting in Jews.

Stan entered the old-fashioned bar, an ambience in keeping with the bunch of senior, pipe-smoking members in brass-buttoned blazers who sat sipping on their gin and tonics.

'Evening, Michael. My usual, please,' Stan said to the youthful-looking barman in a striped waistcoat.

'Coming up, Mr Rose, sir,' he replied in a deep voice, incompatible with his slight frame, and proceeded to pluck a bottle of Bell's whisky from the shelf above him.

'Mr Cole joining you?' he enquired, pouring out a generous measure into a crystal tumbler.

'No, he's abroad,' Stan replied.

'All right for some,' the skinny fellow grumbled. 'I've only had a week off the whole year – and then it rained the whole bleeding time!'

'Might as well keep the tab open, I'll be here for a while yet,' Stan said, moving heavily across with his drink to a weathered chair by the window.

Stan was not in a good way; even Brendan Cole had been sufficiently concerned to advise him to cut down on his drinking. The problem was, alcohol was the only thing that gave Stan any escape from his frequent bouts of melancholia. Dismissing them as no more than a temporary malaise that would soon pass, he carried on as normal. And the strain of doing so was apparent for all to see – apart from Stan himself.

He had shrugged off, or so he thought, the initial shock he'd suffered regarding the revelation about his father, although having refused any further contact with his mother since then, he hadn't really put it to the test. He still found it incomprehensible that Elaine had allowed him to carry on believing his entire life that Arnold Rose was his real father. Not that his sentiments towards Harry were any better; if anything, they were far worse. It was bad enough that his mother had fallen for the smooth-talking younger brother, but then for her to be discarded when it was established that she was carrying the man's child, defied belief. And on top of that, to trick poor Arnold into believing that the child was his . . . Stan felt nothing but disgust towards both Elaine and Harry. He just hoped that Arnold hadn't ever found out. The discovery that his beloved son was not truly his would have destroyed the kindly man.

Stan's mind turned to Tara. So far, in the weeks that followed Elaine's revelation, she hadn't mentioned the dark family secret that she had walked into. Presumably her grandmother had used her good sense not to bring it up.

The girl's excellent A-level results had not influenced her to change her mind about going to university. Naturally, it helped that Stan had agreed to support her with the rent of the one-bed flat she had taken off the North End Road in Golders Green, up by the famous Old Bull and Bush public house, at least until she could stand on her own two feet. How much easier it would have been for him, he thought, if he himself had shown the same initiative by moving out of his parents' house instead of getting married straight from home.

No longer facing resistance from his daughter, he put the house in Hampstead on the market, and within a few days accepted an offer of five hundred thousand pounds. That fact that he had to cough up a cool £1.5 million for its replacement didn't put him off. He had secured a fantastic Victorian residence in prime St John's Wood, two miles away, which would only increase in value. What he needed now was a woman to share it with him. If it meant that she was still young enough to have children, he would have to give the matter serious consideration, although starting a new family in his forties wasn't a prospect that he particularly relished.

At this point in his introspection, Stan held up his empty glass, trying to attract the attention of the barman.

'Same again, Mr Rose?' the young man said, looking up from the evening paper that one of the members had left behind.

'Terrible about that poor woman,' he went on, going over and placing Stan's fresh whisky on a coaster in front of him.

'What's that?' Stan asked, only half-listening.

'I wouldn't be surprised if someone bumped her off,' the barman mumbled, tapping his nose before sloping off.

Stan had more pressing things on his mind, namely the dinner engagement with his interior designer. It hadn't taken long to get over Victoria Rider. To her credit, the agent had been extremely apologetic for messing him around that evening when she wasn't at home, and suggested that they make another arrangement. However, suspicious of her motives, he thought better of it and decided to give the dynamic businesswoman with the long ginger hair a wide berth.

Charlotte Jacobs was a different matter. Recommended to him by Brendan's wife Anne, he was immediately taken with the twenty-seven-year-old Cambridge graduate. Charlotte had quickly deduced that his interest in her extended beyond her suggestions of colour schemes for his new house, and she told him that although she had a long-time boyfriend, the relationship wasn't going anywhere. To his credit, Stan did feel slightly uneasy about dating someone when there was such a large age difference, but so far it remained platonic and they did enjoy each other's company.

Unaware that he had fallen asleep where he sat, Stan got up and tottered over to the bar to settle up before going off to Le Caprice restaurant, a few minutes' walk away, where he had arranged to meet Charlotte. Just as he was about to leave, however, some instinct made him glance at the paper that had been left open on the counter. Stan paused when he came to the short item the barman had talked about.

Following the inquest into the recent death of forty-year-old Alison Brown, information has come to light leading police to believe that criminal activities may have been involved. The former estate agent was found dead at her home in Islington on 17 August. The police are asking for anyone who has information that might assist them to come forward.

At first, Stan thought that it must be a different woman with the same name, except the description exactly fitted the former close family friend. Wondering how he was going to break the news to his daughter, he left the club, making his way slowly up St James's Street to a dinner that had suddenly lost its appeal.

Earlier the same day

Tara tried Alison's number again. Since starting work a few weeks previously, she had made a habit of being first in at the premises under the arches of Southwark Bridge that housed the *Londoner* newspaper. It was just as well, since she didn't want to be seen making private calls. Her arrival had already created a stir with her colleagues, Gareth and Marise, who regarded her presence as an unwelcome intrusion into their space, and she didn't want to give them any further excuse for resentment. Not easy when, from day one, her boss Mark Bailey had made it clear that she had been brought in to liven up the weekly paper, and then had unashamedly given her the pick of the assignments. As far as he was concerned, it created healthy competition.

Tara hadn't thought twice about taking the position as trainee reporter. Having received so many letters of rejection after the offer at *Cosmopolitan* fell through, she was relieved just to be given an interview. It was explained to her that if she was prepared to start at the bottom and accept the £100 a week wage that was being offered, the job was hers.

Even though the paper had a circulation of just 70,000 and a staff of only two other reporters – who were also responsible for their own sub-editing – she saw it as a unique opportunity to gain hands-on experience that wouldn't be available to her at a larger publication.

Putting the phone back down, Tara frowned: something didn't make sense. Recalling how stressed Alison had seemed on the evening of the school dinner, the girl now regretted that she hadn't contacted her again sooner. But she was so busy getting bedded into her new job that Alison's birthday, five days before, had completely slipped her mind.

'Morning!' It was her boss, a rugged man in a grey sweatshirt and jeans, who had just made an appearance. 'Where are the others?' he asked in his mild Irish accent. Mark Bailey was in his early thirties with designer stubble and didn't believe in dressing for work – something which, as editor, he felt was his prerogative.

'Gareth's on his way back from his mother's funeral in Halifax and Marise is covering the aftermath of the Hyde Park demonstrations against the Criminal Justice Bill,' Tara answered competently.

'Bloody good job,' commented Mark. 'How dare they bring in a crap piece of legislation like that! It's an infringement of personal liberty. Soon we'll be living in a sodding police state.' In the same breath, without a pause, he went on: 'Tara, love, how's that piece on the Oasis concert in Camden coming on?'

'Nearly finished,' she replied, checking it over on her desktop a final time.

'Great. If it's nearly as good as your last one on the bigamist in Greenwich, we won't be able to keep up with the rise in circulation,' the editor joked, positioning himself on the edge of his junior's desk. 'Which reminds me, any chance you can stay late? The new format should be ready about six. We can always get something to eat afterwards.'

'I'm afraid tonight's a little tricky,' Tara replied, conscious that her boss was coming on to her again.

'Don't tell me it's that bloke of yours again?' The editor sighed.

'No, it's nothing to do with Ryan. I'm concerned about a close friend whom I've been unable to contact. I thought I'd go around to her house to see if everything's all right.'

It suited her to let Mark think she had a boyfriend, in order for them to maintain an arm's-length relationship; difficult, when she found him so incredibly attractive. However, her career came first, which was why she had ended it with Ryan in the first place.

'I suppose it can wait till the morning,' the Irishman replied, in no hurry to move away.

It was late afternoon when Tara came out of Angel tube station in North London. Remembering the address in the Liverpool Road that she'd been to on a couple of previous occasions, she walked the few hundred yards and knocked on the front door. The front garden of the terraced house had been allowed to fall into neglect, with weeds in the flowerbeds and old plastic toys lying around on the tatty bit of lawn. The door was eventually answered by a rough-looking individual with a young child dangling from his tattooed arms.

'Yeah? What do you want?' he growled.

'I'm looking for Alison Brown,' Tara replied.

'You from the Benefits Office or summink?'

'No, I'm just a friend.'

'Must be the previous lot. They've moved out. It's our

squat now – all right?' He went to slam the door on her.

'Did they leave a forwarding address by any chance?' she persisted.

'Clear off!' was the response from inside the house.

No nearer to finding out her guardian's current whereabouts, Tara checked her watch. If she got a taxi, and the traffic into town wasn't too heavy, there was still a faint chance she could get to Alison's office before they closed. In fact, she walked into the estate agency in Marylebone Lane, just as the clock on the Methodist Church struck six-thirty p.m.

'Do come in,' a huge, jolly-looking man called over from where he'd been manning the empty premises.

'I'm sorry it's so late but I've been trying to contact Alison Brown,' Tara said, trying to spot her desk.

The expression on the man's face instantly became more serious.

'Young lady, please sit down. By the way, I'm Nigel Fitzcrombie,' he said, waddling over to join her.

'Is something wrong?' Tara asked, starting to panic. 'My name is Tara Rose. Alison is a very dear friend and she is also my guardian.'

The large man withdrew the handkerchief from the breast pocket of his jacket to wipe the perspiration from his brow.

'I'm afraid there are some rather sad tidings concerning Alison,' he told Tara.

The girl held her breath, fearful of what was about to be revealed to her.

'You see, she died on the seventeenth of August,' Fitzcrombie said quietly.

'But that's not possible!' Tara protested, refusing to

believe what she'd been told.

'I can see that it's come as quite a shock,' the man sympathised. 'I must admit, it did to us too. Alison was our star negotiator and a lovely person. We all miss her terribly.'

'But what happened? I mean, she was fine the last time I saw her. It just seems so sudden,' Tara said, unable to hold back her tears.

'From what we have managed to find out, she suffered an accident at home – well, that's what we thought until very recently.'

'I'm sorry, I don't understand,' Tara said, trying her best to somehow absorb the terrible news.

'A package came in the post, addressed to Alison, which caused us to alter our opinion.'

'What did it say?'

'It contained a funds transfer to an overseas bank and a plane ticket to Panama,' the agent said tersely. 'For something just to turn up like that, out of the blue, seemed suspicious to say the least. Of course, I immediately took legal advice and called the police.'

'The *police* – but why?' Tara asked, now utterly bewildered.

'They seem to think there's more to this story than meets the eye,' Fitzcrombie prattled on, oblivious to the distress he was causing to the young woman in his presence.

'But you mentioned it was an accident?'

'That was the verdict at the inquest,' the huge man nodded, his cheeks pink, 'but now they're not so sure. Didn't take long for the press to get their hands on it. Apparently, there's a piece about it in tonight's *Evening Standard*. Anyway, I'm confident the police will soon find out what really happened. They're pretty thorough, you know.' Then, glancing at his watch, 'Good gracious, I didn't realise the time. I really should be trundling off. Got a dinner party to go to.' He swiftly manoeuvred his tubby frame out of his chair.

'Perhaps if you hear anything further, you could let *us* know,' he said, escorting Tara to the door then pulling down the blind behind her; she heard the lock click shut.

Nigel Fitzcrombie then returned to his desk to make the last phone call of the day. It was to inform Richard Jeffrey that Tara Rose had finally paid him a visit, and to thank the solicitor for keeping the name of Fitzcrombie's out of the press. The three thousand pounds Nigel himself had received for his co-operation in the matter made a nice change from the everyday bungs that had become the norm in his line of business.

22

Reeling from the visit to Alison's office, Tara wandered aimlessly around the streets, trying to take in this latest cruel blow. After a while, she decided that what she needed was a strong drink to help her calm down. Proceeding with more intent down Wigmore Street, she went into the Pontefract Castle tavern and ordered a vodka and tonic while she tried to work out what to do next.

Her first inclination should have been to go to her father, but it wasn't in him to be supportive, as she had found out to her cost when first her mother and then her Grandpa Ben died. Alison, she recalled sadly, had been both mother and father to her during those painful times of loss. Added to which, since Stan now only mixed in influential circles, he hardly had anything to do with Alison any more.

Tara had hoped, naively, that the shock of learning the true identity of his own father might have brought them closer together, but that turned out to be wishful thinking. Instead, Stan buried himself even further in his property business, intent on becoming mega-rich. Naturally, the girl didn't divulge that she had overheard the entire conversation between him and her Grandma Elaine from her position on the landing. Observing her father with his head in his hands on the sofa, Tara could tell it had been an almighty shock: he couldn't have suspected what was coming because she had never seen him so deflated. Such a contrast with his far more resilient mother, who carried on as normal by taking Tara out for the day as if nothing had happened . . . although the girl liked to think that it was purely an act put on for her benefit.

At this moment, she had no desire to go back to her flatmate Maxine, the out-of-work actress who filled her days being turned down for parts and getting stoned.

There was only one place she could go to which would help take her mind off this devastating news – and that was back to work. For once she wished she had taken her car rather than having to face another journey on the tube. Except it wouldn't have given the right impression to the others, turning up in her new-registration Mini Cooper that her father had bought her after she passed her test.

It was already dark when she entered through the heavy iron door of the former warehouse. There, to her surprise, a box of half-eaten Kentucky Fried Chicken by his side, was her boss Mark, busily typing out the headlines for the following day's edition.

'Didn't expect to see you back tonight,' he said. 'Help yourself to some food, it should still be warm. I won't be much longer.'

'Thanks, but I'm not really hungry,' Tara replied shakily, feeling the emotions welling up inside her again.

'Gareth came in pissed again, stinking of scotch, with a half-cocked piece on the war in Sarajevo – as if our readers know where the hell Bosnia is. And that Marise, her interviews of people injured in the riots yesterday were so long-winded, the poor sods could have taken themselves off to Lourdes and got cured by now,' Mark bitched. He gave a snort of laughter.

Unable to control herself, Tara went up to her boss and burst into tears.

'What's all this? My joke wasn't that bad, was it?' Getting up from his stool, Mark opened his arms and drew her towards him. 'Come on, petal, tell Uncle Mark what the matter is.'

Already regretting her outburst, Tara withdrew from Mark's embrace. It was comforting to know that she could confide in him, but there were no words to describe how devastated she felt by the news of Alison's death or the growing belief that she was cursed.

Settling back behind her desk, she began to feel a little calmer. This space, no larger than one of her school classrooms, had become her refuge.

'I'm afraid it's a long story,' she said quietly.

'Bea's at her sister's, thank the Lord, and won't be back till tomorrow, so we've got all night to talk, if necessary,' Mark said, his smile warm and encouraging. 'You do know it was her father who set me up in this place, after I left the *Mail*. Did I not tell you that?'

'No, you didn't,' Tara answered, wondering why Mark had chosen to speak to her about private matters. He'd never mentioned this fact previously.

'It's only because I dread going back to the house that I stay late,' he went on. 'If Bea would only have an affair, it would make things simpler.'

'Mark, that really isn't any of my business,' Tara responded, alarmed.

The Irishman ignored her. 'It's not that she's all that bad-looking, you know. I'll show you a picture of her if you like,' he rambled on, going over to the metal filing cabinet, taking out a framed photograph and handing it to his young reporter.

Tara was taken aback by the sight of a beautiful woman posing, relaxed in front of the camera.

'She doesn't look that way now,' Mark said, 'not since her depression.'

'I'm sorry,' Tara empathised, knowing from her own bitter experience how debilitating that condition could be.

'Being Roman Catholics is the only thing that keeps us together – you know, the whole sanctity of marriage bit,' Mark stressed, seemingly resigned to his fate. Then in a quick change of mood he said, 'Don't mind me. I've been rattling on about myself again when I was supposed to be hearing *you* out.'

'That's fine,' Tara said flatly, disappointed that she now knew for certain he was married.

'Give me another twenty minutes to finish off, and you can tell me your story while I drive you home,' he said, returning to his desk.

'Mark, you really don't have to. It's only a dozen stops on the Northern Line.'

'Am I letting you go home on your own at this ungodly hour? No, I most certainly am not. Anyway, it'll give me a chance to see where you live,' he grinned.

'It's only a boring first-floor walk-up overlooking Golders Hill Park,' Tara explained.

'You should have seen my first place after university. It was a grand house in Ealing, ruined by some unscrupulous property developer who'd converted it into bedsits. I had to share the toilet with six other people.'

Tara shuddered to think that might be how her father and Grandfather Ben before him had made their money.

'I shouldn't knock it,' Mark said, printing off the finished format. 'Anything's got to be easier than publishing.'

'Everything *is* all right though?' Tara enquired, all of a sudden feeling less secure about her job. 'I mean, now NatWest Bank and Barratt Homes have agreed to take space?'

'We'll pull through. Bea's dad has got deep pockets. The man likes telling the other Masons at his Lodge that he owns a paper. He thinks of himself as some bloody modern-day Citizen Kane!'

Tara fell about laughing; for a brief moment at least, she was able to put her anguish aside.

'I've never asked what your father does?' Mark said next.

'He runs the family company,' Tara replied, careful to avoid mentioning that he was also a property developer.

'And, I'd imagine, makes a shitload of money?' Mark probed.

'I don't really know, but he works very long hours,' was all she was prepared to divulge.

'Right, I'll lock up and see you downstairs,' the editor said, appearing to busy himself with a last-minute chore.

When his employee was out of sight, Mark removed the metal safe-deposit box from the bottom drawer of his desk and withdrew the entire £250 in cash, which he stuffed into his pockets.

'I'm just over there,' Mark told Tara, pointing to an old two-seater Triumph Spitfire that had been parked carelessly.

Soon they had crossed the river and were headed at great speed on the open road towards North London.

Unperturbed by the bumpy ride, Tara felt herself drifting off to sleep. She was totally drained.

'What street did you say you lived in?' she heard a voice say. She opened her eyes and couldn't believe she was nearly home. They were by Hampstead Pond and accelerating past Jack Straw's Castle, the landmark inn.

'It's this turning on the left,' she said groggily, and yawned. 'Sorry about not being great company.'

'Don't worry about it,' Mark replied.

'It's the last house at the end,' she told him.

The car came to a halt. Tara leaned across and pecked her boss on the cheek. Mark looked into her eyes and kissed her back softly, then again, more passionately. She didn't resist. Her heart was racing so hard she thought it was going to burst through her chest. Involuntarily, she got out of the car and walked up to her front door. Taking the key from her bag, she turned and flashed a smile at Mark, then let herself into the house, the usual chilliness of the place replaced by her warm feeling inside.

Later that same evening, at a quiet spot on the edge of Clapham Common in South London, a youth in a black-hooded tracksuit stood loitering, waiting for his customer to show. Before long, another man, with an athletic build, went up to him. In a swift transaction, the customer handed over a roll of twenty-pound notes, receiving in exchange a few packets of a powdery white substance. It was all the money he could scrape together. For how much longer he could put off paying the rest of the five grand he owed to the dealers breathing down his neck was another matter.

The punter then returned to his car and opened one of the packets. Rubbing the excess cocaine on his gums, Mark Bailey leaned back on his headrest and shut his eyes, waiting for the drug to take effect.

23

Stan was in the office early the next day. Perusing the preliminary details that had just come through on the fax from Riders, he smiled in satisfaction. Another building in Covent Garden, just a few doors away from the ones he had purchased from Sammy Talachi – who would have believed it? Out of courtesy, he would talk to Brendan about it, although the probability was that he'd end up doing it on his own again. At just under three million, it seemed like an absolute steal. Confident that the bank would give him the normal 70 per cent loan to value, his mind went to work on how he was going to free up the remaining £900,000 for the purchase. The problem was, none of the company's properties were unencumbered. Then he had a flash of genius: there was still a substantial amount of equity in the house he had bought for himself in St John's Wood near the famous Lord's Cricket Ground that he could use. There was no point in procrastinating – he was going to go ahead!

Just as he was about to pick up the phone to Victoria Rider, however, his secretary Laura appeared, looking concerned.

'Mr Rose, there's some gentlemen outside from West End Central police station to see you.'

'It's probably only to do with security on the building,'

Stan replied casually. There had been a few break-ins recently. 'Tell them I'm tied up and ask them to come back later?'

'They said it was quite important,' Laura stressed, standing her ground.

'All right, you'd better show them in.'

A few seconds later, Stan was looking up at two plain-clothes policemen with humourless expressions.

'Sorry to disturb you like this, sir,' the more senior one said, 'but we are making enquiries into the recent death of an Alison Brown, whom we believe was known to you?'

'I read about it yesterday, in the papers,' Stan replied. 'Gave me quite a shock.'

'And that was the first you knew of it?' the younger one probed.

'Yes, why?'

'How well did you know Miss Brown?' the same one continued.

'Very well,' Stan said immediately. 'She and Carol were friends.'

'Carol?' the older of the two quizzed.

'My late wife.' Stan sighed, looked at his hands. 'They'd worked together a long time ago. Then when Carol passed away, Alison became a sort of surrogate mother to our daughter, Tara. In the end, we made her a legal guardian. To be honest, I don't know how I would have managed without her,' Stan reflected. 'We owe her a lot.'

'So you would say, then, that Ms. Brown was completely trustworthy?'

'Absolutely, otherwise I would never have agreed to her being appointed my child's guardian. I really don't understand what the problem is,' Stan said, wishing they would get to the point and go away.

'Only, documents have just come into our possession which suggest otherwise,' the older officer divulged.

'Sorry, I'm not with you. What documents?'

'We were wondering whether you could clarify how the deceased was able to open a foreign account with twenty thousand pounds?'

'I've got no idea,' Stan said irritably.

'And were you aware that she was preparing to do a runner?' the younger policeman added.

'What?' Stan said, sure it was some act of fantasy or else the figment of someone's over-active imagination.

'That's just speculation at this stage,' the more senior one bumbled, throwing a dirty look to his colleague, who was rummaging around in his jacket pockets for the items in question.

'Here, you can see for yourself,' the younger one said, passing over the bank confirmation and crumpled British Airways ticket. 'First Class to Panama – I'd wager that must have cost a penny or two.'

'Of course, it might all be completely innocent,' his superior remarked, 'but it still doesn't explain why it arrived at her place of work a whole two months after she died.'

There was a short pause.

Stan perused the evidence a second time then shrugged his shoulders before handing back the documents.

'Mr Rose, we're sure you've got a lot to be going on with, so we won't take up any more of your time,' he was told. 'Be assured we'll be in touch – once we've established whether there has been any wrongdoing.'

With that, the two policemen left, heading back to their

station in Mayfair, less than a mile away.

Stan went straight back to work but the visit had unsettled him. There was only one person who might be able to shed some light on the matter, and that was his former solicitor, Richard Jeffrey. The trouble was, there had been no contact between them for a couple of years, not since Stan had followed Brendan's recommendation and gone over to the more established City firm of Broder Evans. Despite his reservations, Stan picked up the phone.

'Can I help you?' enquired an abrupt female voice, which Stan immediately recognised as that of Roz Wilson, the solicitor's secretary.

'Is Richard in?' Stan asked. 'I need a quick word. It's Stanley Rose.'

'Mr Jeffrey is rather busy this morning. He'll have to get back to you later,' the woman said firmly.

'That's not going to be possible. I'm sure he can spare a few minutes,' Stan persisted, refusing to be fobbed off.

The line went dead. And then Richard Jeffrey's voice came through. 'Stanley, it's been a long time. How's that daughter of yours? Tara, isn't it? My goodness, she must be a young woman by now.'

Ignoring the chitchat, Stan came straight to the point. 'Richard, I've just been paid a visit by the police, and I am hoping that you might be able to throw some light on it.'

'I'll try – what's it all about?'

'The police claim to be in possession of an overseas bank account in Alison Brown's name. You remember she was Tara's guardian?'

'Yes, of course, the estate agent – a very pleasant woman.'

'Unfortunately, I learned yesterday that she died.'

'What? How awful! She could only have been in her

early forties,' the other man responded.

'The thing is, Richard, apparently she transferred a great deal of money to an offshore account and was planning to fly to Panama.'

'Good Lord. But I'm not sure what you expect me to do about it?' Jeffrey said carelessly.

'Don't you think it's a bit strange though?' Stan said, hoping for a more helpful response from the lawyer.

'There's really nothing I can say. When I was trustee to the Miller Estate, I only had sporadic contact with her.' His tone became brisk. 'It's good to chat though, and I do hope that business is going well. However, right now I really do have to get to a meeting,' he said, cutting short the conversation. 'Goodbye, Stanley, and do send my best wishes to Tara.' The phone went dead.

What a waste of time. Stan went over to the cocktail cabinet and poured himself a large scotch. To hell with the fact that it was only eleven o'clock, he needed something to get through the rest of the day. As he took a large gulp, he wondered whether Alison might have mentioned anything to his daughter.

That same afternoon, Tara collected her things at the office and negotiated the three flights of stairs down to the ground floor. After not getting a wink of sleep the previous night – unsurprising because Alison had occupied most of her thoughts – she was glad to be able to leave work early. Today had been taken up with trying to control her desire for Mark. From the time she'd got into trouble for making an exhibition of herself with her English teacher at King Edward's School, she had always been attracted to older men, no doubt in search of the emotional support of a paternal figure – something her father had been abjectly unable to provide. In fact, she wouldn't have been at all surprised if he hadn't known about Alison all along and had decided not to say anything.

Proceeding along Southwark Street towards the tube station, she was looking forward to getting home and having a hot bath, assuming Maxine hadn't used up all the hot water, and then eating supper in front of the television with a plate of freshly made spaghetti that she had purchased from a stall in Borough Market.

To her complete surprise, waiting outside her house was her father in his red Ferrari.

'Get in,' Stan said grumpily, opening the passenger door.

Tara eased herself down into the seat of the Italian sports car, which to her mind was as much a response to a midlife crisis as it was to his newfound wealth. She was pretty sure why he seemed so on edge.

'How did you know I was coming home?' she asked, turning to him. 'I might have been going out. Is this about Alison?'

'You could say that,' her father answered bluntly.

'I didn't know what to do when I found out,' Tara said, biting her lip, still unable to fully absorb the terrible tragedy.

'I'm talking about the fact that she'd spirited a large amount of money away to Central America and was about to disappear – not the fact that she died,' came the icy response.

Tara's mind went blank for a moment but then she recalled what the fat man in the estate agency – Nigel

Fitzcrombie – had mentioned about a letter addressed to Alison. That must be what her father was referring to.

'Why are you so cold and callous, Daddy? Is that all you care about?' Tara cried, unable to control herself.

It hadn't been his intention to upset his daughter.

'I'm sorry, I know how close you two were,' he said more gently, 'and I also know how much we owe her as a good friend to us all, but I need to know: did Alison confide in you about what she was up to?'

'Of course not, otherwise I'd have told you. Anyway, I don't believe it!' Not that Tara was going to convey any doubts she might have to her father.

'And she didn't appear different in any way, the last time you saw her?' Stan continued.

'No, not really. She just seemed eager to get me to sign some papers to do with Grandpa's company before we went off to the school dinner event. And yes, there's no need to ask me again – I checked with the solicitors before I signed anything.' She looked at her father and said passionately, 'I've just lost another of the most important people in my life – and your only worry is that she may have done something illegal!'

Tara got out of the car in a temper and slammed the door. She ran towards her front door, and this time, she didn't look back.

25

Stan stood in the pouring rain, sheltering beneath his Riders Estate Agents umbrella, looking up at the scruffy building on which he'd just exchanged contracts. Getting involved in a bidding war was normally against his principles, but even at the £3.5 million he'd been forced to pay, and even though it had stretched him to the limit, it was still a cracking deal. Most importantly, he was determined to secure the former government offices in Covent Garden – to prove to himself as much as anything that he was still *in the game*.

There was no question that the unexpected visit from the police had left him seriously rattled. Not knowing what was going to happen next and with no one to confide in, he had carried on the best way he could, apprehensive each time the phone went that it could only be more bad news.

But that was over three weeks ago. It was late November now, and no further light had been shed on the subject. Gradually, Stan felt better, his enthusiasm for work restored. He decided to put the whole episode with Alison Brown down to the futile attempt of a desperate woman to gain some sort of petty revenge against him.

He just wished that he hadn't been so ready to apportion blame to his daughter. There had been no contact between them since she had stormed out of his car. Deep down, he was hoping that she would back down first, but of course she hadn't. Perhaps they were more similar than he had imagined.

Not feeling as buoyant as he had expected with his latest acquisition, Stan walked back down Long Acre. There was little point sitting in traffic to cover the mile and a half to his office, when he would feel better for the exercise. Passing Leicester Square tube station, he carried on around the Eros fountain at Piccadilly Circus and turned into Regent Street. Just as he was passing Liberty's department store, full of elegant Christmas displays in its Tudor-style windows, he noticed the familiar figure of Howard Barnet walking towards him.

'Oh, hello, Stan. You're the last person I thought I'd run into,' the car dealer said gruffly, devoid of his normal friendliness.

'I'm coming back from a building I've just purchased in Covent Garden,' Stan gloated.

'Still buying up the whole of London then?' Howard said snidely.

'Trying to,' Stan replied, feeling ill at ease. He suspected that Howard was peeved because he had gone to Maranello, the specialist Ferrari dealership, for his new car and not to him. That might explain his aloofness. Though to Stan's mind, when you were spending £90,000, you were entitled to expect the best.

'How's that daughter of yours, or shouldn't I ask?' Howard said, his voice sour.

'Tara's working at a small newspaper – not one that you've probably heard of. She seems quite happy,' Stan chattered.

'You're aware she and Ryan are not seeing each other any more?'

'Actually, I didn't know that,' Stan replied.

'My son couldn't do enough for her when she was ill. You do know it was down to Ryan that she started eating again?'

'Yes, he was very kind,' Stan conceded, slowly recalling the time he had found the lad waiting outside his house with a tray of food.

'That's how much she meant to the boy. Then when something better came along, she dumped him. Ryan's not been the same since. After three years! She broke his heart.'

'Howard, I really . . .'

'You think I don't know the reason?' the other man continued to rant. 'The Roses have always looked down on our family. You've forgotten that time your mum wouldn't let me into your house because she said my father was a spiv? We were only kids! That type of thing leaves a bad taste. All I can say is, I know who Tara takes after.' His lips were quivering with emotion.

'I'm sorry,' Stan muttered, feeling bad about the distress his family had apparently caused the Barnets. 'But we can still be pals, can't we?'

'Stanley, that's not been the case for a very long time,' the car dealer said as his parting comment.

Stan looked on as his former best friend strode off in the other direction. He had had no idea quite how much Howard resented him. But to feel that hard done by because Tara had gotten tired of his son was clearly ridiculous. And unfair.

Feeling hungry, Stan quickened his pace back to

Manchester Square. With a bit of luck Laura would have made up some sandwiches before she went on her lunch break. There was a good afternoon's work ahead and he intended to take full advantage of the number of new deals that had recently come on to the market. Also, now the first phase of La Quinta was well under way, another trip to Spain was definitely on the cards. Brendan was spending most of the year on the Costa Del Sol now, and Stan estimated it wouldn't be too long before his partner would want to dispose of his interest in their joint company. It wouldn't come cheap, but Stan wasn't prepared to take the chance that the portfolio of the seven prime properties they owned between them, would go to someone else.

Just as Stan reached his place of business, a message from the bank came through on his mobile phone.

It simply said, *Facility on hold. Lucas*

It took a moment for the words to register. He had forgotten all about the bank's Annual Review, and now he was being informed that, all of a sudden, they were playing hardball. What the hell was going on?

Stan immediately hailed a taxi to take him to the City. If they thought they could treat him like a nobody, they had another think coming. Unless he received a full apology, he would see to it that both he and Brendan moved their account elsewhere.

When Stan entered the executive offices of the Pretoria Bank, to his surprise, already seated around the boardroom table were the six, all but one male, members of the credit committee, whom he had met on various occasions in the past. Their stony expressions left him in no doubt that he was in a great deal of trouble.

'Take a seat,' Lucas Voss, his Relationship Manager said, clearing his throat.

'Would you mind telling me what this is all about?' Stan exploded.

'Mr Rose, there really is no need to be so aggressive,' responded an authoritative man in a navy pinstripe suit who gave the impression of being the most senior of the group. 'I'm sure you don't need reminding that all loans made are at the discretion of the bank and are repayable on demand.'

'Yes, of course, I'm sorry,' Stan replied, regretting his unseemly outburst. 'But I'm sure you can appreciate that this news has come as quite a shock.'

'As did the phone call we received from a company calling themselves CM Nominees,' put in the youngest in the room, a smarmy upstart with slicked-back hair.

'Giles, would you tell Mr Rose what the chap told you.'

'Certainly, Tim,' the young banker replied. 'He simply said he was introducing himself as the owner of seventy-five per cent of Miller Investments.'

'But that's impossible! The man's obviously an imposter,' Stanley protested.

'That's what we thought at first – but when this Stock Transfer form arrived in the post this morning . . .' Giles held up the document for everyone to see '. . . and saw that it was signed by Tara Rose, we realised that you had been withholding some material information from us.'

'But I've never heard of anybody called CM Nominees,' Stan insisted, feeling he'd been set up.

'We did a check and it appears to be an offshore company incorporated in Belize.'

'Owned by whom?' Stan babbled.

'I'm afraid we've rather come up against a brick wall in that respect,' Giles conceded. 'It seems to be part of a complex network of outfits registered in various jurisdictions but, as yet, we have no idea about the identity of the ultimate Holdings concern.'

'But surely that can't be right,' Stan said indignantly. 'It's obviously a scam and an attempt to deprive my family of what's rightly ours.'

'Stanley, of course we have a great deal of sympathy with your awkward position,' the main board director said, 'but look at it from our point of view. We've lent you a great deal of money over the past three years on the understanding that you had control over the day-to-day running of the company.'

'That hasn't changed,' Stan countered.

'I'm afraid it's rather been superseded by events. The facts are, that now your daughter has transferred her shares, this company, whoever they may be, are the ones calling the shots.'

Stan went quiet, trying to bring some sense of order to the strange goings-on over the past few weeks. First, it was Alison's offshore bank account and now this. Suddenly, he remembered Tara remarking that she had checked up with the lawyers before signing a particular document. It was a certainty that Richard Jeffrey's firm had to be involved somewhere!

'Wait, I think I can throw some light on what's happened,' he said slowly.

'That would of course be most helpful. Nothing, and I'm talking for the rest of my colleagues, would give us greater pleasure than if we were able to reinstate your account.'

'Are you saying that you're foreclosing on me?' Stan gaped.

'Let's just say that it's been suspended. The last thing we want to do is to precipitate calling in a debt, especially one that's running well in excess of thirty million – isn't that correct, Olivia?' the senior director said, addressing his comments to a serious young woman with tortoiseshell spectacles.

'Thirty-one million and forty-nine thousand, including accrued interest at the close of business last night,' she said nasally.

'What the bank proposes is a twenty-one-day moratorium, which according to my calculations, brings us to the nineteenth of December . . .'

'But Covent Garden completes tomorrow!' Stan interrupted.

'. . . in the course of which, if you are able to give us satisfaction that the shareholding in question has reverted to your family's control, we can continue doing business as if nothing had happened. If not, we will expect repayment of our loans in full.'

'But that will mean disposing of the whole portfolio.' Stan started shaking as the reality of his plight began to sink in. 'It'll take time for me to find a buyer,' he said, trying desperately to salvage the situation.

'Time is something, I'm afraid, that will no longer be available to you,' Tim St John reaffirmed. 'The major shareholder has made it perfectly clear that they intend on appointing their own board of directors – something which, I don't need telling you, they are fully entitled to do.'

'So you're saying . . .'

'. . . that they will expect your resignation.'

'And if I refuse?' Stan said defiantly.

'Then you will be forcibly removed.'

Tim St John then got up from the table, followed by the rest of his colleagues, who filed out of the boardroom; the last to leave being Lucas Voss, looking sheepish, having been severely censured by the committee for introducing Stanley Rose to the bank in the first instance.

25

February 1995

Ice had already formed on the windscreens of parked cars when Stan stepped out of his home in St John's Wood for the last time. Carrying a briefcase containing a few important items, he made sure he was out of sight of any of his neighbours, who might question why he was suddenly vacating the place after such a short time. Stan then set off on foot for Swiss Cottage, half a mile away, trying to convince himself that his move to the far less prestigious district would only be temporary.

Ironically, the luxury six-bedroom home that he'd occupied for less than a year had been snapped up just after Christmas by a cocky young property developer in a Porsche who, wanting to put on a show in front of his Barbie Doll-like wife, had no qualms about paying the £2.5 million asking price. Fortunately, Stan had been able to sell on the contract of Talachi's property in Covent Garden at the twelfth hour, freeing up a sizeable amount of equity in his own residence. That had given him breathing space after the bank had called in the personal guarantees he had given on his company's loans. It could have been far worse, had it not been for the major shareholder's willingness to carry on running Miller Investments as a going concern.

Naturally, he had taken separate legal advice from his lawyers Broder Evans, but they came up with the same opinion as Richard Jeffrey: there was no evidence that the transfer had been signed under duress and, as far as they could tell, it had been executed properly. Tara was adamant that she hadn't done anything wrong, recalling that the whole thing had been purely at Alison's instigation as a legitimate way of avoiding tax. Stan then asked to speak to the person at Lowndes Jeffrey to whom his daughter had sought confirmation before she signed the transfer, but was informed that Roger Prince, the seventy-year-old partner in question, had conveniently retired to his native Australia. There had to be an explanation, but with no one else to throw any light on the subject, Stan knew he'd come to a dead end.

His trip to Spain to see Brendan immediately afterwards proved to be an even bigger disappointment. The bond the two men had built up over the last two and a half years appeared to count for nothing.

No longer even trying to keep Luisa, his Spanish mistress, under wraps, Brendan was now living with her in a newly constructed villa he had purchased near the Marbella Beach Club. That brief conversation on the terrace, warming themselves in the winter sun whilst sipping Pimm's cocktails, was still fresh in Stan's mind.

'Sorry to hear about your bit of bother, old boy,' were the words Brendan had used as if he, Stan, had encountered nothing more than a minor inconvenience. 'Though I don't much relish having a bunch of faceless individuals as partners,' he added, with as little conviction.

Stan shouldn't have been surprised that his partner was already in the loop. The bank had obviously filled Brendan in, straight after that fateful meeting. In any case, their gripe wasn't with Brendan; to them, he was still a valued customer.

'I'm really sorry that it's come to this,' Stan had said remorsefully. 'Please believe me, when I tell you it was really none of my doing.'

'Seems that you may have upset someone down the line,' Brendan speculated. 'Maybe it was those Singaporeans who got pissed off when you pulled out of the deal for your company, and they wanted to get their own back?'

Stan knew that behind their polite public-school exterior the Lim brothers were extremely canny, but he was convinced they would be incapable of resorting to such deceit.

'Actually, the major shareholder has made it clear they don't want any involvement in our joint company, so I was wondering whether you could loan me five million just to get the bank off my back,' he asked, thinking naively that he would get a positive response.

'Nothing would give me greater pleasure, matey,' Brendan said airily, 'but the truth is I'm under a bit of financial pressure myself. Anne wants a divorce and she's intent on extracting her pound of flesh. Perhaps you could go in with them, whoever they are? They could do a lot worse than taking someone on with as much knowledge of the market as you possess,' was his final careless suggestion before saying that he had to get going for lunch.

Stan returned to London feeling utterly demoralised. He had tried everything, but knew he had been done over by unscrupulous people, far cleverer than himself, and he had lost control of the company that had been entrusted to him. There were too many similarities with what had happened to H. & R. Rose for it to be just a coincidence. Stanley Rose had to face the fact that perhaps he wasn't quite the astute businessman he imagined.

He arrived back at the small estate of three-bedroom properties that bore an uncanny resemblance to the street where his former girlfriend Jackie lived, just as the removals van containing all his worldly goods was pulling away. Even though he'd been relegated to living in a £300 a week rental, Stan felt strangely sanguine about the prospect of starting up again – which was exactly what he intended to do, as soon as he got himself straight. Admittedly, he'd lost practically all of his capital but he wasn't yet out on the street. The £500,000 he'd received for his 25 per cent holding was a fraction of what it was worth, he knew that, but he was in no position to hold out for more.

All this reminded him so much of that time when Ben Miller had offered to buy back the shares that he'd given to Carol. Stan now learned, first-hand, that no one was lining up to buy a minority stake that afforded no voting rights, however successful the company may have been. Wasn't that also the reason that the major shareholder found it so easy to pass a special resolution to get rid of him? However, the year's severance pay he had managed to negotiate with the Pretoria Bank, who had taken on the role as mediators with their new offshore client, had gone some way to cushioning the blow of his dismissal.

On the plus side, he had got a sort of relationship back with his daughter. They spoke once a week on the phone, although Tara always seemed to be working too late to make an arrangement to see him. After weeks without any communication, they had finally got together for a quick lunch at Balls Brothers wine bar in the City. Barely recognisable as the moody teenager to whom he had found it impossible to relate, Tara had become a confident young woman of almost nineteen, in no apparent need of advice or parental guidance. There was an unspoken agreement that he wouldn't bring up the question of the share transfer again, even though he retained a niggling suspicion that she hadn't told him everything. For her part, she never mentioned Alison, whom he still held fully responsible for the disaster that had befallen his family.

In the early hours of the following day, Tara stirred as the naked man with whom she had just finished making love pulled back the covers and got out of bed.

'Mark, it's still early – please don't go yet,' she implored him.

'I have to. Go back to sleep,' he said, gathering up his clothes.

She knew the routine. Mondays and Thursdays, when his wife was under the impression that they had late-night production meetings, the couple would grab a quick bite and then check into the seedy hotel next to London Bridge, after which Mark would return to his home in Clapham. The news of Alison's death had sent Tara spiralling down to her lowest ebb since her mother died, and Mark was the only one she could turn to. Their affair started soon after.

Mark admitted to having gotten married too young, but coming from a small village near Kilkenny in the west of Ireland, he couldn't wait to escape. A scholarship to Oxford afforded him the opportunity. That was where he was introduced to Beatrice, daughter of the Right Honourable Percy Boothroyd, heir to the giant agricultural equipment company of the same name. Mark was, as he said, just a simple lad who got seduced by all the wrong things and ended up regretting it. In his words, he had 'sold his soul to the devil'.

For Tara, the arrangement wasn't ideal but it was better to have him for a few hours than not at all. She was hoping they might have a future together. She had surprised herself by being sufficiently responsible to take precautions, especially since the prospect of getting pregnant had always quite appealed to her. Ironically, when she found in Ryan someone who adored her, she treated him badly. She just hoped that one day, he'd find happiness with someone more worthy.

'I won't be in till later on tomorrow,' Mark said, putting on his shoes. 'Can I leave it to you to check the copy and then get it down to the printers?'

Still half asleep, Tara grunted her consent. She knew better than to ask where he was going. Mark had simply said that since the source of finance from his father-in-law had dried up, they were losing money heavily and he was doing everything possible to keep the paper afloat. It seemed odd, because both circulation and advertising revenue had steadily increased; that, coupled with the fact that Marise and Gareth had reluctantly agreed to take a cut in wages, made Tara suspect there was more going on than met the eye. Nevertheless, whatever it was, she found she didn't care. Being so deeply in love with Mark, if she had had the money, she would have gladly given it to him herself. How her inheritance could have just suddenly disappeared into thin air, she still didn't understand; nor, for that matter, through what means her father's fortunes could also have changed so dramatically overnight.

Perhaps the two were connected in some way?

There was only one person she could go to for help – and that was her Grandma Elaine. Yawning, Tara resolved to call her when Elaine returned from her Caribbean cruise. Placing her head down on the pillow and falling asleep, Tara didn't hear her lover leave the room.

26

On a clear April evening, the shrill of police sirens permeated the walls of the cheaply built house where Stan now resided. He had spent another frustrating day at home, methodically going through lists of everyone with whom he'd ever done business, in the hope that they might be able to throw some light on the individuals who had forcibly taken control of his company. His efforts had proved futile.

Now he peered through the living-room window at the line of police cars in the street outside. It was the second raid this week. It was definitely a dodgy area. Still, that was none of his concern. He had his own worries, like how he was going to earn enough money to get out of the rabbit hutch that he'd been cooped up in for the last five months. Many residents, lucky enough to sell their properties, had moved to better neighbourhoods. Stan, unfortunately, wasn't one of them. Without the cash to lay out on a decent-sized house, where else could he go? To Stanley Rose, the half a million pounds he had on deposit, not to mention the Ferrari back from the tuners in the garage, didn't count – and certainly didn't equate to the lifestyle to which he had become accustomed.

It was supposed to have been a foregone conclusion that he'd be able to pick up where he had left off – in

Ladbroke Grove, his old stomping ground. His reputation with all the local agents was still sufficiently intact, or so he believed, and his old bank, Barclays, had even offered him a facility – not as much as he had hoped for, but enough to get up and running again. Traipsing around London for several weeks, it came as a huge setback to find himself palmed off with a bunch of junior negotiators, who had never heard of Miller Investments and wasted no time nurturing their own developers with whom they now did all their business. The reaction was the same throughout the entire Borough of Kensington and Chelsea. 'We'll keep you in mind,' were the supercilious words they all used. How many times had he gone back to the small office next to the tube station, convinced that sooner or later someone would show? But it remained boarded up without any sign of life. The only glimmer of hope he'd received was when he stopped in Dantés one day for a bite of lunch and Theresa happened to mention that Mary Cunningham had been up the previous week. For half a second, he'd thought about enlisting the help of the shrewd older woman, but then thought the better of it. Did he really need further humiliation piled upon him, when she learned how he had lost control of Ben Miller's company?

He fared little better in the West End. Victoria Rider's agency had just been swallowed up by Gérard Le Saux's Trumpton Estates, and whilst appearing sympathetic to his predicament, they were unable to provide him with the information he so desperately needed, due to data protection restrictions. How an established business with a portfolio of seventy properties could suddenly fail to exist was the question that occupied all his conscious thoughts. Once again, Stan had failed to learn the following lesson:

that it can take a lifetime to build a reputation, but just a split second to lose it.

If his business career had been left in tatters, he was determined not to let it show. In future, he decided that come six o'clock he would spruce himself up and drive to one of his old haunts in the West End. It was important to be seen in the right places with the right people. He hadn't got to know all the big players in the property business for nothing, and he wasn't about to waste such valuable connections sitting on his backside in Swiss Cottage, feeling sorry for himself. Perhaps Brendan was right: even if he didn't have the capital himself, he had a nose for a deal, so why not take his talents to people like Sammy Talachi or the Lims in return for a piece of the action?

Feeling more buoyant, Stan went into the kitchen and boiled a kettle. Another evening on his own was infinitely better than going to his mother's place and then having to make excuses to leave early because he still hadn't forgiven her for the trauma she had put him through. Elaine, on the other hand, purged of the guilt she had carried for so long, had apparently cleared her conscience and was at peace, Stan thought sourly. The fact that Paul Klein hadn't offered to help him to set up again, despite knowing full well of his recent difficulties, came as another let-down. Stan had always thought of Paul as a decent enough fellow. Maybe Elaine had advised him not to get involved? Stan wondered whether she had even told him about Harry Rose.

He took a carton of eggs and a packet of smoked salmon out of the fridge for his supper. Just as well Sofia, the Serbian cleaner he'd inherited from the previous tenants, had agreed to do his shopping. He had just sat down in front of the television with his omelette, when there was a ring on his doorbell.

There, standing on the doorstep, was a powerfully built man with a black bushy beard, holding a stack of black and white pamphlets. Dressed in an old coat and frayed white shirt under which he wore a strange-looking garment with twisted threads, Stan thought he resembled many of the down and outs he had encountered in the rougher areas of North Kensington.

'Yes. Can I help you?' he said, put out at being disturbed.

'Good evening. I thought you might be interested in learning about our Centre,' came the cheerful response. 'We provide assistance for people in the community with mental and physical illnesses.'

'I'm afraid you've come to the wrong house,' Stan said curtly and began closing the door.

'You have a *mezuzah,* do you not?' The man pointed to the small wood casing containing Hebrew script that was affixed to the doorpost.

'That doesn't mean anything,' Stan replied, made aware of the religious symbol for the first time.

'So, you're a Jew,' the man announced.

'I was born Jewish,' Stan replied guardedly.

'If you will permit me a few minutes of your time, I will gladly explain more about the valuable work we do.' Before Stan had a chance to reply, the impudent individual had entered the house and marched down the hall into the front room. 'We aren't able to attract government funding,' he called to Stan, who was struggling to keep up behind him, 'so we have to look elsewhere for support . . . It's a nice home you have here,' he added, looking around admiringly.

Stan was puzzled. Who on earth was this chap, suddenly conversing with him in the middle of his living room?

'But too big for just one person, no?'

'Actually, I live on my own,' Stan replied, having no idea why he needed to justify himself.

'A family with children should occupy such a space!' the fellow proclaimed. 'What's your line of business, if you don't mind me asking?'

'Property,' Stan answered, saying the first thing that came into his head.

'Ah! So you make a good living, Mr . . .?'

'Stanley Rose,' Stan replied, accepting the firm hand being offered to him. Then: 'Well, I used to until . . . Look, I really don't mean to rude, but— '

'You know, the Almighty pays back many times over when you give to charity.'

'I'm sure He does,' Stan replied, 'but that's really none of my concern. So if you don't mind, I am rather busy.'

'I'll leave a brochure. If you feel it will benefit you to give a donation, our address is on the back,' the religious man said, going swiftly back down the hall. And then he called back: 'Maybe you would like to come and see the work that *we* do? You know Golders Green, Princess Park Avenue? The Lakish Centre is a few yards from the main road.'

'I'll think about it,' Stan lied, showing the man out. He then returned to his meal, without giving the unusual individual another thought.

27

Elaine Rose entered the lounge area of the exclusive Mayfair hotel where her granddaughter was already seated.

'Tara dear, I'm sorry, have you been here long? It's just that Paul hasn't been feeling well since we came back from holiday and I had to take him to the doctor.'

'Don't worry, Grandma,' the girl replied, glancing nervously at her watch. She rarely took time off from the office but Mark hadn't seemed to mind. Unable to come up with a solution to their financial difficulties, he appeared quite buoyed by her suggestion of her grandmother possibly investing in the business. In the circumstances, £25,000 didn't seem too much to ask for and would provide the newspaper, so she was informed, with enough working capital for at least the next twelve months.

'I do hope that this is all right for you?' Valerie remarked with her usual haughtiness. She had first come to the place with her parents in the 1950s and, since then, the Connaught remained her favourite hotel.

'It's absolutely fine,' Tara confirmed, beginning to worry that her pitch wouldn't come out right.

'Mrs Rose, how good to see you again,' the lounge manager said, coming over to greet her. Elaine's polite smile failed to disguise her satisfaction at being publicly acknowledged in the renowned establishment in front of her nineteen-year-old granddaughter.

Soon afterwards, two waiters appeared with pots of tea, silver-tiered stands of finely cut finger sandwiches and delicate French pastries.

'So tell me, how's your job at the paper?' Elaine enquired, as she began pouring out the tea through a strainer, guessing that that was the reason for her granddaughter's call.

'Actually, that's what I wanted to speak to you about,' Tara said apprehensively.

'Well, I didn't expect it was to talk about your father,' the older woman retorted, gratified that she'd been proven correct in her assumption. 'You are aware, of course, that we've made up? Most families have dissension at some time or other. Ours isn't unique.'

Tara was rendered speechless by the words that had just come out of her grandmother's mouth – as if the secret Elaine had revealed a year ago, tearing the family apart, had been nothing more than a minor disagreement.

'I assume your father told you what it was all about,' Elaine continued undeterred, taking a sip of her Earl Grey tea. 'I was practically the same age as you when . . .' She stopped herself.

'Daddy was devastated by what you told him,' Tara said heatedly, unable to restrain herself. 'It's not exactly an everyday occurrence, finding out who your natural father really is, after forty years.' Having to contend with that bombshell, on top of all his business worries was, to her mind, nothing short of cruel.

'I had no idea it would affect him so badly.' The older woman's voice had lowered to slightly more than a strained whisper and her face had become contorted.

'So you're saying that if you had known, you would have kept it from him altogether? What reaction did you expect?' Tara ranted, in full flow now and unconcerned that she was attracting the attention of other people in the lounge area.

An uncomfortable atmosphere gripped the table. Elaine Rose had become a shrivelled version of the proud, chic woman of just moments before.

'I have to go,' Tara said, getting up from her chair.

'Wait, please.' Elaine grabbed hold of her grand-daughter's arm. 'What life do you suppose I had, married for twenty years to a man I was completely unsuited to, having to pretend that everything was hunky-dory? Now my only son can't even look me in the face because he won't forgive me for deceiving him. What's worse is that he only knows the half of it.'

Anticipating that she was about to hear a fresh revelation, Tara sat down again. Elaine took a few seconds to collect herself before carrying on.

'There was bad feeling between us, on the night Arnold died. I remember it as if it was yesterday. My husband was always such an even-tempered man, so when he came home from work with a face like thunder, I suspected something was wrong. You see, Arnold had had a row with his brother. It used to happen quite often. You may not be aware of this but Harry has a temper and it doesn't take much for him to lose it.'

'What was the row about?' Tara asked.

'Oh, the usual complaints about Arnold not pulling his weight in the business. But this time it went too far and Harry ridiculed his brother, saying that he wasn't even capable of producing a child of his own. Of course, Harry realised immediately what he had said, but it was too late to take it back. The damage had been done. A seed of doubt had been planted in Arnold's head.'

Elaine looked as if she was going to break down, as the memories of that long-ago night came back to haunt her. Summoning all her resolve, she took a deep breath and finished her story.

'Instead of occupying his normal seat at dinner, next to me, Arnold moved to the other end of the table. He didn't look in my direction once during supper. It was as if he was disgusted with me – the same way Stanley is now.'

In a great deal of distress, Elaine took a drink of water, her hand shaking.

'Grandma, you don't have to tell me any more,' Tara said gently. Her earlier anger had been replaced with feelings of regret and unease at being subjected to the older woman's confession of blame.

But it was to no avail.

'The thought that I had caused his death will stay with me forever.' Covering her face with her still elegant hands, Elaine began to weep softly.

Instinctively, Tara got up and went around to comfort her grandmother. She hadn't intended it to go this far. What would she have done in the same position? she wondered. She herself was having an affair with a married man, so what did that make *her*?

'You know, I would give anything to go back to where we were, you and your father,' Elaine said, dabbing her face and reaching for her compact, her equilibrium partially restored. She smiled at her granddaughter. 'You're different – you're strong-willed like your mother and grandfather.

You can cope when things in life go against you. My son hasn't got the same toughness, never did have. Strange as it may seem, he inherited Arnold's mild temperament, even though Stanley wasn't his son. That's why I've always protected him – not realising that when he had to stand on his own two feet, thanks to me he wouldn't be capable of it.'

Tara knew what her grandmother was saying was true. And maybe it *was* time for her father to grow up. It was just that she found it hard to comprehend, seeing how he always seemed to give up without putting up a fight when things turned against him. It reminded her of the way he fell to pieces when her mother was dying. If only he had consented to Alison's suggestion of getting professional help from a therapist instead of regarding it as an affront to his male ego, things might have turned out differently. And now he'd gone to ground in a sulk just because he had encountered difficulties in his business, instead of facing up to adversity and dealing with it as she had had to do.

Then in a complete change of mood, Elaine came back with, 'What was it that you wanted to ask me, dear?' It was as if the emotional dialogue that had taken the best part of three-quarters of an hour had never happened.

'I've said all I wanted to say,' Tara replied, changing her mind about asking her grandmother for the money.

'Then I assume that what I told you will remain between us?' Elaine added, inferring it was already a fait accompli.

'Daddy needs to feel good about himself again, if he's to get back on his feet. Showing that you care would make a big difference,' was all Tara was prepared to say. She then got up, embraced her grandmother and went back to work, leaving Elaine in no doubt of what was expected of her in return.

It was already late afternoon, but Tara needed to clear her head so she decided to walk for a while in the direction of Green Park tube. The meeting hadn't turned out at all as she had expected. Now that she couldn't give Mark any positive news about securing an investment for the paper, she wondered just how long the *Londoner* could survive.

28

It was the last game of the football season and Stan was in good spirits, despite the boring 1-1 draw. His Tottenham Hotspur season ticket was something he had always treasured and would never give up, though his earliest childhood experiences of the double team of the 1960s and the magic of their star player Jimmy Greaves were now only a distant memory. Perhaps he wanted to blot them out of his mind because he had been taken to those matches by Arnold Rose, the kindly father whom he'd adored.

The other reason for his welcome change in mood was bumping into Howard Barnet again. This was not in itself totally surprising, since they sat a few rows apart in the new West Stand and, in happier times, frequently went to the Saturday-afternoon games together.

Sharing a beer in the bar at half time, Howard told him that Ryan was now working for him and had found a steady girlfriend, so the boy was much more settled. The men chatted quite happily, two old friends who had rediscovered each other, with a bond that, despite their recent differences, went back a long way. Fortunately, Howard didn't ask Stan about the property business. The fact that Stan mentioned that he still had the Ferrari was, as far as Howard was concerned, sufficient proof that everything was still going well. Why, Stan wondered, did he hang on to a high-performance motor car that ate petrol, cost a fortune to insure and could only pootle along in traffic? Surely it was the act of a stubborn man, clinging on to his last trappings of wealth.

Approaching his home, Stan was surprised by the sight of a beaten-up van parked across his driveway, blocking the entrance. A few seconds later, three youths stormed out of his house, which they had just ransacked. Stan was pulled out of his car with the engine still running and knocked unconscious with a blow from a blunt instrument. Stripped of his wallet and his gold Rolex watch, he was dumped in the front garden with blood pouring from a deep wound in his head.

At nine o'clock that evening, a middle-aged man close to death was wheeled into the operating theatre at Hampstead's Royal Free Hospital, his identity unknown. Not wishing to face charges of murder, the leader of the gang – known as Gerbil on account of his rat-like features – took it upon himself to phone an ambulance from a phone box a few streets away.

An investigation was immediately launched and a door-to-door search of the area undertaken, more out of a need to assuage panic in the locals than in any real expectation that the officers might suddenly stumble on the culprits. The police knew well who they were after, but when it came to grassing up one of their own, no one in the three tower blocks that made up the Shrewsbury Estate would dare to come forward.

*

That same evening, Tara rushed out of her flat, got into her car and accelerated away at speed. Constable Matthew Lyons at Kentish Town police station sometimes gave her leads for the *Londoner*. He was a good friend of Ryan Barnet and she knew he fancied her like mad.

Violent attacks on the streets of North London had become commonplace over the last few years. What attracted her to this particular case, however, was the presence of an extremely rare sports car that had been found at the scene. It could only have belonged to a wealthy businessman or a pop star. Either way, it was just the type of news piece her paper specialised in, and she was determined to get her report in the Monday edition.

Bowling along Chalk Farm Road, it was a relief to have something else to occupy her mind. It was certainly better than waiting around all day in the vain hope that Mark would call. She had begun to think twice about their relationship; if she was honest, the doubts had been there from the beginning. His sudden change in attitude, after she told him that the money from her grandmother would not be forthcoming after all, had hurt her considerably, and it explained his obsessive interest in her family. It was obvious that he had been sizing them up in order to exploit them for his own ends.

Reaching her destination, she found the road closed at both ends. Tara got out of her car, and hoping she would be allowed access, hurried along the quiet residential street. Halfway down, small pockets of police stood chatting outside an unremarkable modern house. Two forensic officers were at work collecting evidence from a luxury car in the drive.

It took only a few seconds for Tara to realise that she

was staring at her father's red Ferrari.

'Sorry, miss, you're interfering with a police investigation. You'll have to move away,' a rough voice boomed.

Completely numb, Tara stood paralysed, unable to move.

'Come on, love, don't play silly buggers. Move along now, please,' the same burly policeman repeated.

'I think that's my father's car,' she said in a voice that was barely audible.

'Come again, miss?'

As the reality of the situation began to take hold of her, she started to panic. 'Please tell me where my father is!'

'Calm down, love, take a deep breath and tell me why you think you know who this car belongs to,' said another policeman with a kindlier disposition, who had extricated himself from his colleagues.

'It just looks like his car. His name is Stanley Rose and I know he lives around here somewhere.' It wasn't her choice that she had never been to the house before. Knowing her father, she could now see that he had kept her well away because he felt ashamed of the modest surroundings that had been forced upon him.

'And you say you're his daughter? Can you describe him to me?' the officer said, taking notes on his pad.

'He's forty-three, tall, salt and pepper black hair . . . Please, will you tell me what's happened to him?' Tara begged.

'A man fitting that description was found badly injured on the ground here at six-thirty this evening; an ambulance was called and took him to the Royal Free Hospital,' the police officer revealed.

'I'd better get over there now – thank you!' Tara said feverishly.

'Sorry to have asked so many questions, I thought you might be a reporter,' the policeman called after her. But she didn't hear him. Running as fast as her legs would take her back to her car, she was already out of sight.

It was after midnight and the activity in the Accident and Emergency Department waiting area of the Hampstead hospital showed little signs of dying down: mothers with fractious children fighting a losing battle to keep them occupied; bad-tempered elderly women taking it as a personal affront that their even more decrepit husbands were still waiting to be allocated a doctor, and teenagers with sickly-white complexions suffering the after-effects of a Saturday-night binge of alcohol or drugs.

Tara sat back with her third cup of coffee waiting anxiously for news of her father's condition. Giving her name as the next-of-kin, all she'd been told by a curt nurse was that a middle-aged man, whom they were now able to identify as Stanley Rose, had been admitted earlier in the evening with a serious head injury and was undergoing an emergency operation. That was three hours ago. Since then, she had heard absolutely nothing.

The distressing image of a horribly disfigured face had been superseded by the terrifying thought that her father might already be dead, or worse – so badly injured that he'd remain a vegetable for the rest of his life.

Tara was suddenly filled with remorse for giving him such a hard time after her mother died, for not being there for him when he had had no one else to turn to. If he failed to regain consciousness before she had the opportunity to tell him how much she loved him, Tara knew she would never be able to forgive herself.

Mercifully, it wasn't long before a slight man with a blue stethoscope around his painfully thin neck approached her.

'Tara Rose?' he said warmly. 'I'm Dr Chaudhry. Please do come with me.'

Tara jumped to her feet and followed the white-coated physician down the corridor, passing patients in hospital robes waiting to be called for treatment. Finding an unoccupied cubicle at the end, she was ushered in by the doctor, who pulled the plastic curtain closed to give them privacy.

'How is my father?' Tara asked nervously. 'He is going to be all right, isn't he?'

The doctor, glancing at the chart that was by his side, didn't answer straight away. Then, choosing his words carefully, so as not to increase the young woman's distress, he began by saying, 'Is it OK if I call you Tara?'

She nodded.

'Very well, Tara. Your father has suffered a fractured skull and a broken collarbone. We didn't know the full extent of the injury until we operated.'

Tara took a deep breath, expecting the worst.

'A blood clot was removed from his brain and a shunt inserted – just a small tube really, to relieve the build-up of pressure.'

'But he is alive?' Tara asked anxiously.

'Your father is in a coma. It's not uncommon after this type of procedure.'

'When can I go and see him?'

'The thing is, he's so heavily sedated, he won't know you're there.'

'Please, Doctor, just for a few minutes.'

'Look, it's not really permitted, but if you don't mind putting on a medical gown and a mask? If anyone asks, just say you're a student nurse, interested at looking in at the Intensive Care Unit.' He winked and went off to find her a uniform.

'Thank you,' Tara called after him, with a great sense of relief.

However, nothing could have prepared her for the shock of seeing the heavily bandaged patient with a shaven head, wired up to a monitor, who bore little resemblance to her father. After a few seconds she fled, needing to be consoled by the kind Dr Chaudhry.

It was past two in the morning by the time Tara got home. Emotionally drained, she collapsed on the bed. Before falling into a deep sleep, she wondered how she would be able to endure the wait of not knowing whether her father would ever regain consciousness.

29

Richard Jeffrey stood looking out from the balcony of his penthouse apartment, wondering why it had taken him so long to leave England. He had bought the home in Florida on plan ten years ago, but there was always a reason for not making full use of it. It would have been easier had he been able to persuade his wife, Julia, to escape the British winter for a few months each year. At least then, the place would have paid for itself. Now, planning on returning to the UK for a mere ninety days a year – which he convinced his wife was for tax purposes – had enabled him to make a new life for himself. Continuing to retain the family house in Highgate, no children to worry about and money in the bank from the sale of his shares in the Lowndes Jeffrey law practice to his fellow partners . . . as far as Richard Jeffrey was concerned, he had the best of both worlds.

Feeling the warmth of the late-afternoon sun on his body, he glanced again at the half-year trading figures of the company that had once belonged to Ben Miller. With profits of £750,000 from the sale of properties and annualised rents of just shy of £1 million, he had good reason to smile. The business was running just the way he wanted it without him being there. There were no employees to ask questions, no company premises to draw attention to his activities. Even Giles at the Pretoria Bank only knew what he had told him. The bank's satellite office in the Antilles, established for clients like himself who wanted to remain off the radar, provided the conduit for all movements of money to and from his company's bank account. Acting as a dummy director, it also allowed Richard to file all the necessary statutory documents, giving him the reassurance of knowing that his company was completely above board and beyond reproach.

In another few years or when the portfolio reached £50 million, whichever was the sooner, he would get out completely, palm off Julia with the smallest divorce settlement he could get away with and spend the whole year in America. With the surfeit of wealthy unattached women living right on his doorstep, he would never be short of female company with whom to enjoy his retirement.

In the meantime, there was the unexpected call he'd received from the person he'd found to purchase Stanley Rose's minority interest. It had left him feeling unsettled, and that was the reason why he'd reluctantly forfeited his Saturday-afternoon game of golf to await the arrival of his visitor on the British Airways flight from London.

Mary Cunningham wiped her brow as the yellow taxi sped off towards North Miami Beach. She hated the heat, which was why she always holidayed in England where she knew what to expect. At least flying first-class made the nine and three-quarter hour flight bearable, especially when someone else was paying for the ticket. Taking full advantage of the complimentary champagne and caviar, she decided that the few days away actually made a nice break from the English coast. However, as she kept reminding herself, it was never a holiday having to do business with Richard Jeffrey. You needed all your wits about you.

It hadn't taken long for the lawyer to realise that he couldn't fully wreak his vengeance on Tara and Stanley Rose without enlisting her help, she thought smugly. Then her smile turned into a frown. No one could blame her for feeling resentful. It had hurt, always coming second in Ben's affections to that Alison Brown woman he'd been besotted with – added to the fact that Mary hadn't been properly provided for in his will, despite his promises. It just wasn't right! True, Ben and Alison had both got their comeuppance – but that didn't change anything: she still had a score to settle.

Naturally, she felt slightly sorry for Stanley Rose. The fact that he'd managed to double the size of Miller Investments within a few years, despite his father-in-law's low opinion of him, had come as a pleasant surprise. Mary knew that in normal cases you didn't need brains to make money in property, especially if you had the agents in your pocket. Ben Miller had always deluded himself that he ran a straight business, when she had been the one who had paid 'dropsy' or bribes to get him the deals in the first place. That's why she had told Jeffrey, when he wanted to get his greedy hands on the portfolio, to bide his time and let Stanley Rose carry on building up the business before he swooped and struck. For a crooked lawyer it was surprising, she thought, that the concept of maximising value seemed to be beyond his comprehension.

The ease at which the company had been whisked

away from Stanley Rose still made her chuckle. It wasn't as if she hadn't warned him about not trusting Richard Jeffrey - but the big lummocks was so intent on making a name for himself, he didn't bother looking over his shoulder. Accepting without question that his daughter had carelessly signed away her inheritance, he still hadn't a clue that he had been set up. And afterwards, running all over Kensington like a blue-arsed fly, too late to retrieve what he'd lost, simply confirmed her initial assessment of him - that he wasn't sufficiently streetwise for the property business. Of course, she had made it harder for him, ensuring, at a price, that none of the people with whom Stan had previously done business would offer him anything that might resemble a half-decent deal.

It wasn't long before the taxi pulled up outside the Ocean Bay condominium at the luxurious Bal Harbor resort. Mary paid the driver, collected her suitcase from him at the door and entered the luxurious residence. After giving her name at reception, she was directed by a bear of a security guard to take the elevator up to the seventeenth floor.

'Mary, how good of you to have come all this way,' Richard said, standing at the open door in his Lacoste sports shirt and cream cotton slacks. 'Let me take your case from you.' Barefooted, he then proceeded to lead the way through a wide marbled hall into an open-plan living area decorated throughout in stark white, making it appear even larger than it actually was.

'See you've done all right for yourself,' Mary remarked, gazing at the stunning view of the ocean from all three sides of the glass-fronted room.

'It's comfortable enough for Julia and me, just the two of us. A cold drink – or would you like something stronger?' the lawyer asked.

'Tea, please,' Mary replied. Forgetting that because of the five-hour time difference with the UK, it was almost midnight, she sank her weary frame into a deep-seated sofa, knowing that if she was to achieve her objective, she had to remain alert.

Richard Jeffrey reappeared from the split-level kitchen carrying a tray with their refreshments.

'Old habits die hard, eh?' he said, passing the visitor her mug of tea. 'I must say I prefer beer, especially in the heat.' Taking his bottle of Becks, he went over to the centre of the room and rested against a life-size bronze sculpture of a female dancer.

'What I was thinking,' Mary began, 'now that things are going all right, is that our arrangement has probably served its purpose, if you see what I mean.'

Richard Jeffrey took a gulp of his beer, to give himself time to think. Despite his outward calm, he felt that he'd been caught unprepared. The 25 per cent she'd got hold of from Stanley Rose had cost her nothing; the old harridan was too smart for that. Since she had pleaded poverty, he himself had funded the purchase of the shares on the understanding that he'd get his money back, plus nominal interest, when the business was eventually sold. In the meantime, her stake had risen several times – and yet all of a sudden, she wanted out. Why? It didn't make any sense.

'You've viewed the latest figures,' she went on. 'Anybody can see the business today is worth twenty million – and in a few years, who knows?'

'I'm afraid, my dear Mary, it's not quite as simple as that,' Richard said, prepared to be as hard-nosed as necessary to ensure the woman continued to run the show.

'I've already taken the necessary steps for someone else to take over the reins,' she continued.

'Really – and who might that be?' Jeffrey enquired dubiously.

'Young Francis Simmonds,' Mary answered.

'I know him. He's one of the owners of Parker's. Doesn't most of our Kensington business go through them?' the lawyer pointed out.

'Which is why he's the man ideally placed for the job,' came the reply from the sofa.

'I'm not with you,' Jeffrey said, looking puzzled.

'With the amount of commission he's been raking in from both sides over the years, you'll save a fortune having him on the books. I've already sounded him out, and with an increase in salary and a small share of the action, it should be a smooth enough handover,' the visitor explained, as if it were already a done deal.

The lawyer remained pensive for a few minutes then went off to get another beer from the fridge.

'So where does that leave us?' he said, returning to the discussion that he hadn't expected to be having. Dispensing with the need for a glass, he took a swig from the frosted bottle.

'That's what I've come to talk to you about,' Mary Cunningham replied, her vibrancy restored. 'I've done my sums, Richard, and reckon seven million sounds reasonable.'

Not usually short of an answer, on this occasion the man was too bemused to offer any response. Not when he had assumed that she was on board to grow the company into one of the largest privately owned property concerns in London.

'Mary, you know that's excessive,' he said eventually. 'You are also aware that, being locked in – as Stanley Rose found out to his detriment – doesn't give you much of a bargaining position.' He was beginning to regain the upper hand.

'Richard, I take it that's just your tactic of trying to talk the price down?'

'No, not at all. I'm just suggesting that you reconsider what sounds to me like a rather rash action. Taking into account the huge upside in business that you yourself mentioned, I would have thought you'd want to stay in, that's all.' He stared at her intently.

Mary Cunningham smiled to herself. She had predicted the lawyer's reaction to a T. The only way to get the greedy bastard to bite was for him to believe he was buying her out cheaply.

'Well, in that case,' she sighed, getting up slowly and painfully from the sofa, 'it looks like I've seriously miscalculated. Ah well, that's what comes with age. Oh dear. Would you mind calling me a taxi?'

'Hold on a minute,' Richard said. 'If you're serious and really do want out, I'm sure I can find someone to take it off your hands.'

'The way you're talking, you are making it sound like a fire sale,' Mary objected, slightly unsteady on her feet.

'Looking at the present value, and applying the normal 40 per cent discount attributable to a 25 per cent shareholding, you're probably right.'

'Richard, you are so much better at working these

things out than me,' the visitor said with false modesty, then worried that she might be overdoing it. 'What does it come out at?'

'I'd say no more than about three million. But you'd be mad to take it,' the lawyer replied, more confident now that he had regained control of the situation.

Mary walked around the apartment, conveying the impression that she was giving the matter serious consideration. To her, the price was secondary. What mattered most was that there couldn't be any comeback to trouble her at a later date. Whether or not it was wishful thinking, she was convinced that one day, Richard Jeffrey was another one who would get what he so richly deserved – which was why she had chosen this moment to sever all ties to him.

'And if I were to agree, how long would it take for the deal to go through?' the shrewd woman asked, thinking she'd be surprised if the lawyer hadn't twice that amount in his private bank account.

'The easiest way would be for the company to buy back its own shares and then effect a reduction in capital,' he muttered and then added, 'If you are sure I can't change your mind, I could get you a banker's draft on Monday morning.'

'Actually, I was thinking of cash,' Mary said bluntly.

'I suppose that might just be possible,' he mused. 'The paperwork should be straightforward enough. Come to think of it, Stanley Rose is still listed as a shareholder. With a bit of creative accounting, it'll be as if neither of you ever existed.'

The words were music to Mary Cunningham's ears, although she would have liked to hear them again just to make sure.

'So – do we have a deal?' Jeffrey looked her in the eyes.

'I suppose so,' she responded heavily, not wanting to appear overly keen.

30

June 1995

Stan awoke from his induced coma remembering nothing about the assault that very nearly killed him. He knew the eight-hour operation had been a success; the doctors told him so but they'd warned him that after such a serious procedure, recovery would, at best, be slow. That was why to avoid any post-operative complications, a further spell in Intensive Care was prescribed so that he could continue to be monitored.

During those early weeks, apart from the West Hampstead police, who were keen to gain any information that would help them with their enquiry into the incident, Stan's only visitor was his daughter Tara, not that he was aware of her presence most of the time. With his best interests at heart, she had attempted to keep everyone else away – no easy feat when it came to Elaine. Her grandmother had apparently turned up at the hospital, dressed to the nines, on her way to the Goodwood races. Armed with a Selfridges food hamper, it was as though she was expecting to find her son sitting up watching television with nothing more than a plaster over his eye. Even when Dr Chaudhry tried to explain about the seriousness of his patient's condition, Elaine's only response was that her son would be better off being moved to a private hospital where he could receive *proper* treatment.

One Saturday afternoon in the middle of June, Stan's stitches were removed, exposing an angry six-inch scar from the left side of his head down to his ear. Gloom threatened to overwhelm him. Even the fresh delivery of white lilies on his bedside table from an anonymous well-wisher, their pollen carefully removed by the nurses, failed to lift his depression. His move to the private ward, shared with just one other patient, only made things worse.

The memory of his attack came in waves and left him feeling emotionally distraught. More than once he had to be given a sedative to calm him down after waking up in the middle of the night screaming. Obsessed with what his assailants looked like, he invented faces for them and engaged them in conversation in a bizarre attempt to become friends. And yet, the next day, he couldn't remember a single thing. When he was told that he was making progress, it didn't have any effect on him whatsoever. Nor was he interested in communicating with those closest to him. The truth was, whether they came or not was of no consequence. The doctors said that his feelings were consistent with post-traumatic stress and recommended an extensive course of therapy – to commence immediately.

Stan was lying back with his head on the pillow, when out of one eye, he saw an individual, wearing a magnificent black coat made of silk, standing over him; a round fur hat placed delicately on his finely shaped head. Stan wasn't sure whether or not he was dreaming, but it seemed that he was in the presence of a character out of a winter's scene in Tolstoy's *War and Peace*.

'Mr Rose! How are you feeling?' the man asked out loud, as though he had just discovered a long-lost friend.

Stan tried to sit up, to get a better look at the person addressing him, curious as to how the visitor knew his name.

'Here, let me help you.' Without further ado, the mysterious individual moved briskly over to Stan and, supporting his body with one strong arm, he propped up his pillows. He then pressed the lever on the bed, to elevate it a little so that Stan could see him better.

'Do I know you?' Stan asked.

'I came to your house a few months ago but you've obviously forgotten.'

'But how did you recognise me?' Stan said, gesturing to the bare patches on his head.

'I noticed you last Sabbath when I came here, but you were resting and I didn't want to disturb you. No matter, the important thing is that you're making a good recovery. By the way, allow me to introduce myself. My name is Rabbi Frankel.'

Stan suddenly recalled the evening when that other, odd-looking fellow had turned up on his doorstep. But that man had been unkempt and looked as if he had fallen on hard times. He certainly wasn't beautifully dressed, like this man. Stan racked his brain, trying to remember the other chap's name, but it escaped him.

'You must have a good memory for faces, that's all I can say,' Stan remarked, 'especially the way I look these days. I've been told I'm lucky to be alive after the injuries I suffered.'

'Have you, perhaps, asked yourself why that might have been?' There was an intensity about the man as he spoke.

'What do you mean?' Stan replied.

'You are querying how you survived, are you not?'

'As I said, it was very much touch and go.'

Leaning over to Stan so their faces were practically touching, the religious man whispered, 'Everything happens for a purpose – for example, us meeting again now. We don't believe that there's such a thing as a coincidence.'

'And what do you suppose that purpose might be?' Stan asked, curious to hear the answer.

'That's a very good question,' the rabbi responded, straightening his powerful frame. 'What I can tell you is that it can be a long and arduous road trying to discover what that purpose is, but with the Almighty's guidance, when you find it, you'll know.'

'And you're suggesting that's a journey I should take?'

'That's for you alone to decide.' The rabbi smiled warmly. Then, without another word, he walked away.

'But where do I start looking?' Stan called after the charismatic man, who had engaged him in conversation for the last half an hour. But it was to no avail, for he had gone off to continue his rounds of the other wards.

That night, Stan lay awake, unable to get to sleep. Rabbi Frankel's words had left him searching for answers. Yes, he could go along with the possibility that he'd been given another chance to make a go of it. But surely the fellow wasn't referring to the property business. There had to be a deeper meaning somewhere . . .

It then came back to him. The dishevelled-looking individual before him had alluded to the same thing, when he suggested that Stan should visit the place for which he, the rabbi, was raising money. Perhaps that had something to do with what his purpose might be.

As tiredness took hold, he was suddenly impatient for next Saturday to come around again, so he could continue his conversation with the man who had left such a deep impression on him. Stan began to sense that his life was destined for a change of direction.

On 30 June, six weeks after he'd been admitted, Stan was well enough to be discharged. In the fresh change of clothes his daughter had brought for him earlier that day, unassisted, he walked slowly out of the Royal Free Hospital and got into the passenger seat of Tara's little green Mini.

'How do I look?' Stan asked, examining himself closely in the rear-view mirror.

'I think the hat makes you look quite cool,' Tara responded, gazing at the white trilby she had managed to find in an Oxfam shop nearby. 'Anyway, your hair's already beginning to grow back so you won't need it for long,' she said, driving off.

'You know, you really don't have to stay with me,' Stan said.

'Daddy, let's not go through that again. Dr Chaudhry said that for the time being, it is better for you not to be alone, and I've already moved my stuff into the spare room. In any case, you can't drive, so who's going to take you to your therapy appointments?'

Stan sat glum-faced, saying nothing. Those twice-weekly sessions he'd been enduring had done nothing to alleviate the mood-swings that were now part of his everyday life. How long, he wondered, could these feelings be put down to the after-effects of his injury? Or was it a permanent change in his personality and outlook, a fact that the hospital had kept from him?

A short time later, the car drew into the drive of the terraced house in Swiss Cottage. Tara bit her lip, scared in case it would bring back the memory of his attack. She certainly had a vivid memory of the scene.

'I've got keys,' she announced quietly. Taking her father's arm, she walked with him slowly along the path to the front door.

'The place must look like a tip,' Stan said.

'Don't worry, your cleaner has been coming in while you were incapacitated.'

'Sofia? But she hasn't been paid!'

'I told her I'd see to it, but she wouldn't hear of it. I reckon she's got a soft spot for you. I can't tell you how many times she asked to come to the hospital.'

'Don't be ridiculous,' Stan protested. 'She's the cleaner, for goodness sake.'

'That's never stopped you in the past,' Tara quipped.

'What's that supposed to mean?' Stan retorted, as Tara bent down to pick up the day's post and handed it to him.

'You had quite a thing for Inge, if I recall. Don't worry, Mummy knew all about it.'

'I was just being friendly,' Stan stammered. 'Look at these bloody bills,' he cursed, trying to change the subject.

'There's more post on your desk – when you feel up to it,' Tara said.

'Tara, I'm fine. Please don't fuss. If you insist on being here, why don't you go out and buy some things for dinner?' Running his hands down the outside of his linen jacket, Stan stopped in a panic and said, 'Have you seen my wallet anywhere?'

'It must have been on you, when you were admitted to hospital,' Tara replied.

Stan remembered the police inspector saying something about how they'd recovered a man's Gucci wallet in the gutter but that it was empty.

'Of course, I was robbed,' he said.

'Don't worry, Daddy, I have money. It's all under control.'

Tara conveniently avoided mentioning that Elaine Rose had insisted on settling all bills herself, including any extras after his BUPA health insurance, she'd had the foresight of checking, had been sorted out. Ever since that fraught tea at the Connaught Hotel, the girl had noticed the change in her grandmother's disposition towards her son. Whether it was because she had genuinely begun to put him first, or was just creating a show because she had unwittingly disclosed something about her past that she feared could be used against her, Tara wasn't entirely sure.

All of a sudden feeling overwhelmed with tiredness, Stan went and lay down on the sofa.

Tara put a pillow under his head, covered him with a light throw and took off his shoes. Her father was asleep before she had a chance to tell him that her grandmother had also ensured that the fridge was well stocked up with fresh, nutritious food for when her son arrived home.

Part Two

31

Stan got off the number 13 bus at Golders Green bus station. A fortnight had passed since his return home and he was now well enough to leave the house and venture out on his own. He had had another restless night but, unlike previous ones when he was reliving his attack, on this occasion in his dream he was continuing his conversation in hospital with the noble-looking man in the round fur hat. They were discussing ways in which he could help out at the Centre that the rabbi was promoting.

'We have many people there for whose lives you could make a real difference,' the man had stressed.

'But why me?' Stan asked.

'The first time we met, I sensed a certain disillusionment with your life. You would have realised it yourself, eventually. But there's a time for everything.'

'And you are saying that time is now?'

The man nodded and then disappeared from sight.

Stan woke early, recalling the dream in detail. Strangely, the disappointment he had felt, having been discharged from the Royal Free before being able to see the finely dressed rabbi again on the following Saturday, had now been replaced with an obsessive desire to recover the leaflet about the Lakish Centre which he had foolishly discarded. The two men whom he had encountered three months apart were, he now knew for certain, one and the same person.

Creeping downstairs, so as not to disturb his daughter, Stan eventually discovered a crumpled piece of paper pushed right down the side of the armchair in front of the television. Fortunately, Sofia, the cleaner, must have missed it when she was tidying the room.

Now, having no idea what he was looking for other than the number of the street, Stan arrived a little while later at a large semi-detached house that had fallen into disrepair. Paint was flaking off the window-frames and there were several tiles missing from the roof. An old wooden board with the name *Lakish Centre* was the only indication that he was at the right place. Hesitantly, he entered the sad-looking premises.

'Good morning, can I help you?' asked the pleasant youth who was manning the front desk.

'Yes, I hope you can,' Stan said. 'I've come to see the gentleman who visited me when I was in hospital. I think he had something to do with raising money for this place.'

'Most of the people involved here are volunteers. Do you have his name, possibly?'

Stan shook his head; his mind had suddenly gone blank.

'I do remember that he wore long black stockings and a prayer shawl under his coat. You know the way those people dress?'

It was clear from the dubious expression on the young man's face that the description he had been given wasn't going to be sufficient.

'Fundraising is organised from our centre in Stamford

243

Hill,' he explained. 'Many of the helpers there are more religious in the way you described. Perhaps they could be of more assistance. Here's their address.' Writing the details down, he tore a page off his pad and passed it over.

'Thank you, but he did specifically mention that it was *here,*' Stan stressed.

'I don't know what else to suggest, but you are more than welcome to have a look around. We're not busy this morning. My name is Saul, by the way.'

'And I'm Stan. Yes, thank you, I'd like that very much,' Stan replied impulsively, accompanying the volunteer on a tour of the ground floor, where six small treatment rooms were situated.

'This one's for occupational therapy,' Saul pointed out, knocking on the door in front of them.

'Hi Rachel, sorry to interrupt you,' he said, addressing a plump lady in a dark blue nurse's costume. 'This is Mr . . .'

'Stanley Rose,' he said, introducing himself

'I'm just showing Stan the work we do here,' the adolescent said.

'Pleased to meet you,' the therapist responded with a smile. 'Reuven, who is eleven, suffers from Muscular Dystrophy,' she explained, looking affectionately at the lanky boy with an alert expression who sat perched perilously on the edge of the treatment table. 'This morning we are trying to improve his circulation,' she said, without more ado beginning her massage on the inert limbs in front of her.

'Thank you,' Stan said. Glancing at the wheelchair by the bed, he had seen enough and was eager to get away.

Just as he was about to leave, the young patient called out after him, 'Can *you* take me to the park?'

'Pardon?' Stan said, stepping back into the room.

'It's Wednesday,' the boy affirmed. 'There's always a game on Wednesdays.'

'Reuven, we don't want to trouble Mr Rose. Judith will be here after lunch – she'll take you,' the physiotherapist said.

'It's not the same! Women don't know anything about football,' the boy protested. 'Do you like football, Stanley? I support Spurs, though I've never been to the White Hart Lane ground.'

'Yes, Reuven, I do. And Spurs are my team too,' Stan answered, establishing an immediate rapport with the child. 'But surely your dad could take you?'

'Most of the matches are on Shabbos,' the boy said.

'Reuven's from a religious family,' the therapist said quietly. 'Going to a match on a Saturday would be out of the question.'

'I'm sorry, I didn't realise,' Stan said.

'Rabbi Frankel is his father. You may have heard of him. The family only live a few streets away.'

Hearing the name, all of a sudden it came back to him – the distinguished man in a fine black coat, who was the cause of him being here at the Centre today. It had to be the same person. Everything now seemed to fit. The reason why the rabbi had been so keen on Stan's assisting at the centre was because his own son was being treated here.

That afternoon, Stan accompanied Reuven Frankel in a specially adapted minibus to Lyttelton Playing Fields, the recreational park in Hampstead Garden Suburb, to watch a seven-a-side football match. To his surprise, he had the most fun he'd had in a very, very long time.

*

Deeply affected by the day's experience in the company of such a special young man, Stan returned home early that evening to find his daughter waiting anxiously for him, gazing out of the living-room window.

'Where on earth have you been!' she exclaimed as he walked through the door.

'I must have forgotten the time,' Stan answered thoughtlessly.

'But it's nearly seven o'clock,' she said agitatedly. 'The hospital called twice about your missed therapy appointment. At least you could have taken your mobile.'

Oblivious to the worry he'd caused, Stan washed his face and hands at the kitchen sink and sat down at the table, which Tara had already set for dinner. He was feeling far too elated from the day's encounter with Rabbi Frankel's son to get involved in an argument with his daughter. The joy on Reuven's face, watching boys just a few years older than him on the field of play, knowing that unlike them, he would never be able to kick a football, filled him with humility.

'So where *have* you been?' Tara enquired, more calmly.

'You wouldn't believe it if I told you,' Stan said. He didn't really know where to begin. In the end, he simply said: 'I went to a Centre in Golders Green for physically impaired children.'

'What?' Tara was surprised.

'I was told about the place when I was in hospital.'

'They were probably just looking to raise money,' she said, not particularly interested.

'So I went to have a look, that's all.'

'And that took up the whole day?'

'I met an eleven-year-old child and he wanted me to stay around.'

'Why, what was wrong with him?' Tara asked, now more curious.

'He has a muscle-wasting disease. From what I understand, it's an upward struggle trying to keep it at bay.'

'And how about his family?'

'We didn't talk much about them, apart from the fact I found out that he is one of five children and his father is a well-known rabbi.'

'Bit of a departure for you, isn't it? I thought you detested anything to do with religion,' Tara said, serving up the homemade shepherd's pie, with a bowl of salad.

'We seemed to get on really well so I went with him to watch a football match in the park where Mummy and I took you to play on the swings. It's near where Grandma used to live.' Stan took a mouthful of the delicious hot food. 'Do you know, the lad supports Spurs? What are the chances of that?' he beamed.

'Sounds like you've got quite attached,' Tara commented with just a hint of envy.

'I don't know about that, but he did invite me to his house for tea tomorrow.'

The meal continued in silence, Tara sensing that the closer relationship she had recently developed with her father had regressed again, and Stan now too preoccupied with the young disabled boy to notice.

'So, what did *you* do today?' her father asked finally.

'I got some research done for a feature I'm working on,' Tara replied without elaborating. The fact was that, outside of her normal working environment, she still felt as if she was falling to pieces. She wondered how much longer it would be before she could get her own life back together.

Stan came away from the Frankels' home – a former workman's cottage in a dreary cul-de-sac – and travelled back to Swiss Cottage feeling privileged for having been party to something very special. Expecting the atmosphere to be strained, with a family of seven living on top of each other in such cramped conditions, plus having to suffer the extra burden of a seriously disabled child, he couldn't have been more wrong. Their home was a revelation, so full of joy and love for each other. Most evident was the sense of tranquillity; not a cross word passed between any members of the family for his entire stay.

The four daughters, clothed identically to their mother in black skirts falling to just above the floor, their upper bodies covered to the neck with long-sleeved shirts, were together in the kitchen preparing the evening meal. Reuven wasn't treated any differently from the others. When he didn't require treatment, he went to Kisharon, a special needs school in the area where, because of his exceptionally high IQ, he was able to get individual attention.

Confined to his wheelchair, the child observed everything and participated like any other member of the household. The highlight, as far as he was concerned, was being granted permission to attend a Spurs match in the new season. How Stan was going to get him there was another matter, especially as he hadn't been anywhere near the sports car that lay in the garage; he was still holding it responsible for what had happened to him.

The one disappointment, as far as Stan was concerned, was that their father, Rabbi Frankel, wasn't at home. Even though he wasn't any closer in deciding which path to follow in life, Stan was looking forward to thanking the rabbi for unwittingly putting him in contact with his son Reuven; an experience which, even though they had only just met, had already and undoubtedly enriched Stan's life.

There was no question that their beliefs had given the family the strength to deal with the adversity to which, in his mind, they had been unfairly subjected. Perhaps a spiritual dimension was what had been missing in his own life? If the only reason he had survived his injuries *was* to be given a second chance . . . surely it now behoved him to make proper use of it?

As soon as he got home, he picked up the phone and tapped in the still familiar number.

'Hello, Howard, it's Stan. Look, can you get hold of two tickets for the first game against Liverpool? Money no object.' And then he added, 'I don't suppose you feel like taking the Ferrari off my hands?'

The next day, Stan enrolled as a full member in South Hampstead United Synagogue. His transformation had started.

32

The weather was glorious that July morning and Tara was feeling upbeat as her Mini sped down Southampton Row towards the Aldwych, a route that during the morning rush-hour would normally be congested with traffic. Now that the holiday period had kicked in, however, the roads were empty.

Things were improving. Her father was well enough for her to move out of his house and back to her flat in Golders Green, and she was excited about getting her career on track again. Living with him these past six weeks hadn't been easy, taking into account that they only ever had a strained relationship at the best of times. But the fact that he'd become so philosophical about the trauma he'd suffered, practically forgiving of those who had so nearly taken his life, had come as a surprise.

Whether it was the on-going shock of the attack, she couldn't honestly say, but remarkably, he also appeared to have completely lost his obsession with money. However, it was the relationship he had formed with Reuven Frankel, the disabled child whom he had volunteered to help look after, that had had the most effect upon him. As he said, he learned more about himself in the few hours taking Reuven out on a Sunday afternoon in the second-hand Fiat car he'd found advertised in the newsagent's window, than during any of his expensive therapy sessions. If only her father could have given her the same level of attention, Tara thought. She felt sad but was resigned to the fact that it would never happen.

Her mind turned to her job. At least she'd been able to rely on the others to cover for her while she was away from the office. Marise had been unusually supportive, knowing the challenges Tara had to contend with, from her own experiences of caring for her chronically ill mother. This was more than could be said for her boss. Mark's interest in Tara these days was no greater than it was in the paper he was supposed to be running. One brief phone call was the sum total of his concern during her continuing absence. Tara had learned a painful lesson: their relationship should never have strayed from a professional level.

Fortunately, being at home with her father and with time on her hands, Tara could keep abreast of what was going on in the capital. That meant she was able to submit her piece in time on John Major's re-election as leader of the Conservative Party. Her article should have appeared in the most recent issue of the *Londoner*. Strangely, when she tried to buy a copy at any of the news-stands in her area, none seemed to have one.

Guiding the Mini into Stamford Street, she parked and got out. The front door of the building was unlocked. That was odd. Shrugging, Tara climbed the stairs to the third floor, thinking that whoever had been the last to leave the previous night had forgotten to lock up. Entering the darkened office, she switched on the lights and was disturbed to see that all the desks, including her own, had been cleared out. The place appeared abandoned. Why? What had happened? And why hadn't she been told?

Admittedly, she hadn't been in contact since the middle of last week, but she'd spoken to Mark, who had sounded jollier than he had for a long time. Apart from asking when she was coming back to work, he gave her no indication that there was anything untoward going on.

Tara pondered for a moment; there must an explanation. She took out her mobile phone and dialled her employer's number. It went straight to voicemail. She was just about to look up Marise's number, when she heard the sound of dull footsteps. Expecting it to be Gareth, struggling to sober up from another night's bout of heavy drinking, she was taken aback to see instead the stooped figure of their printer Harold Mayes. The expression on his moon face and the fact that he wasn't, as usual, dragging bundles of the latest copies of the *Londoner* out of the service lift, confirmed that something was seriously amiss.

'Mr Mayes, is something wrong?' she asked.

'You could say that,' the printer replied grimly.

'Perhaps you'd like a cup of tea or coffee?' she asked, hoping that it was only a minor problem that could be resolved.

He grunted. 'I'd prefer to be paid, if that's at all possible.'

'What do you mean? I thought your invoices were settled promptly on the first of the month?'

'Up until eight weeks ago, they were. But I've received nothing since April. I didn't want to let you down so, to maintain goodwill, I went ahead and printed the May and June issues – only because Mark told me that there was a temporary cash-flow problem, which he was sorting out.'

'I didn't know anything about it, you have my word!' Tara gasped, unable to hide her shock.

'I'm not saying you did, but I need the money, otherwise

I can't pay the wages. As it is, I've had to ask my bank to up the overdraft. Not right, is it, miss?'

Tara went over to Mark's desk. She knew the cheque-books were kept in his top drawer and that there were normally several blank ones ready signed for emergencies.

'I'm afraid I'll have to insist on cash,' the man said immediately. 'The last couple of those blighters bounced.'

Tara's mouth fell open. The only thought that flashed through her mind was that she had to keep the paper going.

'How much are you owed?' she asked.

'Three thousand pounds, give or take a few quid.'

'Let me see what I can do.'

Harold Mayes pulled a doubtful face. 'I don't mean to be rude, but where's a young girl like you going to find that sort of money?'

'Don't worry, Mr Mayes, I will get it for you somehow. But what about the July issues?' she heard herself asking, now realising why she hadn't been able to obtain a copy. It was already the last week of the month, which meant that the first two weekly issues hadn't appeared. The position was far worse than she'd imagined. While looking after her father, she had obviously lost all track of time. What was certain, however, was that Mark had been leading her on – and that Gareth and Marise must already have left.

'You see what you can do about getting me paid, and I'll rush the next ones through,' the printer replied. 'Not much I can do about the others – I never received the copy.' He shuffled off disconsolately.

*

253

Tara put down the phone, unable to fully comprehend what the bank had just told her. She'd been hoping to be able to pay off some or all of the printer's invoice from her own account – but instead had found that the latest rental payment on her flat had left her account with just £125 to her name. She had received no pay for the last three months. It didn't seem possible! Usually so good with money, she berated herself for being so lax with her financial affairs.

She remained in the empty office for another few hours in the hope that she might have got it all wrong and that one of her colleagues would suddenly make an appearance. No one did. Just after midday, she collected her things and left the building, wondering if it was for the last time.

The previous afternoon, an Irish car ferry set sail on the trip from Holyhead to Dublin. Sat amongst the scores of families off to Ireland for their summer holidays was a pale unshaven man in a leather jacket and, snuggled up against him, a woman of the same age with a mop of black hair and tinted sunglasses.

'Mark, I really don't think this was such a great idea,' she said, turning to her companion.

'Marise, you worry too much, love,' came the reply.

'But surely it would have been better to come clean with all those people you owed money to?'

If it had been down to her, she would have stood her ground. Running off with a married man who had a serious cocaine habit and who had left honest working people in the lurch, was not her idea of a basis for a happy future. But Mark was in a whole lot of trouble, and for what they had once had together, she felt she owed it to him. Naturally, the offer of a £20,000 lifetime annuity from Percy Boothroyd, in order to get his son-in-law as far away from his family as possible, had helped sweeten the pill. With nothing to keep her in England now her mother had died, perhaps they would be able to make a go of it, she tried convincing herself.

'Fuck that!' Mark snorted. 'They'd have to find me first!'

33

Stan looked at his watch again and adjusted his skullcap. He had selected to meet his date in the lobby of the unobtrusive Regents Park Hotel. Tucked away by the side of Lords Cricket Ground, it was a safe bet that at 9 p.m. on a cold Monday evening in late November, he wouldn't be recognised. Confronted with a large crowd attending a property gala dinner, however, he realised that he had seriously miscalculated. Acknowledging several familiar faces from the past, of people he'd rather have forgotten, he was shown to the last available table, trying to work out why he felt so uncomfortable. He thought he'd learned his lesson for the years he'd wasted in the single-minded pursuit of money, so it had to be something else – but since he couldn't pinpoint exactly what it might be, he applied his mind instead to the woman he would shortly be meeting.

Although all he had to go on was a simple photograph that probably didn't do her justice, he had still agreed to meet Naomi Weiss. There had been a void in his life, created by the absence of a respectable woman. The thirty-nine-year-old widow had come highly recommended by his mentor, Rabbi Frankel, who had known the family for over twenty years and had considered it a perfect match.

Stan had eventually seen Reuven's father the next time

he called around to their house.

There was so much he had planned to say to the rabbi, were they to encounter each other again, yet when it eventually occurred, it just didn't seem to matter any more. Strangely, the boy's father never mentioned the bond that had been formed with his son. It was as if he, Stanley Rose, was already considered part of the family and had, therefore, been taken for granted. Then a few weeks later, an offer came out of the blue to learn with the esteemed scholar, for which he wouldn't take any payment. It had cemented their friendship and brought Stan a basic level of knowledge in religious observance.

A quick transition took place from his previously purely secular existence. He moved to the suburb of Hendon, an area which, with its sense of close community, was more in keeping with his newfound spirituality. With his neat beard and new wardrobe of sombre suits, Stan had adapted once again to the new circumstances in which he found himself - or so he thought.

Stan's heart sank as he caught sight of a shapeless woman, her hair gathered up in a crochet snood, advancing towards him with intent. Perhaps she might give him a wide berth and go to one of the other tables, he hoped, but he was out of luck.

'Hello, sorry if I've kept you waiting, I'm Naomi,' she said. Unbuttoning her thick winter coat, she plonked herself down opposite the man she'd heard so much about. 'No need to look so nervous, I don't bite,' she laughed. 'At least not on the first date.'

'I didn't realise it was that obvious,' Stan said, forcing a smile.

'When you've been on as many of these things as I have,

you learn not to take them too seriously.'

'I'm afraid it's my first time,' Stan admitted.

'I would never have guessed,' the woman teased.

'What can I get you to drink?' Stan asked, suddenly remembering his manners.

'Coffee's fine. But don't let me stop you if you'd prefer something a little stronger, like a whisky, maybe?' That sounded more like a recommendation than a suggestion.

'I'll have coffee too,' Stan said, summoning over a waitress to take their order.

'So what on earth persuaded *you* to agree to come tonight?' Naomi Weiss asked.

'Rabbi Frankel thought I needed to find a wife,' Stan said, seeing no reason to hold back.

'You don't look to me like a person who's in need of help in that department.'

'I'm not sure how to take that,' Stan said, surprised at the woman's outspokenness.

'It was meant as a compliment.' She laughed warmly.

'Oh, I see . . . thank you.'

'The introductions I normally subject myself to are to much older gentlemen, mostly widowed.'

'Well, in that case, you can include me in that category,' Stan replied.

'I'm sorry, that wasn't particularly tactful of me.'

'That's all right. It was five years ago.'

'A long time for a man to be on his own,' the woman sympathised.

'I have a daughter, Tara. She's a journalist,' Stan said proudly.

'And she lives with you?'

'She has her own place, but we stay in touch regularly.

And how about you?' he prompted, trying to show an interest.

'My husband died eighteen months ago, but he had been ill for a long time.' She sighed. 'Jacob was in insurance,' she added. 'Fortunately, both my sons took over the business.'

'They must have been young,' Stan remarked, trying to work out their ages.

'I got married at nineteen. Avi, the eldest, will be thirty next birthday. It's what happens in our circles. Girls get married young and then spend the next ten years having hordes of children!'

At that point, a harassed-looking waitress arrived with a coffee percolator and two china cups, which she dumped down on the table and then hurried off.

'I'm afraid this is all fairly new to me,' Stan said.

'You mean about becoming more observant?'

Stan nodded, wondering how much more she already knew about him. 'I have to say, not growing up that way, it takes some getting used to.'

'So what persuaded you?'

'I suppose I must have been looking for something.'

'You mean after your wife died?'

'Actually, I was the victim of a serious assault.'

'Ah,' Naomi said gently. 'That often happens when a person suffers post-traumatic stress disorder.'

'You're familiar with it?' Stan said, surprised.

'I've treated countless patients with PTSD,' Naomi replied, taking the initiative to pour the coffee.

'So you're a doctor?'

'Psychiatrist actually.'

'I'd better be careful what I say,' Stan remarked light-heartedly, wondering what other surprises this unusual woman had in store for him.

'No, not really, you seem quite well adjusted in the circumstances. The only thing I would say is that, although you think that now you've found what you've been looking for, in my experience it rarely rests there.'

'You mean, apart from praying three times a day and keeping kosher, there's more?' Stan asked, looking worried.

'I couldn't care less what you keep and what you don't. That's not what I'm talking about.'

'Oh, I thought . . .'

'That I was passing judgement? What a nice man you are,' Naomi said, producing a smile that lit up her previously plain face. 'Frankly, if I wanted to meet someone at that level, there is no shortage of rabbis in Hendon, Temple Fortune and Golders Green. Believe me, I know – I've treated most of them at one time or another. With the issues they've got, I think I'd rather convert than be married to one of them.'

Stan laughed out loud.

'I can see I'm not at all what you expected,' she teased.

'Well, to be quite honest, no, not really,' he replied, feeling a great affinity with the woman. He felt confident enough to ask her: 'So what exactly did you mean when you implied that I might still not have found what I've been looking for?'

Naomi smiled again. 'Life is rarely plain sailing. Wouldn't it be wonderful if it were? An incident comes along – when you least expect it – that makes you query the true meaning of life, and so you go down a spiritual path to find it. In cases such as yours, however, where you have suffered a severe trauma, without something else to fall back on, faith might not always be strong enough to keep you going. In my case, I was lucky to have my career. Although it's not the complete answer, it helped me get through a very dark period when I was left on my own.'

Stan took a little time to think through what Naomi had said. It made a lot of sense. Hadn't his preoccupation with becoming more religious taken him away from being part of the real world? And if so, what sort of life could he offer a new wife? Not having a proper job for nigh on two years, his savings had already been substantially eroded, and that was with only himself to look after.

The two carried on talking for another hour. Stan paid for the coffees and they parted, agreeing to stay in touch, but each doubting whether the loneliness that had brought them together was going to be sufficient for them to remain anything other than good friends. This friendship, however, was going to prove of more value than Stan could possibly have imagined.

The months rolled by and Stan's life continued unchanged. He had taken no action after the conversation with Naomi Weiss. Still without any desire to get a paying job, and just about managing to get by financially, as far as Stan was concerned his time was put to better use immersing himself in the community that had welcomed him into their fold. He repaid them, accordingly, by working tirelessly on their behalf. Appointed to the board of his local synagogue and taking personal charge of the project for a complete refurbishment of the out-of-date premises, he had even less time for his previous activities. In particular, he had had to cut back on seeing Reuven. He missed the youngster.

Stan had kept up his Wednesday learning sessions with Rabbi Frankel and was now fluent in Hebrew reading, and familiar with many of the biblical texts. He had enormous respect for his teacher. Recently, however, he had noticed that there had been a change. The rabbi's normal exuberance had inexplicably disappeared and he had become withdrawn. Without warning, he would suddenly drift off into his own world, or else become tetchy at the slightest error that Stan might make.

Matters came to a head on a balmy night in the summer of 1998, when the rabbi called unexpectedly at Stan's house in a very distressed state, to divulge that his son Reuven had died in his sleep. Stan had known from the beginning of the child's diminished life expectancy, nevertheless his passing came as a huge blow. For the first time in a very long time, he wept – a torrent of tears that left him feeling washed clean.

Several sessions followed where the rabbi would open up and talk about himself. Their roles reversed, Stan would listen attentively, often just giving in return much of what he had gleaned from his teacher in the first place. Even though it had been the most severe challenge to his faith, Rabbi Isaac Frankel eventually learned to accept what had happened to his son and was able, with the rest of his beloved family, to move forward.

It was during their time together – and at his former mentor's insistence – that Stan decided to put his new talent of listening and counselling to proper use. His life, as Naomi Weiss had predicted, was destined for yet another change of direction.

34

With the midday sun beating down on him, a bushy-haired man in faded white chinos and Ray-ban sunglasses stood with his suitcase in front of the coral-coloured building, wondering whether he was at the right place. Set deep amongst the fragrant orange groves of Andalusia, with its Moorish-style arched windows and three-cornered open courtyard, it gave the impression more of a hacienda than a private nursing home.

The notification from the hospital to him as the next-of-kin, forty-eight hours earlier, informing him that his father had only a few days to live, had upset Stan greatly. Firstly, because his mother, with whom he'd resumed his former close relationship, could no longer bring herself to communicate with Harry Rose directly and secondly, because Stan feared there would be insufficient time to make amends for the pride that had, up till now, prevented him from burying the hatchet with Harry Rose.

Stan gave his name and was directed to a room on the first floor. If it was an inconvenient time to visit, he could always come back. With the number of small hotels he had passed on the way from Malaga airport, he could see that finding accommodation would not be a problem.

At home in London, work was always quiet in August, so his absence was not a problem to the business. Naomi Weiss, who had helped him considerably when he decided to train as a psychotherapist, and from whom he subsequently received a good number of his referrals, had recently got married to a retired South African dentist and was away on honeymoon in Israel. In any case, Sylvie Gertler, the other partner in the practice, could always step in if necessary. She and Stan had studied at Birkbeck College together, and although the six-foot redhead from Munich was a good fifteen years younger than him, they had embarked on a romantic relationship that lasted the entire three-year course, after which she took up with her personal trainer. As they had remained good friends, Sylvie and Stan decided to go into business together after qualifying and took over a vacant doctor's surgery on Haverstock Hill, near Hampstead Heath.

Stan tried knocking again, a little harder this time.

'Come in,' a frail voice called out.

The emaciated figure of Harry Rose was sat up in an armchair, wrapped in a thick blanket and facing an open window, when Stan entered the sun-drenched bedroom.

'Do I know you?' Harry asked, looking the stranger up and down suspiciously.

Stan went over and placed his hand on the old man's bony shoulder. 'Hello, Dad,' he said, tears running down his face.

'Stanley?' the old man gasped.

'Yes, it's me.'

'I didn't think you would come,' Harry Rose said, reaching for his son's other hand. He coughed. 'Fetch me some water, son, there's a jug by the bed. I would have preferred something stronger, but they won't allow it,' he said with a glint in his eye. For a brief moment, the charmer of old, lodged permanently in Stan's earliest memory, returned.

'I really didn't want you to see me like this,' Harry said, sipping slowly through the straw protruding from the top of the closed plastic glass.

'I should have come earlier – please forgive me,' Stan told him. After recovering from the initial shock of learning who his real father was, it had been easy to put the matter out of his mind – especially as there were more pressing affairs preoccupying him at the time. But when he eventually thought about it, he recognised that it rested upon *him* to get in contact. The fact that he still chose to stay away, however, was something with which he couldn't come to terms.

'What have you got to be sorry for?' Harry replied. The colour had returned to his shrivelled face and he momentarily regained much of his vitality. 'It was only because I was ashamed to tell you myself that I allowed the secret to drag on for so long.'

'You don't owe me any explanation,' Stan replied, not wanting to bring up the past.

'Stanley, there are some things you don't know. I haven't got much time left and I need to clear my conscience before I die . . .' There was a short interlude, as the old man appeared to drift off to sleep. 'I get very tired,' he said, opening his eyes. 'Perhaps you could help me,' he asked, reaching out to his son.

Stan bent down and, lifting up his father in his arms, he placed him gently down on the hospital bed.

'I would never have recognised you. You look different,'

Harry said, his still-piercing blue eyes focused on his boy.

'Because of the long hair, you mean?' Stan replied light-heartedly.

'We had some like that in the sixties. Hippies, they were called. Turning up for work in their headbands and open sandals – untidy lot,' Harry said disparagingly. 'But *you* were always dressed smart in a suit and tie.' He frowned, seemingly put out by the inexplicable change in his flesh and blood. 'Of course, Elaine was always well turned out. And your daughter – what's her name, my granddaughter – is she going that way too?'

The change in himself wasn't something Stan wanted to get into. Suffice to say, once his mother got over her initial surprise, she had accepted his laid-back approach to life. But somehow this was different. He felt the need to justify himself to his father and so he began to explain.

'After I suffered a serious injury, realising I'd been given a second chance, I decided to do something meaningful with my life. I can truly say that I've finally stumbled on my true vocation.' Stan was about to ask if his mother had informed Harry about the six weeks he had spent in hospital but he then thought better of it.

'And you can make a decent living doing whatever it is you do?' the old man probed.

'It's not about money; I'm in a profession.'

'None of the accountants I ever knew looked like that,' Harry said, with a hint of the old disapproval.

'Actually I'm a psychotherapist,' Stan clarified. But his words didn't register with Harry, who had drifted off again.

Stan sat patiently waiting for his father to regain his strength. There was so much he still had to say; he just hoped he would be granted the opportunity before it was too late.

After a short time, the old man stirred.

'It's that damned medication they put me on,' he said croakily. 'It's supposed to control the pain but it's so strong it sends me off to sleep. The cancer is in my lungs. Fifty years of Montecristo cigars – has to catch up with you sometime!'

Stan feared as much. He had witnessed the same cruel illness so often – first with his wife Carol, who in her last days just withered away, and then again, during his long stay in hospital, the sorry souls he'd see shuffling along the corridors, wired up to their intravenous drips, on their way to their next chemotherapy treatment. Irrespective of how cheerful they appeared, for most it was only a question of time before they succumbed to the inevitable.

'I treated Arnold very badly, may his soul rest in peace,' Harry confessed. 'It wasn't his fault that he wasn't cut out for business. He could have been a footballer except that he had this blood-clotting problem, which meant he bruised easily. It must have been inherited because our dad suffered from it too.'

'Didn't my mother know?' Stan asked, surprised that she had never made mention of it in the past.

'He probably didn't tell her. You see, Arnold didn't want to admit that he had it. For him, it was a sign of weakness. He thought he could beat it on his own. I'm convinced that's what killed him.'

'But we were told he had a stroke,' Stan stated.

'Yes, that's what the post mortem showed. In fact, it was a common symptom of his disease, especially if it isn't treated. I suppose they didn't bother looking into it any further.'

'But if you knew about his condition, weren't you ever tempted to say something to my mother, to warn her?' Stan asked, spellbound by the revelation that had remained in Harry's exclusive domain for so many years.

'Arnold made me vow that I wouldn't. He was deeply in love with your mother. Irrespective of what occurred between her and me later, I kept my promise.'

Stan felt an odd sort of admiration for his father, knowing that in spite of his indiscretion, he had not prevented his older brother from achieving happiness.

'The other vow I made – to Elaine – was that I would never disclose to you that I was your father. That was why I resisted you coming into the business. There were times that I found it impossible. Despite what you may imagine, I've never been as strong as your mother.'

With such a conflict of varying emotions, there were no words that could adequately describe how Stan was feeling at that moment. Now the truth had eventually emerged, seeing the old man in bed fighting for his life, he only wished that it had come out sooner.

As if reading his mind, Harry said, his breathing laboured, 'Stanley, you didn't know any different. At least you had a father who loved you. I, on the other hand, have been deprived of my son until now, when I only have a short time left. So you see, if anyone should be sorry, it's me.'

Stan took his father's head in his hands and kissed him.

'The only way I can make it up to you is that you will inherit everything,' the dying man wheezed.

'Dad, that's not important,' Stan butted in.

'Let me finish,' Harry said, short of breath. 'You've still got a life ahead of you; the money will come in useful.

You're probably not aware of this, but I bought out that partner of yours, Brendan Cole. He said he was hard up – not that I believed him. Anyway, I had these two brothers from Singapore – Lim, I think their name was. They wanted to go in with me and we split the profits. Come to think of it, I'm certain they said they had had some dealings with you.' Harry conveniently omitted to mention that he had arranged a back-to-back deal with Brendan to buy Stan's stake in La Quinta, which had allowed Brendan to dispose of his own interest, albeit at a knockdown price, and had enabled Harry to end up as the largest investor in the development.

'I reckon there's about five million in cash, and the apartment.'

These were the last words that Harry Rose would ever utter, but Stan had stopped listening. It was time to leave the sick man to rest, but he would come back again. There was so much he still had to say, and he just hoped he would be granted the opportunity that no amount of money could buy.

In the early hours of the following day, Harry Rose passed away. After completing the formalities, the nursing home released the body to his son's care. The funeral took place immediately afterwards at the pretty Jewish cemetery in Casabermeja, in the hills high above Malaga. Now familiar with the religious proceedings, Stan took the service himself. In attendance was his mother, Harry's granddaughter Tara and the close circle of Harry's friends, established over the last twenty years in Spain, together with Audrey Isaacs, Teddy's widow, who had somehow heard the sad news and had travelled all the way from England to pay her respects.

At the conclusion of the traditional seven-day mourning period, Stan caught a flight back to London, leaving his father's affairs in the capable hands of his English lawyer, Anthony Blendford. He was completely unaffected by his newfound wealth, but haunted by something else entirely: the surreal image of his mother's visible grief for the man she would clearly have preferred to have married.

35

It was snowing hard that March morning in 2003, when a fit young fellow in a green baseball cap and tracksuit, carrying a new Nike sports bag, arrived for his therapy appointment. By now familiar with the routine, he entered through the sandblasted glass doors of the former medical practice, gave his details to the dopey-looking receptionist with the irritating high-pitched voice, and passed quickly across to the waiting area and the soothing sound of the gurgling aquarium filled with colourful tropical fish.

After a short while, a stocky man in a creased suit appeared from the floor above to summon his next patient.

'Jamie, I'm so sorry to have kept you waiting,' Stanley Rose said, leading the way to his consulting room, where they both sat down in their accustomed places.

'So . . . how have things been?' he asked, giving the young man his full attention.

'Had a cool gig in Brixton on Saturday night. This producer bloke came up afterwards and offered us a recording contract,' Jamie said, leaning back precariously on his chair as if he didn't have a care in the world.

'I was referring to the thoughts that have been troubling you,' Stan said, removing the patient's file from under a pile of buff folders.

'Actually, I've got a theory about that,' Jamie declared.

'I'd be interested to hear it.'

There was a short pause while the young man sorted out what he wanted to say. Then sitting up, he began. 'It's like I've been on this guilt trip.'

Stan waited. When Jamie didn't go on, he prompted: 'What drew you to that conclusion?'

'You know I told you that I've always done my own thing?'

'Forming your rock group, you mean?'

'Yes, unlike my older brother, Rick, who did what was expected of him – going into the old man's business straight from school.' Jamie snorted. 'I couldn't exactly envisage myself spending the rest of my life flogging Persian carpets in a warehouse off the Highgate Road.'

'From what you've told me before, I assume that's what caused the tension with your father?'

'Yeah. It's also why I moved out at the first opportunity, even though it meant dossing with a couple of mates for a while, till I earned enough money to get my own flat.'

'We have never talked about that,' the therapist pointed out.

'I thought I mentioned that I had taught guitar at a few schools?'

'Yes. That's really admirable,' Stan remarked, regretting that he hadn't continued with the instrument himself, after Arnold died.

The client heard the sincerity in Stan's voice, and felt supported by him. 'It paid the bills and still gave me time for my own music,' he said proudly.

'And your mother – didn't she have a say in the matter?'

The boy's demeanour changed and darkened. 'I've told you, it doesn't work like that in our family.'

'Jamie, I'm not with you,' Stan said patiently.

'My father's the one who calls the shots. Apparently, it's the Middle Eastern mentality thing. *We* just have to go along with it. At least we had to – before they split up.'

'Was that hard?' Stan asked.

The patient shrugged, showing his indifference, and then continued: 'Through coming here, I've been able to work out what exactly the problem is – that I haven't been able to fully break away. Maybe part of me didn't really want to.'

'Go on . . .'

'That's the reason I suddenly became obsessed with thinking I've done something wrong. It happens several times a day.'

'So you believe the two are connected. Can you give me some recent examples?'

'Let me think . . . I might be in a restaurant, and I've walked out without paying, or I've left the gas on in my flat and the whole place has gone up in flames while I've been away. You know, crazy things like that.'

'And when you're driving,' Stan said, suddenly unable to control himself, 'do you ever, for example, return to the scene because you think you might have knocked someone over? Or maybe at a crowded tube station, you have to stand well away from the edge of the platform, just in case you might be the cause of an accident?'

'That happens a lot!' the young man exclaimed, gaping at the therapist as if he had managed to read his mind.

Stan pulled himself together. 'It sounds as if these thoughts are still really intrusive,' he said quietly.

'Yes, it's hideous. In fact, it often reaches a point where I can no longer differentiate between fantasy and reality,'

Jamie said, his voice hoarse with emotion as he described his torment.

'And the exercises we went through last time?' Stan enquired. 'You know, doing a deal with your subconscious to leave you alone in return for confessing what you imagined you had done wrong?'

'I've tried all that stuff, but it doesn't work, especially when I'm uptight with my girlfriend, or the band hasn't been able to achieve the right sound. It was my girlfriend Pandora's idea that I went to seek help in the first place.'

'I'm glad you agreed,' Stan said.

'She didn't leave me with much of a choice. She kept whingeing on that I was putting my phobias on to her and that I was making her life a misery. She doesn't understand that I can't help myself. Going into the studio is the only way I can get relief – that, and the occasional spliff.'

'If that's what makes you feel good,' Stan nodded. 'What we need to work on is how to achieve the same effect without having to resort to such extreme measures.'

'I don't think you can call banging out our version of "Money" on my Fender Strat particularly extreme. I take it your generation were more into Stones or Bowie?' the young fellow said, stung.

'I'm sorry, that wasn't meant as a criticism,' Stan said. 'Music is a great form of self-expression – if one has the talent.' Feelings of resentment regarding his own missed opportunities resurfaced briefly. 'It's just that we need to find a way of curtailing a thought in its tracks before it becomes obsessive and kicks the whole process off again.'

'You mean by thinking of something else?'

'Exactly. But it needs to take over as the predominant thought, then you'd be surprised how quickly the worry will disappear.'

'Sounds easy enough. I'll give it a try.'

Having treated many patients with Obsessive Compulsive Disorder over the years, Stan knew it was anything *but* easy. Although the symptoms varied widely from person to person, unresolved trauma and low self-esteem were common features in most cases. Didn't he suffer from the same anxiety disorder himself – the result of the horrific injury he had suffered? It manifested itself in a variety of ways, not too dissimilar from those of the young patient he was presently treating. Perhaps that was the reason why he had chosen to specialise in the illness – so he could find out more about himself.

Stan hadn't forgotten the hours of therapy he had been subjected to, when he was recovering in hospital, then later, as part of his training as a psychotherapist. None of it had made any significant difference to his own condition. Ironically, the peace of mind he thought he would obtain by becoming more religious had merely been offset by the increased guilt he was made to feel for his own shortcomings as a person and in particular as a father.

'Stanley, don't you think it's strange that I don't know a thing about *you* after all these weeks?' Jamie said, completely unexpectedly.

'What do you mean?' Stan replied, taken aback.

'Well, there are no photographs of your family here – you know, none of the normal things that one would expect,' the client noted, gazing at the bare walls. 'It looks as if you've covered up your past for some reason.'

'That's deliberate,' Stan replied firmly. He had anticipated this eventuality and blamed himself for becoming too close to the lad. But Jamie Green had such an incisive mind and was so different from the couples with their matrimonial issues who comprised the majority of his patients that Stan actually found himself looking forward to their fortnightly sessions. More often than not, these took the form of an informal discussion. Now he knew he had no choice but to re-establish a proper distance between them.

'Why is that?' the young fellow asked innocently.

'I'm not at liberty to discuss anything about myself that doesn't directly benefit your treatment,' replied the therapist.

'Oh I see. So you're saying that we can't be friends?' Jamie said tightly. The disappointment on his face was that of a child who had just been denied his favourite sweets.

'As long as I continue to treat you, I'm afraid not. It's a question of ethics – I'm sure you understand.'

There was a pause while both therapist and patient were adjusting to the new ground rules of their relationship.

'It just seems a bit ridiculous, that's all,' Jamie said, being the first to break the silence. 'I mean, how can you expect to learn about yourself, if you don't know how the person you have entrusted to help you ticks?'

'But that's the point – my professional position requires that I maintain the required level of objectivity, which would be impossible if I started talking about myself. Think of a judge knowing the plaintiff or the defendant. He would be obligated to excuse himself from the case.'

'I just reckon you were running away, a bit like me,' the young man continued, undeterred.

'We're short of time,' Stanley said at this point, unwilling to be drawn. But the remark had penetrated his whole being. Running away – wasn't that exactly what he had done? By hiding behind a vocation that had taken most of his working life to discover, he had once again withdrawn from the real world. And now he was being reminded of it, in the most poignant way, by a lad young enough to be his son.

'OK,' Jamie replied. 'As a matter of fact, I'm off to the gym. I told everyone I had a doctor's appointment and wouldn't be in until eleven. Well, it's partly true,' he added, giving Stan a mischievous look.

'So I'll see you next week,' the therapist responded, seeing his patient out. 'And remember, however alienated you feel from your father, try not to allow yourselves to drift apart.'

'Sounds like you're talking from personal experience,' were the young man's cheeky parting words as he left the room.

When he'd gone, Stan sat back in his chair, thinking over the events of the last three-quarters of an hour . . . only to be jolted back into action a few minutes later by the arrival of his next patient.

36

On a sunny June morning, a pretty young woman in a baggy jumper and leggings strolled along the Euston Road on her way to the British Library As a freelance, no longer saddled with having to go to an office, she found the BL a most conducive working environment.

Tara Rose was a young woman in demand and it showed. Since she had won an award for her piece called 'The Kosovo Train for Life' in 1999, her career as a journalist had gone from strength to strength. With a substantial five-figure income and her own mews house in Notting Hill, life for the most part was good. She reflected on how different things were now from that low period she went through after the *Londoner* closed down. That debacle had left her feeling completely devastated. On top of her father's near-death experience, it came as an awful blow. But, as always, she had picked herself up, aware that if she wished to salvage her career, there was no time to sit around and mope. That was seven years ago, and since then she'd moved onwards and upwards.

Her normal routine was to spend the day in one of the many reading rooms, working on her laptop. At the moment, she was researching the recent visit to London of the Russian man called Ganjorig, a former circus performer who had become the most powerful political leader in north-east Asia. The feature was just up her street and had helped take her mind off one of her periodic bouts of melancholy. Contrary to what she had been told, the pain of her mother's passing had not lessened with time. Tara still missed her terribly.

Today, the young woman had come well prepared with the latest copies of *Pravda* and the *Moscow Times*, the two English-language papers that understandably gave a somewhat prejudiced account of Ganjorig – a figure they regarded as a threat to the Russian Establishment. She was keen, therefore, to discover a less biased local perspective from the region that regarded him as their Messiah.

'Good morning,' Tara said, entering the Asian and African Studies Reading Room, and showing her Reader Pass to a strikingly beautiful black woman with long braided hair who stood behind the counter. Instead of moving away, she then waited.

'How can I help you?' the librarian said, smiling pleasantly.

'Do you by any chance have any copies of the *UB Post*? It's Mongolia's English-language newspaper. I haven't pre-ordered it, I'm sorry.'

'I'll have to check, although I must admit I'm not familiar with that publication,' the woman said. 'Why don't you find somewhere to sit and I'll let you know if we have it.'

Tara put her laptop on a desk in the corner of the huge room and started to work. It wasn't long before the woman came over to her seat, carrying a few editions of the paper she had requested. The expression on her face had, however, changed to one of extreme anxiety.

'Is something wrong?' Tara whispered, concerned

about the change in her demeanour.

'You don't know me, but I know who *you* are,' the librarian said in a voice so quiet she could hardly be heard.

'Sorry?' Tara replied, politely but impatiently. She had a lot of work to get through and she couldn't afford to be distracted. Fortunately, this part of the room was deserted, so they could speak quietly without being overheard.

'The name Tara Rose didn't register at first. It's been a long time.' The woman's almond-shaped eyes had misted over.

'I'm pretty sure we've never met before. Perhaps you're muddling me up with someone else?' Tara said, still polite but beginning to feel annoyed.

'There was only one young girl of that name who was so close to Alison Brown,' the librarian said. Handing the Mongolian newspapers to Tara, she then walked away without saying another word, her large gold disk earrings swaying with every step.

The mention of her guardian, without any explanation to go with it, left Tara perplexed and unable to concentrate fully on the job in hand. Even more mysterious, when she went looking for the woman at lunchtime, she was nowhere to be seen.

The British Library closed at 5 p.m. By the time Tara had packed up her things and set off down the starirs, the incident earlier in the day was still playing on her mind. As she came through two sets of double doors to the outer courtyard, she found the librarian waiting outside for her.

'Hello again,' Tara said, pleased to have found her.

'I hoped I'd see you on your way home,' replied the woman, who seemed to have regained some of her original poise. 'I needed time to think. Can we go somewhere and

I'll tell you everything?'

Tara nodded. She wasn't seeing her friend Trevor until later on, when he was coming round to the house. Since that lunch at Stromboli, the colourful Italian restaurant in Portobello Road, when she had been on a consignment for the *Kensington and Chelsea Times*, she had become good friends with the forty-seven-year-old surveyor who, with his prematurely white hair and schoolboy grin, looked the double of the American actor Steve Martin. Of course, having never been married and living in his mother's house in Paddington, she suspected he might be gay – but she enjoyed his company and found they could talk uninhibitedly about the most intimate aspects of their lives.

'There's a place that serves great Caribbean food – it's only a short walk away. I don't know about you, but I'm starving. By the way, my name is Syrenna Raphael.'

'And you already know my name,' Tara said with a smile.

The two women headed up the Euston Road and found the cosy restaurant tucked away in a backwater behind University College Hospital.

'I'm vegetarian but they serve chicken and pork,' Syrenna said, settling at a table near the window.

'I'm not fussy, I'll have whatever you have,' Tara said amenably.

The librarian gave their order then, taking a deep breath, she sat perfectly upright for several minutes with her eyes closed.

Tara began to feel that it had been a big mistake to have come here. The woman was obviously disturbed. The fact that she had known Alison was neither here nor there. It had purely been an overreaction on Tara's part to hope that Syrenna was in possession of some new information about her guardian that had suddenly come to light.

The aroma from the two steaming plates of yam curry that had been placed in front of them stirred the older woman from her stupor.

'When I'm stressed, meditating is the only thing that helps,' she confided, sufficiently recovered to take a forkful of her food. 'It wasn't fair of me to have just disappeared like that. But you have no idea what it's been like – the strain of having to keep a dreadful secret to myself for all these years.'

'I'm not sure I understand,' Tara mumbled, her mouth full. She was thoroughly enjoying the spicy dish that she was eating for the first time.

'How well did you know Alison?' Syrenna asked cagily.

'She was my mother's closest friend and looked after me after Mummy died. She became my legal guardian, in fact. We were extremely close.'

'That's not what I meant. Please don't be cross. I'm referring to her private life.'

Tara frowned, unsure what was going on.

'Alison and I lived together,' Syrenna said, coming straight out with it. 'You probably are not aware that she was a lesbian?'

'Yes – and?'

'You don't seem surprised.'

'My mother told me that years ago. It's hardly a revelation.'

'I see. Oh my God. That would have changed everything,' Syrenna muttered. She had stopped eating; trying to absorb what had been said to her. Then, after a short pause, she burst out with a confession. 'Alison was being blackmailed!'

Tara was astonished. 'By whom?' she enquired, taking a drink of her Coke.

'What I'm about to tell you is going to sound far-fetched, but you have my word of honour that it's all completely true.'

Tara sat back and listened, the frown still on her face. Could she trust this strange woman?

'Are you familiar with a lawyer named Richard Jeffrey?' Syrenna began.

'Yes, of course – he's our family's solicitor. He's been looking after our affairs for years,' Tara replied, wondering how the woman knew his name.

'Huh! Only so that he could benefit himself,' the librarian snorted.

'In what way?' Tara asked.

'You see, I saw the letter that Alison wrote to you the night she died, when she explained everything and asked you to forgive her for what she had made you do.' The woman's lips were quivering as she unburdened herself of the first part of the painful secret.

'Syrenna, you're not making any sense. Alison didn't make me do anything I didn't want to,' Tara said firmly, her appetite gone.

'I'm afraid that's where you're wrong. She instructed you to transfer the shares you'd been left, didn't she?'

'Yes, that's true, but as I told my father, I checked with the solicitor's office that it was all right before doing anything.'

'Those shares ended up in Richard Jeffrey's sole possession,' Syrenna said bitterly. 'He set the whole thing up because he wanted to get his hands on your inheritance.'

'*What?* I don't believe it. What you're saying can't possibly be true. He's a lawyer, for heaven's sake!'

'And, as it happens, an exceptionally dishonest one.' Syrenna's voice was grim with the hatred she felt for the evil man, whom she blamed for Alison's downfall and death. Murderer!

'So you're saying that he used Alison . . .'

'Yes, to carry out his dirty deed and betray you.'

'And she agreed to it because she thought he had something on her that he could blackmail her with? I'm sorry, you've lost me.' Tara was pale and in shock, but wanted to get to the bottom of this.

'It happened like this.' Syrenna sighed. 'Richard Jeffrey got hold of some letters that Alison had written to your mother from years ago, and was threatening to show them to you.'

'About the fact she was gay, you mean?'

'And how she felt about your mother.'

'But I knew all about those letters! Mummy and I often joked about them. She loved Alison dearly, but my mother was never interested in other women.'

Syrenna's eyes were full of tears. 'The thing is, Tara darling, Alison didn't know that. She thought that if you found out, you would reject her. She couldn't bear that, which is why she agreed to go along with that man's ploy. In so doing, of course, she cheated you of your rightful inheritance and it weighed heavily on her conscience.'

Tara was silent, then she said slowly: 'I think I'm beginning to understand.'

'Afterwards, Alison couldn't live with what she'd done. I witnessed her go mad with the guilt of it.'

'So she killed herself,' Tara said, her voice dropping to a whisper.

The librarian nodded.

There was a long pause, both of them deep in their own thoughts about the woman they had loved in their separate ways, and lost.

'If you're curious to know why I didn't come forward and say anything at the time, it was because I too was being blackmailed. Richard Jeffrey told me that if I delivered Alison's suicide note to his office, he would arrange for our joint mortgage to be paid off. Since there was no way I could afford to carry it on my own, if I hadn't agreed to his proposal, I would have ended up homeless. What else could I do? It only occurred to me later that I could have been accused of destroying vital police evidence.'

'Then what did you do?' Tara asked, totally immersed in the story.

'My first thoughts were to move to Jamaica. I've still got family there and it was far enough away to make a new start.'

'So what stopped you?'

'The usual thing, money – or more specifically, the lack of it. After Alison died, I couldn't bear the thought of being in our house on my own. We'd put so much into it together. Stupidly, I moved out to stay with a friend before it was sold. A day later, squatters forced their way into the premises. Someone must have tipped them off. It took a very long time to get them out.' She shuddered.

'That must have been awful,' Tara empathised, recalling the extremely unpleasant individual who'd answered the door, that time she had turned up at the property. 'I only found out what had happened to Alison three months later and I had started work by then,' she said, still feeling guilty that she hadn't done more to stay in touch.

'Alison didn't leave a will so half of the proceeds of the house sale belonged to her family,' Syrenna said. 'It was the least they deserved after all they've been through.'

'She never talked much about them,' Tara mused.

'I felt I owed it to Alison to go up to Scotland to tell them in person what had happened, but in the end I couldn't go through with it. I was in a terrible state. Looking back, I think I had a breakdown. I'm so sorry, Tara, for not finding you before and telling you everything. I felt so ashamed of what I'd done.'

Syrenna wiped her eyes. 'I thought about you many times over the years,' she said, 'probably because you were often the main topic of conversation between Alison and me. I know you are a journalist, but is there anyone special in your life?'

'Trying to establish a career hasn't left much time for close relationships, I'm afraid,' Tara said, choosing not to elaborate. Well, it was partly true. Starting up on her own, sending articles to every publication imaginable, had been a full-time occupation for the first few years – then, when she had finally established herself, remaining at the head of the game became her main focus. Of course, there had been the odd liaison, mostly with older men with whom she had always found more in common, but none of these affairs lasted more than a couple of months. The other thing was that it had taken her a long time to get over Mark Bailey and the way he had just dumped her and disappeared. The experience had left her badly scarred. Anyway, she now had Yul, her Chocolate Point Siamese cat, for company. He never let her down!

'At least you're lucky to have a father like yours for support. Alison always told me how much he adored you,' Syrenna went on, obviously unaware that the two had never enjoyed the easiest of relationships. Tara didn't think it worthwhile putting her right. What was the point? She loved her father but had become used to the fact that she would never be his main priority.

Tara finished her meal, which was now lukewarm but still tasty. A thousand different thoughts were flashing through her mind. They needed to be put into some semblance of order, but there was just too much to take in. Her companion had just spent the best part of an hour baring her soul about her involvement in the deception, but what she had told her about Richard Jeffrey had far wider implications. For a moment, Tara wished she hadn't met Syrenna, so she could have carried on believing that Alison's death had been a tragic accident. The trouble was that now she knew differently, she had a responsibility to do something about it.

'I suppose you're going to have to report me to the police?' Syrenna said, appearing stoical about her fate. 'It's what I deserve.'

'Syrenna, why didn't you inform them yourself? After all, you could have claimed mitigating circumstances for not handing over Alison's note.'

'Don't think I didn't consider it, but I didn't want to go to prison.' The gold earrings shook. 'Apart from the fact that I'm a black woman and they wouldn't have believed anything I said or did, the other problem was that there was no proof that I was being blackmailed. Anyway, knowing that bastard of a lawyer, he probably destroyed the evidence,' she said bitterly.

'In that case, there's no way of ascertaining that you were involved, is there?' Tara didn't go on to say that Richard Jeffrey was probably far too shrewd not to have the letter tucked away somewhere so he could produce it to his advantage, if need be.

'That's why I thought the whole matter would just disappear,' Syrenna said. 'I had enough money from my share of the house for a decent flat in Tooting. I met someone else and gradually got my life back together. Heather and I have been a couple for five years now. So, as far as I was concerned, the whole sorry episode was in the past – until today, when I met you.'

Notwithstanding that the librarian had just contradicted her earlier comment about the strain she'd been under, having to keep the truth to herself, Tara couldn't help feeling a great deal of sympathy for the woman.

Rejecting Tara's offer to pay her share, Syrenna picked up the bill for dinner, after which the two women left the restaurant.

'Well, Tara, it's been good to meet you at last. I hope you didn't find what actually happened to dear Alison too upsetting because you really *did* need to know. I'm so glad we found each other today.' There was no sign of the anxiety that had been present earlier on. It had been replaced by the serenity of one who was finally at peace with the world.

Then, going up and giving Tara a hug, the woman disappeared down the steps into Warren Street tube station.

Tara looked on while her friend Trevor went to get his

jacket. They had stayed up talking into the early hours and she was ready to drop.

'Sorry I've been such lousy company. My mind was just elsewhere,' she said, showing him to the door.

'With what you've been through today, that's completely understandable,' he said, stroking her face affectionately with the back of his hand. 'However, I still think you should at least try and talk to your father.'

'What, Dad? Now he's reinvented himself as a psychotherapist, he's on another planet from the rest of us,' Tara scoffed. 'His own mother can't even get through to him because she's convinced he's gone completely weird.'

'So you're close to your grandmother, then?'

'She likes to think so.'

'That sounds pretty ominous.'

'She's got a lot to answer for – family secrets, if you know what I mean.'

'Don't worry, we've all got skeletons in our cupboards,' the surveyor grinned.

'That's why she tries to keep on the good side of me, in case I spill the beans.'

'And how does she do that?'

'By trying to fix me up the whole time. In her words, *it's about time I found a suitable young man.*' Tara burst out laughing.

'I think I'm beginning to get jealous,' Trevor replied.

'I only wish you were,' Tara countered, making the two of them laugh together.

'Anyway, going back to your father, the horrific injury you told me he sustained can have that effect on people,' Trevor told her. 'I remember this big butch foreman chap, massive beer belly, on a building site I was supervising in White City, who got knocked unconscious by a loose piece of scaffolding. The last I heard, he had joined the Samaritans.'

The image of the burly man lying spark out cold, his hard hat by the side of him, made Tara giggle.

'Though I have to say, the way you've described him, it hardly seems possible of the Stanley Rose I met after your grandfather passed away,' the surveyor remarked, stepping out of the door.

'I didn't realise you had actually come into contact with each other when he was in the property business.'

The look on Trevor's face said it all.

'Oh yes, many times. He was very much involved in a lot of renovations and schemes.' Trevor turned to face her. 'Look, Tara, knowing you as I do and being aware that you are intent on pursuing this case, just remember that with Richard Jeffrey, you're going to be up against a highly skilled professional who knows all the tricks in the book. You will need proof, not just the word of an unreliable witness with an axe to grind. Sleep on it, and give me a call tomorrow.'

His advice was unnecessary. Tara was already busy formulating a plan, one that would outwit the thief of a lawyer and fully substantiate the allegations of Alison's former lover, whom she had met for the first time today.

37

Stan was in a queue at the check-out counter of the Europa supermarket in St John's Wood High Street when he spotted the familiar figure of Jamie Green, his former patient, leaving the store. It had come as no surprise that the young man had discontinued his course of therapy, especially after that last session, and not having heard anything from him for the last three months, Stan merely assumed that the young fellow had managed to overcome his anxiety issues and got on with his life.

Then: 'Hi Stanley, I didn't expect to bump into you here. It's not your normal neck of the woods,' Jamie called over to Stan when he emerged with a small bag of shopping.

'That's right, but I've been to see my mother in hospital and I needed a few things,' Stan explained.

'Can I give you a lift?' Jamie asked, gesturing to a high-performance motorbike parked carelessly a few feet away.

Stan hesitated for a moment, not fancying the idea of being on the back of one of those things, which he'd always regarded as a death trap. However, he didn't want to seem ungrateful.

'If you're sure, that's very kind,' he replied, drumming up the courage.

'Here, put this on,' Jamie said, passing him a helmet and taking the supermarket bag from him and stuffing it into the luggage box at the rear of the bike.

Within moments, the black Harley Davidson roared away.

'Right, where to?' the driver shouted, heading north up the Finchley Road towards Swiss Cottage.

'I'm still at the same address,' Stanley shouted back nervously, trying to make himself heard and bitterly regretting that he hadn't taken the bus.

'Didn't know that you actually lived there,' Jamie bawled to the passenger behind, who was hanging on to him for dear life.

Stan didn't see the need to explain himself. It wasn't unusual for those in his profession to work from home. Anyway, since the space at the top of the practice was surplus to their requirements, Sylvie had decided to convert it to a two-bedroom flat and let it out. Neither of them realising, at the time, that it would be to Stan.

'And how have *you* been?' Stan enquired of the young man whose visits he had sorely missed. They had stopped at a red light and so it was easier to be heard.

'Great! Just been putting down the final tracks of our first album,' Jamie told him.

'So, you're now playing full-time?'

'Yeah. And there's a European tour in the offing.'

Without any warning, Jamie suddenly manoeuvred his bike diagonally into the inside lane and accelerated away, leaving two lines of stationary traffic in his wake.

'Can't be there all bloody night!' he exclaimed, trying to justify his rash action. Then, calling behind him, 'Are you all right?'

Stan was too busy mumbling a silent prayer to offer a response.

'You still dedicating your time to other people's problems?' the biker tried asking again.

'Afraid so,' the therapist roared back. It was, he thought, a fair assessment of what he had been doing for the last eight years. They came to a halt at some temporary traffic lights, allowing the young man to reach into his shirt pocket and take out the butt end of a joint.

'Heavy session at the studio,' he said, lighting up. He took a couple of quick drags before passing it to the man behind him. 'You don't mind, do you?' he said, moving off.

'No, of course not,' Stan replied, trying to juggle the spliff while holding on to Jamie at the same time. 'That's me over there on the right,' he called out, reminding the boy as they travelled at speed up Haverstock Hill.

'I remember it well,' the young man replied, pulling up behind a black Mini Cooper that was blocking the drive. 'Looks like you're in demand,' he added, after switching off the engine.

Stan removed his helmet and gave it to Jamie, who jumped off and put it back in the storage box. Stan frowned. He was sure he'd checked that he had no late appointments before he left the house.

'Jamie, it was good seeing you again,' he said, easing his ungainly frame from the motorbike, grateful to be alive.

Rather the worse for wear from his experience, he was walking unsteadily away when he suddenly heard a familiar voice call out: 'I was beginning to give up hope!'

Stan turned around – and it took him a moment to realise that the young woman hidden behind the large-framed sunglasses was his twenty-seven-year-old daughter. He had completely forgotten that she had wanted to see him today.

'I didn't know you'd taken up dope smoking,' she teased him, 'although I suppose it is in keeping with the bohemian image.'

Stan gazed down, horrified to see the smouldering roach still clutched tightly in his fingers.

'That's not mine,' he spluttered, looking in Jamie's direction to help him out. But the young man, still at the Harley's controls, had fallen about in peals of laughter at the obvious embarrassment he had caused.

'Who is *he*?' Tara asked with more than a cursory interest in the grinning chap on the motorbike.

'That's Jamie – he gave me a lift home,' Stan grunted, stamping on the joint to put it out.

The rider took off his helmet, swung down from his bike and went over to introduce himself. 'Hi, I'm – wait a minute, I know you,' Jamie said to the young woman in the Chanel leather jacket and tight-fitting jeans. 'It's Tara, isn't it?'

'Josh? It can't be! It's been ages. How on earth did you recognise me?'

'You know each other?' Stan said, showing his surprise.

'It's Josh Gohardi, Paul Klein's grandson.'

'W-what? But that's impossible,' Stan stammered, trying to make some sense of it all.

'Jamie Green's just my stage name,' his former patient revealed.

Stan suddenly felt woozy. He wasn't sure whether it was the effects of the marijuana or the sudden realisation that he had had no business treating the fellow in the first place. Recalling that his mother's friend, Regine, had recommended him, Stan berated himself for not conducting sufficient checks. More seriously, taking into account the family connection, it had gone against the entire ethics of his profession, endangering him – if it ever got out – of being struck off.

Turning to the young man, practically whispering his words, Stan said, 'Did *you* know of the connection?'

'I must split,' Jamie said, without offering a reply. His expression indicated that, not only had he been aware of the family links, but also that he had thoroughly enjoyed the whole charade.

He went over to say goodbye to Tara. They talked light-heartedly for a few moments; their body language unable to hide an obvious mutual attraction. Then, tapping a number into his mobile phone, Jamie fastened on his helmet, got back onto his bike and sped off with a wave, leaving Stan glued to the spot, still trying to get over the bizarre last twenty minutes.

Somewhat recovered, he turned to his daughter and said, 'What was *that* all about?'

'Jamie – apparently that's what he calls himself these days – has invited me to one of his gigs.'

'And you're going to go?'

'I might. By the way, how's Grandma?' Tara asked, changing the subject and accompanying her father inside the practice that had already finished for the day.

'It was only a minor procedure. She should be home tomorrow,' Stan replied, negotiating the two flights of stairs up to his flat. 'Tell me, is anything wrong? I thought you'd still be at work,' he puffed, soon out of breath.

'What – gone six o'clock? No journalist I know works past five these days. Anyway, there's something we need to talk about.'

'Couldn't we do it another time? I have to be at the Lakis

Centre in an hour for the unveiling of the new Reuven Frankel Wing – you remember the little boy I used to help look after?' Stan said, picking up and perusing the messages that the receptionist had put through his door.

'Yes, of course I remember, and I know it's important that you're there. But this is important too. The fact is, I've discovered some very significant information that happens to concern *you* – and me.' Tara wore the determined expression that Stan knew meant she had no intention of being fobbed off.

'All right, come in.'

Tara gazed admiringly at the uninterrupted views of London from the two dormer windows on either side of the irregular-shaped room, thinking how little resemblance the flat bore to the house in Hendon that seemed to have been left intentionally drab to match the severe lifestyle her father had previously embraced.

This place couldn't have been more of a contrast. Tastefully decorated in pastel colours, and showing great attention to detail – right down to the geometric patterns on the scatter cushions enhancing the smart couch they sat upon – it was obvious that, at some stage, this place had had the benefit of a female's touch.

If there were a new woman in her father's life, she wouldn't have known; they had never enjoyed that type of close relationship – although she knew her father had been really keen on Sylvie, the German woman with whom he shared the practice. The three of them had been out to dinner on several occasions and had got on really well, but that was some time ago now. More recently, whenever they'd got together, her father would come on his own; both trying their best to convince the other that life was treating them well but each probably wondering whether happiness was destined to elude them.

'Won't be long, I've just getting changed,' a more relaxed voice shouted out from the other end of the flat.

Tara sat down and got out the file that she had patiently built up over the last three months She had started with the police officers in charge of the investigation, nine years ago, but had found them particularly unforthcoming. As far as they were concerned, the case concerning Alison Brown was closed and they were not interested in hearing anything new that would persuade them to reopen their inquiry. If she didn't know better, she might have suspected that someone had paid them off.

Next, she spent hours at Companies House trying to locate a copy of the stock transfer form she had signed on that fateful evening, all those years ago – along with anything else that might provide a clue as to where her shares had gone. Instead, under the name of CM Nominees, she found nothing untoward. On the contrary, Annual Reports, accounts and all statutory returns had been meticulously filed. It was as if Miller Investments, her grandfather's company, had never existed.

She was ready to give up when a fortuitous visit from her friend Trevor revived her hopes that all might not be lost. Trevor, coincidentally, had just been at a meeting in town attended by Nigel Lowndes, Richard Jeffrey's former partner. The man had apparently been forced to seek alternative employment when the firm he had co-founded was pulled from under his feet. Aware of Nigel's understandable resentment towards his former partner, the surveyor went out of his way to see what information he could glean.

The ensuing outpouring of bile was followed by an assertion – which Nigel said he was prepared to put in writing – that Jeffrey got involved in lucrative deals on the side that he kept secret from the other partners. This explained how he had managed to retire in luxury. His lust for wealth knew no bounds, it appeared, and he had no qualms about stepping on anyone who got in his way. For example, Nigel was willing to confirm that a senior Australian colleague, who had been leaned on by Richard Jeffrey, was forced to quit the firm in a hurry. Tara knew that the Australian lawyer had to be Roger Prince – the man she had trusted and whose confirmation she had sought before signing over her inheritance.

Now Tara knew for certain that she and her family had been fraudulently deprived of millions of pounds, she couldn't wait to tell her father that it *hadn't* been her fault; that he had been wrong to blame her and that they had both been victims of a carefully devised plot engineered by Richard Jeffrey, their family solicitor.

Although she couldn't yet prove it, she was convinced the same man was also responsible for the untimely death of her beloved guardian. As she brooded on this, her father appeared in a newly laundered shirt and pair of dark grey slacks.

'Right, I'm with you. What's on your mind?' he asked, joining his daughter on the settee.

'That sounds like the opening gambit to one of your patients,' Tara replied.

Stan, still shaken up after his flying trip on the back of a Harley and from finding out about the family connection with Jamie, gave a nervous cough.

Tara took pity on him. 'Actually, I've always wondered

what it would be like being psychoanalysed, especially by one's own father.'

'You went into therapy after Mummy died, didn't you?' Stan replied, now more alert.

'That's what I would have had you and Alison believe,' his daughter admitted slyly. 'The truth is, I wound up those poor guys something rotten! After a few sessions, they gave me up as a hopeless case. There was only one of them I quite liked – Felix – but he was married with a child, more's the pity.' She enjoyed teasing her father. In any case, it was an opportunity to lighten the mood before embarking on what she anticipated might be a difficult discussion.

Stan stared at his daughter. Had he really been that naïve in those days, not noticing that he was being misled? In fact, as it had later become apparent, it was he, rather than his daughter, who had been the one in need of therapy.

'Look, can we make a start? We really don't have a lot of time,' he said, becoming edgy.

'Sorry, I forgot you were watching the clock. How much do you shrinks charge, by the way?'

'Tara, I'm a psychotherapist not a psychiatrist and as I've told you before, it's not about money.'

'But I'm afraid this is,' she stressed, her smile disappearing. 'In fact, quite a lot of it.'

Stan saw that she was serious, and he waited for her to explain.

'You remember the argument we had when you accused me of signing away my shares?'

'That was several years ago,' he said vaguely.

'Well, I found out recently that there was a lot more behind it than originally appeared.' Tara decided not to mention her meeting with the librarian, whose revelations concerning Alison Brown might sound a bit too far-fetched to her father and she didn't want that clouding the new dirt she had dug up on Richard Jeffrey.

'I looked into everything very carefully at the time and there was never any proof of any wrongdoing,' Stan sighed.

'Well, I happen to be in possession of an affidavit that says otherwise. It states, unequivocally, that I was misled.'

'I'd forget all about it if I were you. It's probably a hoax,' her father said dismissively.

'So, you don't even want to hear that there might be a way of getting back what we lost?' Tara demanded crossly.

'A lot of water has passed under the bridge since then. We've moved on to bigger and better things. You've got your career to think of and I've . . .' As he spoke, Stan was already getting up, preparing to leave without finishing his sentence.

'How can you be so fucking callous?' Tara shouted, unable to control herself. 'You're doing all right because *your* father left you a fortune. Well, this is *my* inheritance we're talking about here!'

Stan's face dropped. He had been under the impression that no one else knew about the contents of Harry's will other than his lawyer. Not wanting to get involved personally, he had instructed Anthony Blendford to deal with everything on his behalf. Death duties were paid, together with the large number of legacies to members of Harry's extensive social circle; he had been particularly generous to Audrey Isaacs, Teddy's widow, to whom he left the apartment in Marbella and the sum of £100,000, making Stan suspect that they might have been more than just good friends. Even taking into account the depressed

300

property market in Spain, Stan had become a rich man – not that it meant anything to him since he proceeded to give the majority of it away to charity.

His daughter was obviously under the false impression that he was loaded. There was only one person who could have fed that idea to her, and that was her grandmother, Elaine.

'I have to say, I never realised you were that interested in money,' Stan replied, showing his disappointment.

Tara lost it. 'How can *you* accuse *me* of being materialistic?' she screamed. 'Have you forgotten how you thought of nothing else other than business when Mummy was seriously ill? And afterwards, when I had no one, you were only interested in proving to yourself that you could be as successful as Grandpa!' Her face had gone pink with outrage.

'They were difficult times for all of us,' Stan spluttered, attempting to defend himself. The trouble was, his daughter was right. Trapped in a corner by his own refusal to admit to, and come to terms with, the way he had let his family down, it was now threatening to damage the one relationship that should have been most dear to him.

'How can you possibly claim to have found religion when you care more about total strangers *as usual* than your own family?' Tara continued ranting. She burst into tears. 'Mummy may not have been religious in the way you claim to be, but I'll tell you this: everybody loved her because she had a good heart – and *that's* what really matters in this world.'

'I'm sorry you think that way,' Stan mumbled. In his mind, he was reaching out to his daughter, telling her that he loved her ... but the words never passed his lips. 'If you feel you want to go back on the past, I'm afraid I'll have to leave that up to you,' were the words that did come out, cold and devoid of any emotion.

Dashing away her tears, Tara collected her things. She felt deeply aggrieved, not so much by her father's lack of interest in getting the company back: what really hurt was that by treating her inheritance in the same way – which he had no right to do – he had once again, as always, put himself first.

Her initial thoughts as she slammed the door on her way out were that she never wanted to have anything more to do with him. Ever.

Driving back to her home in Notting Hill, Tara felt certain that there had to be another way of pursuing justice. Later, reading the notes again over dinner, it suddenly hit her. Her story would make a great exposé. She couldn't wait to get started.

It was well after midnight when Tara had completed the first draft. She knew she was taking a huge risk with her reputation – *if* anyone had the balls to print it. Now she had to hope that Nigel Lowndes's resentment ran sufficiently high to help bring a case against his former partner. And, if she was really up against it, she could always turn to Syrenna Raphael.

38

Stan, his linen prayer shawl over his head, swayed back and forth, reciting his prayers whilst trying to ignore the clamour outside in the street. Early morning was his time for self-reflection and he had to make the most of it. Striking his chest with his fist, he was asking for the Almighty's forgiveness for his sins. There were many things of which he'd fallen short, not least within his own family. In particular, he felt deeply ashamed of the way he'd allowed his pride to get the better of him, the last time he'd seen his daughter. Not listening to her, not helping her as a father should, not taking the initiative to get in contact. It was unforgivable, and starting that very day, he was going to make amends.

It was no different with his mother. When was the last time he could truly say that he had shown her sufficient deference? Never picking up the phone to her and always finding an excuse to decline an invitation to any of the Sunday-afternoon teas for family get-togethers. Certainly, he had not done much in the years since Harry had died. Yes, he was probably still affected, if only subconsciously, by her admission of Arnold Rose not being his real father – and true, he might have disapproved of her living with Paul Klein – but who was he to judge?

The sound of voices getting louder was causing Stan to

become distracted. He carefully removed the phylacteries, the first from his head and then the other that had been wrapped seven times around his left arm.

Suddenly, there was a ring at the doorbell. Still in his dressing gown and slippers, he went down to see who could possibly be calling at seven thirty in the morning. There, lolling around outside, was a band of individuals in anoraks. Some were drinking from flasks of coffee while others were taking time out to have a quick smoke, waiting for him to show. Before he could react, cameras flashed in his face.

'Mr Rose, what have you got to say about the allegation that the police were involved in a cover-up regarding the death of your family friend Alison Brown?' quizzed a more clued-up member of the crew with his notepad at the ready.

'Is there any truth that it was your family's money that was spirited away?' asked a gamine reporter, who barely looked old enough to have left school.

'There m-must be some mistake!' Stan stuttered, wondering why *he* was suddenly the centre of attention.

'You obviously haven't seen this morning's paper,' the first one said, holding up the tabloid.

Stan gazed at the headline:

London Solicitor Misappropriated Trustee Property

to Line His Own Pockets

'What's any of this got to do with me?' he protested, stopping briefly before he continued reading. The article went on to say: *Richard Jeffrey, 56, is accused of abusing his position of trust to hi-jack a substantial inheritance belonging to former client Tara Rose. The property in question represented a majority holding in a company, Miller Investments, run by Tara's father Stanley Rose.*

'So you're saying there's no truth in the claim that this Richard Jeffrey had a grudge against you?' another one of their number called out from the back. But seeing his name in print had shocked Stan and he was unable to react.

'Come on, mate, give us something!' they all shouted, none wanting to be the one to go back to their editors empty-handed. But it was too late. Stan had regained his wits and moved swiftly back into the house.

'You know, you *are* going to have to give your side of this if it comes to court!' a young female reporter said as her parting shot, which was followed by acerbic mutterings and looks of resignation as the rest of the posse moseyed off in different directions.

Stan, now safely behind closed doors, sat down to eat his breakfast, still trying to make some sense out of the harrowing experience. It didn't take him long to realise that Tara had been the catalyst; this was her logical response to their last fraught encounter. After he had foolishly underestimated his daughter's resolve, she had gone to the press with the findings that he had dismissed out of hand. He hadn't wanted to get involved and this was her way of ensuring he didn't have any choice in the matter.

Tara stared at the mobile she had thrown down on the bed, producing a hiss from her Siamese cat Yul, none too pleased about being disturbed. That morning, the shit had truly hit the fan. The managing directors of the *Sun* and

Mirror, the two biggest daily newspapers, had already been on the phone to inform her that they were facing threats of multi-million-pound lawsuits from a firm purporting to represent Richard Jeffrey. It seemed ironic that after the initial stir the article had created, it had all gone quiet. She had actually felt aggrieved that it had probably been perceived as just another wild story without substance that would soon get forgotten. Now she worried that her reputation would be left in tatters and she'd never work again.

Of course the papers had said, unequivocally, that she had their full backing – not surprising when they had been jumping through hoops to get the exclusive. However, she didn't have to be told about the capricious nature of their loyalty if the tide turned against them. At the end of the day, it was her head on the block if the allegations she had come up with couldn't be substantiated.

Trying to take her mind off her troubled situation, she settled down to the piece she was writing on the Middle East after the fall of Saddam Hussein. Nevertheless, she couldn't help feeling that perhaps her father was right and it had been foolish to dig up the past.

For the next month, putting her job on hold, Tara occupied herself in attempting to compile sufficient evidence to refute Richard Jeffrey's libel charge. The reason was simple: with her career at stake, apart from Nigel Lowndes's testimony, there was precious little else to go on. Roger Prince, on whom she had relied to come forward, had changed his mind at the last moment, for fear of being accused of complicity in depriving her of her inheritance. To add to her woes, she had been unable to make contact with Syrenna Raphael, who had abruptly left her position at the British Library. Tara surmised that the woman had simply panicked after seeing the news.

The advice offered by the lawyers representing the newspapers was to reach an out-of-court settlement, since if the case went to trial, it was likely they would lose and suffer substantial damages.

However, Richard Jeffrey's counsel had other ideas. Claiming that their client had already suffered irreparable damage to his reputation, they intended to have their day in court and in their own words, 'take the press to the cleaners'. That was now just under a week away.

The one plus point was that she had made up with her father. His hysterical voice at the other end of the phone, the morning the press had descended upon his home once they'd found they couldn't get anything out of Tara herself, did bring a smile to her face and brought some much-needed light relief.

The black cab pulled up outside the imposing building in the Strand that housed the Royal Courts of Justice. Stan and his daughter got out and passed apprehensively under the two elaborately carved porches for the hearing that was forecast to last no more than a week.

At that very moment, Stan caught a glimpse of a tanned, well-dressed man walking confidently towards him, accompanied by his sleek-looking brief. It was Richard Jeffrey. As Stan entered the courtroom and the memories flowed back of the harm his family had suffered, Stan experienced a profound loathing, an emotion he had thought he was no longer capable of feeling.

It was time, he realised, to make a stand.

39

Richard Jeffrey took another sip of champagne from the complimentary bottle of Laurent Perrier. That's what you got for a £1500-a-night suite in a luxury Mayfair hotel. In his mind, the Dorchester was the only place to stay in London, and since he could afford the best, he intended to make full use of the comforts it offered, even if it was in the company of the well-worn blonde woman for whom he cared next to nothing. Still, since she was Bill Malone's widow and had inherited the largest privately held hotel group on the Eastern seaboard of the United States, he was prepared to make allowances. That was, until he was installed as its CEO – then she could keep the emerald engagement ring he had enticed her with after they met at a party three years ago, and, for a price, he would vacate the sprawling mansion in West Palm Beach that she had insisted on putting in both their names. He was lucky in that respect; not being bothered by a conscience, he could move on to someone else as easily as changing into a new set of underwear from Saks 5th Avenue.

Looking out over Hyde Park on that grey September morning, Richard was in a buoyant mood. Not having been back to London since his divorce, seven years before, he did wonder whether the place in which he had spent most of his life still held any attraction. There was no denying that there was a vibrancy here that had not existed before, largely due to the deregulation of the financial markets. This had transformed the City skyline and turned London into a global economy, second only to New York as the financial centre of the world. However, now he'd received his Green Card, granting him his permanent US residency, he felt just like any other tourist would who had crossed The Pond on vacation, except that *he* had a score to settle.

A snarl transformed his face. The image of himself on the front pages of the gutter press, insinuating that he had been involved in some wrongdoing, had caught him by surprise. He had wracked his brain, trying to establish who could have had it in for him . . . but each time he came up with a blank. Eventually finding out through discreet inquiries that the whole episode had been instigated by that silly bitch Tara Rose, he had gone on the offensive.

Two days into the libel case, things had gone even better than he'd expected. It was for good reason that he had declined the services of a barrister and decided to represent himself. Seeing how easily he'd torn into Stanley Rose and his snooty daughter, so reminiscent of her mother before her, it had proven the right course of action. Now, unless the defendants were somehow able to produce a rabbit out of a hat, with only the flawed testimony of Nigel Lowndes, his incompetent ex-partner, to go on and Stanley Rose's half-cocked recollection of how he'd suddenly found himself thrown out of a company he had no right to be running in the first place, the case would be done and dusted by tomorrow afternoon. He'd then be on his way back to Florida, a few million pounds in damages to the good.

The other reason that Richard was feeling so pleased

with himself was that he'd been able to finalise the sale of his property interests in London to the Lim brothers from Singapore: the deal would be signed off before he left for the States. Not that the Lims had any idea that *he* was behind the £50 million transaction. All they knew was that the business, being registered offshore, hadn't paid a penny in tax since its incorporation.

Jeffrey retired to the bedroom, relieved to see that Davina was already fast asleep. Tomorrow was another day and he was impatient for it to arrive so he could bury the Roses once and for all.

Stan smiled affectionately at the anxious young woman drinking tea with him in his flat. This time, it had been *his* suggestion that she come and stay so they could support each other during the stress of the legal proceedings. To his delight, the offer was accepted straight away.

'Tara, please try not to worry,' he said, reaching for his daughter's hand. 'I know our prospects don't look particularly bright, but it's not over yet; something may still come up.' Which was more a case of wishful thinking than any real belief that they could salvage what they both knew was a lost cause.

'Daddy, I don't know what else I would do if I was forced to stop being a journalist,' Tara wailed.

Stan regretted his rashness in disposing so liberally of the money Harry had left him – money that he could now well do with, to help Tara re-establish her career. How ironic that now he had got his daughter back, the only thing he could offer her was love. He hoped it was enough.

And the day had started off so well, giving a good

account of himself when he was called upon in court to provide evidence to support the newspapers' claim. Hadn't he been methodical in preparing his notes in the weeks before the trial, taking specific account of Richard Jeffrey's continued animosity towards him ever since he became engaged to Carol? It was clear to Stan, at least, that a pattern had been established of the grudge his solicitor held against his family, even though there was no actual proof of his direct involvement in causing their loss.

'I didn't expect to see Grandma in court,' Tara said, her spirits somewhat lifted. 'Wouldn't have thought she wanted the publicity.'

'Then you don't know your grandmother. She told me she's convinced we're going to win – that's why she, or should I say Paul – has offered to pay all our legal costs if we lose.'

'You kept that quiet,' Tara said in surprise.

'Darling, she just wants to do anything to help; especially since she knows how important the case is to you.'

Tara forced a smile. She knew her grandmother well enough to be aware that any acts of kindness were normally tempered by acts of self-interest. Elaine had been trying to keep on her good side for years. It was as if she was still trying to buy her silence about that fatal argument with her husband, the confession of which she had once let slip. Pushing her together with Paul's grandson Josh was a prime example. Not that Tara was going to admit to her father that they had been seeing each other for eighteen months and that the chance meeting outside his house was merely acted out, to throw him off the trail.

Whatever her grandmother's motive, the young woman knew that Paul's contribution would make scant impression on the huge sum of damages their side were potentially facing – unless there were to be a dramatic, last-minute change in their fortunes.

Broadstairs, Kent

Mary Cunningham leaned back on her fireside chair, enjoying the final moments of the sunset through her living-room window before reaching for the television control, to catch the news. She immediately found she had tuned into a kerfuffle that was taking place outside the Royal Courts of Justice near Fleet Street in London.

Jeremy Chatham, the BBC Legal Affairs correspondent, appeared on her screen and began reporting on the day's proceedings.

'There were raucous scenes and howls of disbelief, a short time ago, from the public gallery after Judge Peter Sampson proceeded to strike out the libel case brought by retired solicitor Richard Jeffrey against the *Mirror* and *Sun* newspapers. From what we understand, a new piece of evidence from an unknown source was produced that immediately threw doubt on what seemed to have gone in favour of the claimant. When Mr Jeffrey, up till now a self-assured individual, was asked to comment on the matter, he became flustered and refused to do so, on the grounds that he would be incriminating himself. We will bring you any further developments . . .'

The report was interrupted by some information being transmitted through the newsman's earpiece. He then continued: 'News is just emerging about a suicide note handed to the Clerk of the Court. It is purported to be written by Alison Brown, the Roses' close family friend. Ms. Brown died several years ago – ostensibly from a fatal accident. The handwritten note apparently tells another story. It describes, in some detail, the intolerable pressure Alison Brown had been subjected to by Richard Jeffrey. That pressure, it now appears, forced her to take her own life. Most saliently, Ms. Brown claimed that she was being blackmailed by Richard Jeffrey, in order for him to get his hands on a substantial inheritance belonging to Tara Rose, whose guardian Ms. Brown was at the time.

'The identity of the mysterious witness is being withheld. But it is known that a woman walked into Charing Cross police station a short time ago, saying that she was in possession of valuable information relating to the case currently in the High Court.'

Mary sat back and chuckled to herself. Retribution had a way of making an appearance when you least expected it, and in the case of that crook Richard Jeffrey, it was long overdue. Just such a pity that with her sister Celia having passed away, she had no one with whom to share the news that had done much to brighten up the start to the weekend.

It had been Mary's decision to move to Kent fulltime. Her asthma wasn't getting any better and the doctor said she would benefit from the sea air. She had kept the family house in West London for sentimental purposes, plus it was convenient for her son Trevor's work. That property, together with the ten million pounds spread around various banks in the City, would be his one day, while she herself had more than enough to be able to take life easy.

Mary wondered how she'd managed to miss the reports in the papers – most likely old age creeping up on her. After all, she was the wrong side of seventy. It was inevitable that the sharp mind which had stood her – and Ben – in such good stead all these years, had lost some of its edge.

As she tried focusing her attention on the rest of the day's news, she had a niggling sense of worry. There was, of course, nothing that could possibly implicate her in any wrongdoing. Her role had simply been as the anonymous buyer of Stanley Rose's 25 per cent, a holding that like Stanley before her gave her no rights into the running of the company and equally no responsibility – sufficient reason to have declined to join the board as a non-executive director in the first place.

It was bad enough that she was the only one who knew that the scumbag Richard Jeffrey had swindled the Rose family out of its inheritance – but the thought that he had caused the death of Alison Brown to achieve his purpose went, despite Mary's resentment of the woman, far beyond what was acceptable.

On 30 January 2004, in the packed court, at the end of a four-week trial, the foreman of the jury delivered a guilty verdict against Richard Jeffrey. The former solicitor was handed down a seven-year prison sentence for fraud. At the collapse of the libel action brought by the defendant four months earlier, once the police had completed their investigation the case was referred to the Crown Prosecution Service.

In the interim, several new witnesses came forward

– most importantly, once she had received immunity from prosecution for withholding police evidence – was Syrenna Raphael. The so-called mystery woman had, it turned out, had the nous to keep the original copy of Alison Brown's letter, which was verified by a handwriting expert as genuine.

However, it was Mary Cunningham whose testimony finally nailed Richard Jeffrey. With tears in her eyes, in a vintage performance worthy of actress Dame Peggy Ashcroft and describing herself as his first unsuspecting client, she told the jury how the defendant had, for years, systematically cheated her and her partner Benjamin Miller out of huge amounts of money, in order to feather his own nest. By the time she finished, Mary had convinced everyone present, including the judge, that Richard Jeffrey should have been on trial for the murder of that poor, unfortunate Alison Brown – instead of the lesser crime of fraud.

40

Stan breathed a huge sigh of relief as the heavily-made-up woman disappeared back downstairs to her Range Rover parked outside, leaving behind the overpowering scent of Dior's Poison. Sneezing, he opened a window and gratefully breathed in the fresh air of hilly Belsize Park.

Stan hoped he'd finally seen the back of Angela Kravitz. The woman wouldn't leave him alone once she had discovered that he was unattached. It had taken weeks after he'd told her that he could no longer continue treating her for the lonely divorcée to finally get the message. Except that she hadn't: the hand-delivered invitation for Stan to attend the charity dinner she was hosting revealed that his optimism had been premature.

Stan glanced at his watch. It was only half past ten in the morning, and he was already feeling as if he'd done a full day's work. The last few months had taken their toll on him. Now predominantly grey, his heavy-set jowls convinced him that he looked much older than his fifty-two years. More disconcerting was his mistaken belief that he could just pick up where he had left off with his psychotherapy practice. That was proving completely unrealistic. The truth was that the two high-profile court cases had left him feeling unsettled. Naturally, he was happy for Tara, who had been able to resume her career with her reputation intact – a far greater priority than reclaiming her inheritance.

Stan, however, had since found himself reliving the past with such frequency and intensity that it was as if the last nine years had never happened. He became obsessed with the thought that now the gross injustice suffered by his family had been corrected, it behoved him to make good its future. The prospect of going back into business terrified him since from a moral standpoint it represented a world from which he thought he had escaped. On the other hand, in his willingness to abandon it for a safer existence he had forfeited the financial security that he owed to his family.

Faced with what appeared to be an unsolvable dilemma, Stan reacted as he always did in such situations: he put it out of his mind, in the hope it would leave him alone. The unexpected phone call from Richard Jeffrey's former partner, Nigel Lowndes, asking whether he was free to attend a meeting at their firm, propelled him into rethinking his stance.

At lunchtime the following day, Stan entered the modest offices situated above an Indian restaurant in a grubby part of Camden High Street. Huddled around a table in the solitary meeting room with Nigel Lowndes – a man with whom, before the recent court cases, Stan had only ever exchanged pleasantries – were two familiar-looking gentlemen, although he couldn't immediately place them.

'Stanley, thank you so much for agreeing to come at such short notice. You remember Michael and Vincent Lim,' the solicitor said, introducing the two immaculately dressed Asian men whom Stan now recognised as the Singaporean businessmen with whom he had once had dealings.

'Yes, yes, of course – although it's been many years since I had the pleasure,' Stan replied, having fond memories of the non-identical twins.

'Please help yourself to some refreshments,' the lawyer said, gesturing to a platter of sandwiches and some cans of soft drinks. 'I'm afraid there's not much of a selection, but I hope it'll suffice.'

'Thank you. In fact, if I remember correctly, I think the Lim brothers and I were quite close to concluding a transaction,' Stan observed, feeling more relaxed.

'Which is why I thought it would be a good idea for the four of us to meet,' Nigel said.

'I'm not sure I'm with you,' Stan responded, taking a large bite out of an egg mayonnaise sandwich.

'I'll come straight to the point. Michael and Vincent were, up until recently, in advanced discussions to purchase a substantial property portfolio in Central London. It was only late in the day when they discovered who the ultimate owner was – and at that point, the deal fell apart.'

'I see. But I don't understand what any of this has got to do with me,' Stan replied, glancing at the two brothers whose impassive expressions gave nothing away.

'Yours was the company they wanted to buy.'

'I haven't been involved in business . . .' Stan began

'Since Richard Jeffrey swindled you out of it, you mean,' the lawyer interjected.

'We thought something was a little strange, when some of the buildings were the same ones that we'd viewed several years back,' Michael Lim said, speaking for the first time.

'You were kind enough to show them to us yourself,' his

brother Vincent added.

'So you see,' Nigel said, taking over, 'even though the operation was supposedly undetectable in an offshore company, our two friends here put two and two together and soon realised that they were being offered Miller Investments. What they didn't know, until the libel case, was that Richard Jeffrey had obtained the company through underhanded means. That's when they approached me to act for them. They remembered that Lowndes Jeffrey used to be your lawyers so I wasn't *that* difficult to track down.'

'Now there is no one for us to deal with,' said Michael Lim.

'You mean you still want to buy it?' Stan quizzed.

'But of course! It has many very valuable properties in the most prestigious parts of London,' Vincent emphasised.

'Now CM Nominees has been wound up, the legal position is that, without any directors to run the company or shareholders to appoint one, Miller Investments has reverted to the Crown,' Nigel Lowndes clarified.

'So what does that mean?' Stan asked.

'In simple terms, it has to be bought out in order for your family to reclaim its interest.'

'But surely that will require a substantial sum of money?'

'That's where the Lims come in,' the lawyer beamed.

'We will provide the funds in return for half of your company,' Michael Lim said shrewdly.

'Just enough to satisfy the royal coffers,' Nigel Lowndes put in.

'And what happens to the remainder?' Stan enquired instinctively.

'We will be partners with you, fifty-fifty,' Vincent

answered.

'You mean you want me to be involved?' Stanley said incredulously.

'The deal depends upon it, Stanley,' the lawyer affirmed.

Stan put down his sandwich. 'I have to say this has all come as a bit of a shock. I'll need some time to mull it over.'

'Take as long as you like. The company's not going anywhere without you,' Nigel said warmly and the Lim brothers nodded, smiling.

After shaking everyone's hands, Stan got up from the table to leave, when another thought occurred to him.

'There's one thing that doesn't make sense: how did Vincent and Michael learn that the portfolio was for sale?'

'We keep, as you say, our ears close to the ground,' Vincent replied cagily, not prepared to reveal his source.

'Your properties were always a strategic purchase for us,' the other brother said, trying to offer Stan comfort.

Nigel Lowndes summed up: 'Richard Jeffrey had made his money, or the people running it for him did, and so the sooner he got rid of the company, the less likely it would be that he could ever be accused of any wrongdoing. Unfortunately for him, the legal case had caught him by surprise. If he had had any sense and had settled without it going to court, he might well have got away with it. But knowing the man as I do, I could have predicted that his pride wouldn't allow him to do so.'

'Goodbye, gentlemen, it's been good to see you all again. I shall now go home and think about all this,' Stan repeated on his way out.

*

Tara joined the taxi queue at Glasgow Central station, going over again in her mind the carefully prepared speech she would shortly have to give to the Brown family. The urn containing Alison's ashes was inside her luggage. Syrenna Raphael had eventually agreed that it should be returned to Alison's family, together with the official death certificate. She had kept the ashes all this time, unable to part with what remained of the woman she had loved, but now it was time to surrender them.

Tara herself had come to understand that the reason none of Alison's family had been at the funeral was because Richard Jeffrey had made sure it was carried out expeditiously, before any questions could be asked as to the true circumstances surrounding her death. Now they deserved to be told the truth about Alison, and how much she had meant to the Rose family, who had adopted her as one of their own.

When the cab drew up at a grim housing estate in the south of the city, Tara picked up her bag, retrieved the address from her raincoat pocket and prepared herself for the emotional ordeal ahead.

41

Stan nodded approvingly at the surveyors' drawings, spread across the boardroom table in the new Ladbroke Grove office. He was suitably impressed. The mixed development of fifty shops and the block of a hundred and seventy flats would completely regenerate the entire northern part of the area, which hadn't been touched for years.

He had deliberated long and hard about his quandary and eventually sought the help of his mentor Rabbi Frankel. The latter's advice was unequivocal. It was, he said, Stan's duty to his daughter and himself, to go back into the enterprise that had been left in his care by his father-in-law, so that it should not again fall into the hands of strangers. It was good advice, and Stan took it.

That was in February, and it was now July. Fortunately, since the Lims placed no requirement on him being involved fulltime, Stan was able to continue working as a psychotherapist three days a week, which helped him to keep a proper sense of perspective. Overwhelmed by the trust they had shown in him, he resolved to do everything in his power to safeguard the brothers' interest in the multi-million-pound company that had been brought back to life. In return, when the time came for him to retire, they had agreed to pay the full market price for his

50 per cent holding.

Stan was embarrassed by how naturally he'd fallen back into the world of property. Suddenly, everyone wanted to do business with him again. Those agents who had seemingly suffered bouts of amnesia when he was trying to re-establish himself, were now trampling over each other to offer him deals. Most surprising, however, was the delegation of senior executives that arrived from the Pretoria Bank. They had obviously been following the court case against Richard Jeffrey with trepidation, expecting to be implicated in the fraud he had committed. Not taking any chances, the parent company in South Africa had replaced the entire board of the London office with new faces. Now they were offering him incredibly competitive terms on a new facility. But the Lims were too smart for that and had already secured a substantial line of credit with a bank in Singapore run by their cousin, James.

'Great scheme, Trevor,' Stan said to the handsome man standing beside him.

'It seems to work all right and I don't envisage the council will raise any planning issues,' the chief surveyor replied.

'I'm just surprised it took so long for us to get to work together,' Stan commented. 'Although you say we met when I was married to Carol?'

'Just after, actually,' Trevor corrected him. 'It was when you had suggested to Ben about joining his company.'

'And his response was wanting to buy my shares!' Stan shook his head. 'I remember now. We never did see eye to eye.'

'Ben probably just thought you weren't really cut out for the rough and tumble of the property game,' Trevor

323

said tactfully. He chose not to remind Stan that he hadn't given him, Trevor, the time of day once he'd taken over the reins of Miller Investments.

'He wasn't wrong. Unfortunately, it took a lot of pain and heartache to find that out for myself,' Stan conceded.

'This business – if you can call it that – has always been full of rogues,' Trevor remarked.

'And dishonest solicitors,' Stan added.

'Can't say I've come across too many like Richard Jeffrey – you must have been unlucky. Though my mother did warn me about that chap. The thing is, Ben was loyal and couldn't or wouldn't see the fellow for what he really was.'

'We have a lot to be grateful to Mary Cunningham for, don't we?' Stan said. 'But I really had no idea that you were her son.'

'Mum reverted to using her maiden name. My only regret is that I'll never provide her with grandchildren, although my partner Robin, who is ten years younger than me, says that we should adopt. But you are right; she is a remarkable woman. Fortunately, we've always been close. When my dad ran off with that usherette at our local Odeon, Ben became like a surrogate father. Mum was working at a betting shop in Westbourne Grove at the time – that's where she and Ben met. He liked his flutter on the horses, did Ben.'

'I didn't know that either,' Stan answered. 'But then I only found out about Mary when I met her in Richard Jeffrey's office, after Ben passed away.'

'Mum and I were his other family. Of course, in those days my mother looked the spitting image of the young Joan Collins. How Ben was able to keep us apart for so many years must have taken some doing. But then he fell for that Scottish lady.'

'You're referring to Alison Brown?'

'Yes. Apparently, he was besotted with her – you know, the younger woman thing. My mother didn't take too kindly to that,' Trevor said ruefully.

'I'm sure she didn't,' Stan muttered under his breath, having witnessed at first-hand how intimidating the woman could be when she was crossed.

'But nothing ever happened between them. Alison just saw Ben as a father figure.' Trevor looked at his watch. 'Right, I'd better be going. I've got to get these plans lodged at the Town Hall. Then I've arranged to meet a certain young woman.'

'Really?' Stan sounded surprised.

'It's nothing like that. I'm taking Tara to lunch.'

'Yes, she told me that you've become close friends. That was a bit of a coincidence.'

'Not really. Being on the panel of most of the building societies in the area, I carried out the valuation on the house she purchased – then we bumped into each other again in that restaurant Ben introduced me to. Apparently, he used to take Tara there sometimes when she was a little girl.'

'I suppose you're right,' Stan said, scratching his head. 'But I do worry whether she will ever meet someone special.'

'What's wrong with Jamie? He seems a nice enough fellow and she does seem quite smitten with him.'

'Who did you say?' Stan replied, clearly in the dark about his daughter's private life.

'I'm sorry – I thought you knew. Please don't mention

I said anything,' Trevor blustered, embarrassed by his faux pas, leaving Stan to ponder on what else he didn't know about his enigmatic daughter.

Stan looked enviously up at the stage from his front-row seat in the renowned jazz venue, Oscar's Club, Soho. That was the reason why he never went to gigs. Imagining what might have been still left him pining for the excitement that only a live performance could produce. But as Jamie was appearing with his new seven-piece band, Tara had asked him to make up a table with a few of their friends and he wasn't going to disappoint her. He and Jamie had actually jammed a few times together, after it came out in conversation one day that Stan also played guitar. He'd finally got over using Arnold's death as an excuse to give up the instrument when, in truth, it had been disenchantment with himself because of a lack of talent. How he'd risen so high in Jamie's estimation, when he had only a limited repertoire, he couldn't say. Perhaps it had something to do with the three vintage guitars that until recently had remained locked away in their cases – a crime!

Even though Stan had a genuine affection for the young man, when it involved his daughter that was different. Maybe it was because he was being overly protective of her, albeit late in the day. Or perhaps it was the fact that Tara was a few years older than Jamie that had made Stan initially dismiss what Trevor had let slip. But then, when he found that she and Jamie were living together, he knew he would have to adjust to the situation.

Elaine readily admitted that she had encouraged the friendship. Maybe she had seen the error of her ways by having been against his marriage to Carol, Stan thought, and this was her way of ensuring that she wouldn't make the same mistake with her granddaughter.

42

It was just past six in the morning and the residents of London's fashionable Holland Park hadn't yet stirred from their slumber. Not so for the handful of fitness centres that had sprung up in the area, the most exclusive being The Conservatory, a private members' club tucked away behind a façade of opulent Victorian villas.

'Right, Stanley, remember about loosening up first,' Jamie reminded the lean man in a pristine white sports outfit as they entered a huge loft space, already occupied by several well-toned young men and their female counterparts working out on the impressive range of equipment.

'Don't worry, I'll catch up with you later!' Stan shouted back. Then, arms and legs working furiously on one of the three cross-trainers, he began his circuit in time with the high-energy music being played through the two wall-mounted plasma screens situated at either end of the windowless gym.

At first, he had dismissed his daughter's gradual prodding, that he needed to get into shape, as a nuisance; he thought she would soon get tired of harping on about it. Then, nine months ago, when Tara announced that she was expecting Josh's child, her anxiety for her father's well-being became more, not less intense. Stan came to understand that this was because Tara saw him as the most vulnerable part of the new family unit she was creating.

In the end, it was Jamie's less emotional approach, which had persuaded Stan to drastically alter his lifestyle.

Stan was halfway through his floor exercises, when he glanced up from his mat and saw Jamie standing over him, holding his mobile phone and looking concerned.

'What's wrong?' Stan panted, irritated at being interrupted.

'It's Tara, she just called to say she thinks the baby's coming!'

Stan paced up and down the empty waiting room in St Mary's Hospital in Paddington, trying to control his anxiety. He had been at the hospital all morning, and there was no sign yet of mother or baby.

Tara had wanted Jamie to be present at the birth, so Stan was relegated to the visitors' room along the corridor from the maternity ward. The prospect of being a grandfather filled him with a sense of pride. It was no longer just Tara and himself, but a new dynasty emerging of which he desperately wanted to be a part.

It hadn't been a straightforward pregnancy. As his daughter said, nothing in her life had ever come easy – and the baby girl now being delivered by emergency caesarean was unlikely to be an exception. Not that Tara had helped herself, working up till the last minute. With her reputation massively enhanced as a result of the court case, there was an ever-greater demand for her services as a features writer, and she was determined to take full advantage while she could.

Being fiercely independent and steadfastly refusing to have anything to do with the sizeable inheritance that had been recovered, and which her father was looking after on her behalf, Tara was also conscious that hers was the only regular source of income, since Jamie was only receiving a trickle of royalties from his album sales and one-off payments from the occasional live performance.

Stan found himself thinking again about Carol and the loss that Tara rarely showed outwardly but must be feeling inwardly, especially now. Fortunately, after some initial judgmental comments, Elaine had, as Tara predicted, become a hands-on great-grandmother – to the extent of accompanying her to the evening antenatal classes and shopping for a wardrobe of flattering new clothes to accommodate her changing figure.

The one thing that didn't add up, however, was the apparent lack of contact from Jamie's family, the Kleins. It was as if they were deliberately remaining aloof. Certainly, that seemed to be the case whenever Stan was around.

At that moment, a tall bespectacled man poked his head around the door. 'Mr Rose, I'm Piers Dillon, Tara's obstetrician. Congratulations, your daughter has just given birth to a beautiful seven pounds baby girl.'

'That is wonderful news, but how is my daughter?' Stan asked, the agitation showing on his face.

'Tara's still in recovery, she has had quite an ordeal. Had a hell of a job pulling the blighter out; seemed to be content staying where she was. Still, all's well that ends well. Give it another half an hour and your daughter will be back in her ward,' were his last words before departing.

A few seconds later, an out-of-breath Josh arrived.

'Congratulations!' Stan told him.

'Thank you. By the way, Tara thinks our daughter looks just like you,' the young man said, beaming with pride.

'I shouldn't imagine that's going to make her very happy,' Stan replied dryly.

'You're wrong about Tara. She really does love you, you know.'

Stan sighed. 'Sometimes I'm not so sure.'

'It's just that she doesn't show it. Behind the tough exterior, she's the warmest person I've ever met. You've got to get to know her, that's all.'

'I think I'm just learning to do that,' Stan confessed.

Impulsively, Josh went up and threw his arms around the older man. The two unlikely allies stood together in a tight embrace, caught up in the emotion of the moment.

Then, regaining his composure, Jamie said, 'For what it's worth, both of us – no, the *three* of us – think we're extremely fortunate to have you in our lives.'

'I love you too,' Stan responded to the young man he had begun to look upon as his son.

43

Looking around to make quite sure he wasn't being spotted, with his coat collar pulled up high, Stan entered the premises of the *Temple of Fortune* agency. He had thought long and hard before resorting to what still seemed a desperate course of action but the truth was, he was lonely. Seeing less of Tara, who was now fully occupied in the day with three-month-old baby Florence, and by the evening too exhausted to be able to make any arrangements, he had started to dwell on his empty life. He did his best to keep occupied. It wasn't that there was a lack of opportunity to meet other women – especially as his friend, Howard Barnet, finally separated from his long-suffering wife Giselle and living with a showroom model half his age, always included him in their busy social lives.

But he wanted something more.

'Yes, can I help you?' asked the fat-faced woman, sat at a desk in front of a giant yucca plant, like some castaway on a desert island.

'I would like to see Regine, if that's possible,' Stan replied, already regretting coming to the tiny half shop that appeared to have been pruned from the florist's next door.

'Sorry, she's abroad,' came the short reply. 'I'm her daughter, Penina. You'll just have to deal with me.'

'On reflection, it can wait till your mother returns,' Stan said, wanting any excuse to leave.

'Please yourself,' the big woman shrugged, inspecting her terrifyingly long nails, 'though you might be waiting a long time.'

'Oh, I see,' Stan replied, thinking Regine might be ill.

'No, you don't!' the woman snarled.

Stan flinched. He wondered why this Penina woman was being so aggressive towards him – and putting on his psychotherapist's hat, concluded she was in definite need of help. Then he reminded himself that *he* was the one who had come seeking guidance.

'Husband number four cleaned out their joint account, took off back to Malta and left her with a pile of debts – and so she's gone looking for him. I told her she was wasting her time, but would she listen?'

'It must be very difficult,' Stan said, trying his best to sound sympathetic.

'Dumped this place on me,' the woman grumbled on, ignoring him. 'Good thing I only do mornings, otherwise I think I'd shoot myself. I do have a life, you know.' And she stared at him challengingly.

'I'm sure you do,' Stan replied, wondering why he was still there.

'Right – let's get one thing clear. If you're like all the rest, after a gorgeous thirty year old with a figure to die for who wants your looks rather than your money, I'm afraid you've come to the wrong place. Don't get me wrong, it's just our clientele need to be more realistic in that department, if you get my drift.'

'That's exactly why you were recommended,' Stan remarked, completely missing the inference. 'My mother,

Elaine Rose, is a very good friend of Regine's.'

'Why didn't you say so? Pull up a chair,' the large woman replied, adopting a much friendlier attitude.

'Thank you.' Stan sat down opposite the marriage broker, unsure whether he should mention that it was entirely at his mother's volition that he was there.

'She talks about you to Mum the whole time, and says how close she is to her granddaughter and great-granddaughter. How is baby Florence, by the way?' Penina cooed.

'Very well, although I don't see as much of her as I should like,' Stan explained, conscious that he was sounding just like his mother before him, harping on about being denied her rightful access to Tara, when *she* was growing up.

'It just so happens I have got one or two very nice ladies with whom you might have quite a lot in common,' the fat woman muttered, licking her plump little fingers and flicking through her index cards. 'Of course, the right one for you would have been Sara Klein – but she's been deleted for some reason. Perhaps she's found someone through another source.'

'Wait a minute. I know that name!' Stan exclaimed.

'You should, since it's Paul's daughter – her son Jamie and your Tara?'

'Yes, yes, I'm aware of the connection, but I didn't know . . .'

'What, that she was on our books? Such an elegant lady – what a shame! She would have been ideal. Still, we'll see who else we have, shall we?' Penina stared at him appraisingly. 'You're a nice-looking man, a sort of Sean Connery with hair, I'd say.'

A bit of a comedown from Omar Sharif, and even from

Tom Selleck, Stan thought to himself.

'Fill in our fees agreement, Stanley, and we'll get on the case straight away,' Penina said, all business now, handing the form to her new applicant. 'Yes, Sean Connery,' she repeated. 'All the older women are mad about him.'

Never having been compared with someone twenty years his senior before, Stan came away feeling uncomfortably self-conscious. Perhaps he had aged far more than he'd imagined.

Instead of concentrating on the portfolio of student accommodation in Earl's Court that was just coming up to auction, Stan spent the rest of the day preoccupied with thoughts of Sara Klein. They had always liked each other but practically being family, he never gave it another thought. Even when he found out she was getting divorced it never occurred to him that they might get together. But now he had to find a way of getting close to her – easier said than done, since any time he'd asked after her, he never got more than a cursory response.

Over the next few weeks, Stan called on the agency more than once, on the off-chance that the situation with Sara might have changed. That brought him as little joy as trying to prise any information out about her from Josh or his daughter. He'd heard from his mother that the break-up from her husband had been acrimonious, so he just assumed that as far as the Rose family were concerned, she was *persona non grata*. Of course, he had plenty of excuses to get her on the phone and, on several occasions, had been quite close to doing so. What prevented him, however, was the fear of being rejected.

In an attempt to put Sara out of his mind, he decided to focus his attentions instead on introductions to the two middle-aged ladies arranged by the agency. Unfortunately, it didn't take long to establish that he didn't have the slightest thing in common with either of them. The only saving grace about the first one, Mavis Blumenthal, a painfully thin woman with alopecia, who spent the whole evening talking to him about her neuroses, was that she became a patient. The second, Lorraine Goodkind, was a different kettle of fish entirely. A dynamic businesswoman with her own PR company and villa in Tuscany, although not at all unattractive, she was so overpowering that it came as no surprise that, despite being in her mid-fifties, she had never been married.

It took the arrival of a formal invitation in the post a week later – to a party to celebrate Paul Klein's eightieth birthday – to lift his spirits. However, Stan was the last to arrive at the dinner party, having been delayed by a distraught elderly patient, shocked and grieving, and unable to come to terms with his beloved pet dog having to be put down.

With a heightened sense of expectation about seeing Sara again, Stan went straight into the overheated dining room, where the extended family were already well into their first course, fussed over by two bored female staff in uniform, provided by the caterers for the evening.

'Sorry I'm late,' he said, going up to his mother to kiss her.

'You're here now – that's all that counts,' she answered, her tight expression showing her true sentiments on the matter.

'Happy Birthday, Paul,' Stan said, addressing the frail-looking man sitting next to her, whose vacant look indicated that he might have been setting eyes on Stan for the very first time.

'Hi, Stanley,' Jamie called over, his mouth full of smoked salmon mousse. 'There's a place next to me as Tara couldn't make it. The babysitter let us down at the last moment. She's well pissed off.'

Stan moved up the table, spotting Sara in conversation with a thin-lipped fellow in a tweed sports jacket, who reminded him of a headmaster at a boys' boarding school. Just as he took his seat, he was sure he caught her smiling at him, and found himself thinking that she was far more beautiful than he remembered.

'That's Laurence Horwood,' Jamie pointed out. 'Apparently, he's a top immunologist. Bit of a pompous twat if you ask me, but Mum seems to like him.'

Stan forced a smile as a wave of despondency swept over him, seeing that she had somebody else. He now wished he hadn't bothered to come; at least he could have continued to delude himself that there was still a chance. Stan picked at his meal, drank little and engaged in trivial conversation with the other people at the table.

After a couple of hours, Paul began to tire. So after the cutting of the birthday cake and the perfunctory champagne toast, the party started to break up. Stan couldn't help but notice that Sara's gentleman friend was holding his stomach and appeared to be in some considerable degree of discomfort. Struggling to get to his feet, he quickly left the room, presumably in search of the lavatory.

Stan seized the opportunity to go over to the woman he

337

had been pursuing, in his mind, for the last three months.

'Is everything all right?' he asked with genuine concern, taking possession of the vacant chair next to her.

'Laurence has a delicate constitution. Actually, he's been a bit off-colour all evening,' Sara whispered, not wishing to be overheard. Then: 'How have *you* been anyway?' she went on, more perkily.

'Me? Oh, fine. You know, rushing around as usual.'

'I must say you're looking very well. Losing the beard has taken years off you.'

'Thank you.' Stan was pleased that the drastic action he'd undertaken, after advice from the marriage broker, seemed to have produced the desired result.

'And I hear from Josh that you're still regularly working out?'

'That's right, and I have your son to thank for that, although when he's away on tour, it's not that easy to stay motivated, if I'm honest.'

'I don't think I've seen you since the hospital when Tara gave birth. You had just come from the gym, someone said. I don't think you even noticed me.'

'I was in a bit of a state,' Stan explained. He smiled sheepishly. 'It was a very emotional moment.'

'Yes, of course,' Sara said softly. 'I would have been the same if I had a daughter, and with Tara not having a mother to be with her, it must have been difficult. Though she seems to be coping really well. It certainly seems that way, every time I go and visit her and Florence.'

'I'm afraid she's had to learn how to cope,' Stan said resignedly, wondering whether Sara had been told how badly he had behaved in the past towards his daughter. 'But she and Josh do seem really well suited.'

'Stanley, I have to tell you, I've never seen my son so happy,' the woman said animatedly. 'I was really worried that he'd gone off the rails, especially after David and I split up. But, of course, you knew all that since he was your patient at the time.'

'Yes, he was,' Stanley acknowledged, assuming that it had been her idea that the boy sought help. 'Although I didn't know of the family link,' he added hastily.

'He's a different person since he's been with Tara,' Sara commented.

'The influence of an older woman,' Stan said light-heartedly.

'Obviously it's what he needed,' she agreed.

'Though I can't say I prescribed it,' Stan joked.

'You didn't have to – you can thank your mother for that.'

'Really?' Stan frowned. What had Elaine been up to now?

'Don't look so surprised. Elaine's been trying for years to bring our two families closer together,' Sara divulged quietly, giving Stan a lingering look.

At that point, Laurence Horwood came back into the room, looking even paler than when he'd left.

'Must have been the chicken liver pâté snacks that we had before dinner,' he grumbled, in earshot of the owner of the catering company, a short bald-headed man with an unfortunate twitch, who had come to pick up the balance of his payment.

'Good evening, sir. I do hope you're not insinuating that any of the food we provided was substandard.'

'Depends whether you include salmonella as not being up to scratch,' the specialist retorted. 'I reckon only a top-quality strain of the bugger could have got to work that quickly!'

'I do assure you, we've never had complaints about any of our dishes before,' the owner said, getting hot under the collar. 'Chef makes everything fresh in our own kitchens; you're welcome to inspect them yourself!'

Concerned that the evening was ending on a sour note, Elaine Rose went discreetly over to see what was going on.

'Mr Rudolfski, would you care to tell me what you are doing, upsetting my guests?'

'Mrs Rose, I do apologise. It's just a simple misunderstanding,' said the proprietor, who had come out in a sweat. 'I trust the meal was to your satisfaction?'

'Very good actually. I thought the roast lamb was particularly delicious. Though it appears something has disagreed with that gentleman,' Elaine said, gesturing towards the specialist, who had had to rush back to the toilet.

'I think we should call him a taxi,' she suggested, taking Sara aside.

'I'd better go with,' replied the younger woman.

'I don't think that's necessary,' Elaine said smoothly. 'You'll see Sara home, won't you dear?' she told her son. 'Anyway, you can't go yet, you've only just got here.'

The two of them looked at each other, neither objecting to the unsubtle way in which they had been thrown together.

Stan saw Sara to her front door and kissed her gently on the cheek. 'I don't suppose there's a chance I can see you again?' he said, drumming up the courage.

'Why not ask and find out?' she replied, touching his arm affectionately.

'But how about Laurence? I thought . . .'

'What – that we were together? He's just a friend and, actually, quite amusing when you get to know him. However,' she went on, 'I shan't be sending *him* bouquets of lilies until he gets better.'

It took a few moments for Stan to get the connection. Then it came to him. When he was recuperating in the Royal Free, the scented white flowers had been from Sara.

'Please believe me – I had no idea that they were from you,' he replied, deeply touched by her great kindness.

'How many other secret admirers have you got?' Sara teased.

'If you'd seen what I looked like in hospital, very few,' Stan riposted.

'Just as well I was prepared to be patient, then.'

Suddenly, overcome with desire for the woman who had waited for him for the best part of ten years, Stan drew her towards him and kissed her passionately on the lips, a little voice telling him that this was the person with whom he wanted to spend the rest of his life.

Marble Arch Synagogue, November 2005

Men in black dinner suits on one side and women in colourful evening gowns on the other, sat chatting cheerfully in the resplendent prayer hall adorned with tall stained-glass windows depicting scenes from Exodus, while a young violinist on a dais played haunting melodies reminiscent of the shtetl. The arrival of the bride prompted the all-male choir, in an exalted position behind the Ark which held the holy scrolls, to break into full voice.

The wedding party made its way slowly towards the *chuppah*, a white canopy embellished with white roses under which the ceremony was to be administered by a smiling Rabbi Frankel.

Stan stood proudly, while his bride circled him seven times in accordance with ancient Hebrew tradition. The past six weeks since he had proposed were a haze. He had thought it only right to first seek his daughter Tara's approval. It transpired there was no need. Of course, he hadn't known at the time that it was merely a charade orchestrated by his mother, in cahoots with her granddaughter, to test his keenness, which had prevented Stan from getting to Sara earlier.

Fortunately, Sara accepted his proposal straight away and immediately set about making the arrangements. Looking at the ailing individual in the wheelchair a few feet away, there was good reason to have acted without delay. Paul's health had deteriorated and, being close to her father, Sara wanted him to be able to witness the occasion in the short time he had left.

Jamie, acting as the best man, handed Stan the simple gold band which, after reciting the marriage proposal, he placed on his bride's finger. The couple were now officially married. Rabbi Frankel then read out the *Ketubah*, the ancient marriage contract, followed a few minutes later by the groom stamping on a glass to roars of '*Mazel Tov!*'

Stan leaned across and kissed his bride, which brought enthusiastic response from the hundred and twenty guests, with the notable exception of a bickering mother and daughter, fully engrossed in an argument as to which family, the Roses or the Kleins, their *Temple of Fortune* agency should invoice for their introductory commission.

Acknowledgements

I would like to thank my family for their unwavering support and for being prepared to share in my journey.

My thanks also go to everyone at 2QT for agreeing to publish this book. To Balcony Art & Design Studio for the original illustration. Last but not least to my editor Joan Deitch for her continued guidance and help in giving *The Temple Of Fortune* a voice.

Lightning Source UK Ltd.
Milton Keynes UK
UKHW020951241120
373991UK00006B/250